KU-134-432

WEAVEWORLD

'All that you expect from Clive Barker and more – terrifying, shocking, audaciously imaginative, moving and ruthlessly unputdownable.'   RAMSEY CAMPBELL

'His new dark fantasy, an epic tale of a magic carpet and the wondrous world within its weave, towers above his earlier work . . . it manages, via its powerful and giddy torrent of invention, to grasp the golden ring as the most ambitious and visionary horror novel of the decade . . . a raging flood of image and situation so rich as to overflow. Barker has unleashed literary genius.'   *Kirkus*

'Prodigious imagination . . . *Weaveworld* is beguiling for its imaginative power.'   *Today*

'*Weaveworld* is pure dazzle, pure storytelling. The mixed tricky country where fantasy and horror overlap has been visited before – though not very often – and *Weaveworld* will be a guide for everyone who travels there in the future. I think it'll probably be imitated for the next decade or so, as lesser talents try to crack its code and tame its insights.'   PETER STRAUB

'His most ambitious and imaginative work . . . strands of Joyce, Poe, Tolkien . . . an irresistible yarn.'   *Time*

'*Weaveworld* confirms Clive Barker as a formidable talent in British dark fantasy.'   Q

'Recommended . . . a fantastic tale of imagination.'
JONATHAN ROSS, *Sunday Express*

THE GREAT AND SECRET SHOW

'Clive Barker's career has been building up to *The Great and Secret Show*. With each book, he's been moving toward a sort of fiction that is grander than the usual horror novel but that is also a paradigm of horror fiction. If you thought Thomas Pynchon's *Vineland* was disappointingly tidy and coherent, by all means latch on to *The Great and Secret Show*. In its vast, loopy sprawl, it is nothing so much as a cross between *Gravity's Rainbow* and *Lord of the Rings*: allusive and mythic, complex and entertaining . . . extravagantly metaphorical, wildly symbolic, skillful and funny.'

New York Times Book Review

'A massive and brilliant Platonic dark fantasy that details an eruption of wonders and terrors – as the veil between the world of the senses and the world of the imagination is rent in a small California town. The torrent of invention is astounding, the total impact is staggering, as Barker creates one of the most powerful overtly metaphysical novels of recent years.'   *Kirkus*

'Rich and absorbing . . . the images are vivid, the asides incisive and the prose elegant in this joyride of a story.'

Time

'The best thing he has ever written . . . pure narrative simplicity . . . gore fans will get their chills, subtle horror readers will have theirs and the lighter fantasy readers will be entranced . . . what wonders are in store as he develops his themes?'   *Fear*

'There is such intensity and scope to this work that I can find no flaw in this utterly perfect novel. *The Great and Secret Show* is a horror story, it is mythology, and it is a story about people, real people . . . one of the most original and important works of horror fiction in a long, long time.'   *Rave Reviews*

Also by Clive Barker

The Books Of Blood, Volumes I - VI

The Damnation Game

Weaveworld

Cabal

The Great And Secret Show

The Hellbound Heart

Imajica

The Thief Of Always

Everville

Incarnations

Forms Of Heaven

Sacrament

Galilee

The Essential Clive Barker

Coldheart Canyon

Abarat

Abarat II

Mister B. Gone

CABAL

Clive Barker was born in Liverpool in 1952. In addition to his work as a novelist and short story writer he also illustrates, writes, directs and produces for sstage and screen. In 1987 he made his debut as a film director and writer of the highly successful Hellraiser, bades on his *The Hellbound Heart.* He is the worldwide bestselling author of numerous novels including *Weaveworld, The Great and Secret Show, Sacrament, Imajica,* and his latest *Mister B. Gone.* Clive Barker lives in Los Angeles.

CLIVE BARKER

Cabal:
The Nightbreed

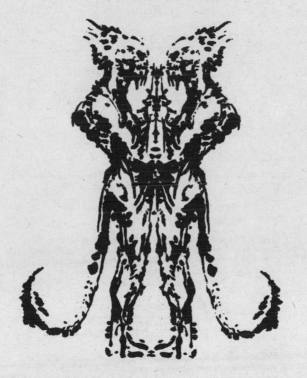

HARPER
Voyager

This novel is entirely a work of fiction.
The names, characters and incidents portrayed in it are
the work of the author's imagination. Any resemblance to
actual persons, living or dead, events or localities is
entirely coincidental.

HarperVoyager
An imprint of HarperCollins*Publishers*
77–85 Fulham Palace Road
Hammersmith, London W6 8JB

www.voyager-books.co.uk

This paperback edition 2008

1

First published in Great Britain by
Fontana 1989

A catalogue record for this book is
available from the British Library

ISBN 978-0-00-785510-0

Set in Trump Mediaeval by Palimpsest Book Production Limited,
Grangemouth, Stirlingshire

Printed and bound in Great Britain by
Clays Ltd, St Ives plc

Mixed Sources
Product group from well-managed
forests and other controlled sources
www.fsc.org Cert no. SW-COC-1806
© 1996 Forest Stewardship Council
FSC

To Annie

'We are all imaginary animals . . .'
DOMINGO D'YBARRONDO
A Bestiary of the Soul

CONTENTS

PART FIVE: THE GOOD NIGHT

PART ONE

LOCO

'I was born alive. Isn't that punishment enough?'
Mary Hendrickson, at her trial
for patricide

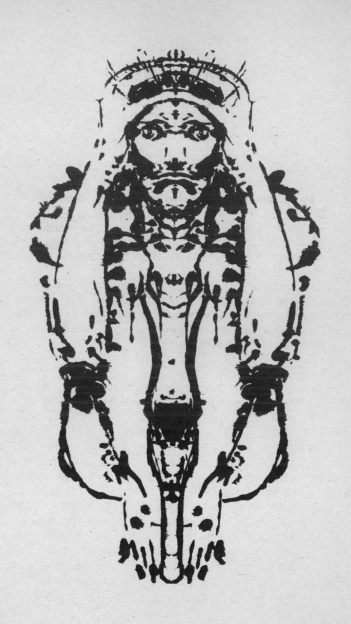

I

The Truth

Of all the rash and midnight promises made in the name of love none, Boone now knew, was more certain to be broken than: *'I'll never leave you'*.

What time didn't steal from under your nose, circumstance did. It was useless to hope otherwise; useless to dream that the world somehow meant you good. Everything of value, everything you clung to for your sanity would rot or be snatched in the long run, and the abyss would gape beneath you, as it gaped for Boone now, and suddenly, without so much as a breath of explanation, you were gone. Gone to hell or worse, professions of love and all.

His outlook hadn't always been so pessimistic. There'd been a time – not all that long ago – when he'd felt the burden of his mental anguish lifting. There'd been fewer psychotic episodes, fewer days when he felt like slitting his wrists rather than enduring the hours till his next medication. There'd seemed to be a chance for happiness.

It was that prospect that had won the declaration of love from him; that: *'I'll never leave you,'* whispered in Lori's ear as they lay in the narrow bed he'd never dared hope would hold two. The words had not come in the throes of high passion. Their love life, like so much else between them, was fraught with problems. But where other women had given up on him, unforgiving of his failure, she'd persevered: told him there was plenty of time to get it right, all the time in the world.

I'm with you for as long as you want me to be, her patience had seemed to say.

Nobody had ever offered such a commitment; and he wanted to offer one in return. Those words: 'I'll never leave you'. Were it.

The memory of them, and of her skin almost luminous in the murk of his room, and of the sound of her breathing when she finally fell asleep beside him – all of it still had the power to catch his heart, and squeeze it till it hurt.

He longed to be free of both the memory and the words, now that circumstance had taken any hope of their fulfilment out of his hands. But they wouldn't be forgotten. They lingered on to torment him with his frailty. His meagre comfort was that *she* – knowing what she must now know about him, – would be working to erase her memory; and that with time she'd succeed. He only hoped she'd understand his ignorance of himself when he'd voiced that promise. He'd never have risked this pain if he'd doubted health was finally within his grasp.

Dream on!

Decker had brought an abrupt end to those delusions, the day he'd locked the office door, drawn the blinds on the Alberta spring sunshine, and said, in a voice barely louder than a whisper:

'Boone. I think we're in terrible trouble, you and I.'

He was trembling, Boone saw, a fact not easily concealed in a body so big. Decker had the physique of a man who sweated out the day's *angst* in a gym. Even his tailored suits, always charcoal, couldn't tame his bulk. It had made Boone edgy at the start of their work together; he'd felt intimidated by the doctor's physical and mental authority. Now it was the fallibility of that strength he feared. Decker was a Rock; he was Reason; he was Calm. This anxiety ran counter to all he knew about the man.

'What's wrong?' Boone asked.

'Sit, will you? Sit and I'll tell you.'

Boone did as he was told. In this office, Decker was lord. The doctor leaned back in the leather chair and inhaled through his nose, his mouth sealed in a downward curve.

'Tell me . . .' Boone said.

'Where to start.'

'Anywhere.'

'I thought you were getting better,' Decker said. 'I really did. We *both* did.'

'I still am,' Boone said.

Decker made a small shake of his head. He was a man of considerable intellect, but little of it showed on his tightly packed features, except perhaps in his eyes, which at the moment were not watching the patient, but the table between them.

'You've started to talk in your sessions,' Decker said, 'about crimes you think you've committed. Do you remember any of that?'

'You know I don't.' The trances Decker put him in were too profound: 'I only remember when you play the tape back.'

'I won't be playing any of these,' Decker said. 'I wiped them.'

'Why?'

'Because . . . I'm afraid, Boone. For you.' He paused. 'Maybe for both of us.'

The crack in the Rock was opening and there was nothing Decker could do to conceal it.

'What *are* these crimes?' Boone asked, his words tentative.

'Murders. You talk about them obsessively. At first I thought they were dream crimes. You always had a violent streak in you.'

'And now?'

'Now I'm afraid you may have actually committed them.'

There was a long silence, while Boone studied

17

Decker, more in puzzlement than anger. The blinds had not been pulled all the way down. A slice of sunlight fell across him, and on to the table between them. On the glass surface was a bottle of still water, two tumblers, and a large envelope. Decker leaned forward and picked it up.

'What I'm doing now is probably a crime in itself,' he told Boone. 'Patient confidentiality is one thing; protecting a killer is another. But part of me is still hoping to God it isn't true. I want to believe I've succeeded. *We've* succeeded. Together. I want to believe you're well.'

'I *am* well.'

In lieu of reply Decker tore open the envelope.

'I'd like you to look at these for me,' he said, sliding his hand inside and bringing a sheaf of photographs out to meet the light.

'I warn you, they're not pleasant.'

He laid them on his reflection, turned for Boone's perusal. His warning had been well advised. The picture on the top of the pile was like a physical assault. Faced with it a fear rose in him he'd not felt since being in Decker's care: that the image might *possess* him. He'd built walls against that superstition, brick by brick, but they shook now, and threatened to fall.

'It's just a picture.'

'That's right,' Decker replied. 'It's just a picture. What do you see?'

'A dead man.'

'A murdered man.'

'Yes. A murdered man.'

Not simply murdered: butchered. The life slashed from him in a fury of slices and stabs, his blood flung on the blade that had taken out his neck, taken off his face, on to the wall behind him. He wore only his shorts, so the wounds on his body could be easily counted, despite the blood. Boone did just that now, to keep the horror from overcoming him. Even here, in this room where the doctor had chiselled another self from the block of his patient's condition, Boone had never choked on terror as he choked now. He tasted his breakfast in the back of his throat, or the meal the night before, rising from his bowels against nature. Shit in his mouth, like the dirt of this deed.

Count the wounds, he told himself; pretend they're beads on an abacus. Three, four, five in the abdomen and chest: one in particular ragged, more like a tear than a wound, gaping so wide the man's innards poked out. On the shoulder, two more. And then the face, unmade with cuts. So many their numbers could not be calculated, even by the most detached of observers. They left the victim beyond recognition: eyes dug out, lips slit off, nose in ribbons.

'Enough?' Decker said, as if the question needed asking.

'Yes.'

'There's a lot more to see.'

He uncovered the second, laying the first beside the pile. This one was of a woman, sprawled on a sofa, her upper body and her lower twisted in a fashion life would have forbidden. Though she was presumably not a relation of the first victim the butcher had created a vile resemblance. Here was the same liplessness, the same eyelessness. Born from different parents, they were siblings in death, destroyed by the same hand.

And am I their father? Boone found himself thinking.

'*No*,' was his gut's response. 'I didn't do this.'

But two things prevented him from voicing his denial. First, he knew that Decker would not be endangering his patient's equilibrium this way unless he had good reason for it. Second, denial was valueless when both of them knew how easily Boone's mind had deceived itself in the past. If he was responsible for these atrocities there was no certainty he'd know it.

Instead he kept his silence, not daring to look up at Decker for fear he'd see the Rock shattered.

'Another?' Decker said.

'If we must.'

'We must.'

He uncovered a third photograph, and a fourth, laying the pictures out on the table like cards at a Tarot reading, except that every one was Death. In the kitchen, lying at the open door of the refrigerator. In the bedroom, beside the lamp and the alarm. At the top of the stairs; at the window. The victims were of every age and colour; men, women and children. Whatever fiend was responsible he cared to make no distinction. He simply erased life wherever he found it. Not quickly; not efficiently. The rooms in which these people had died bore plain testament to how the killer, in his humour, had toyed with them. Furniture had been overturned as they stumbled to avoid the *coup de grace*, their blood prints left on walls and paintwork. One had lost his fingers to the blade, snatching at it perhaps; most had lost their eyes. But none had escaped, however brave their resistance. They'd all fallen at last, tangled in their underwear, or seeking refuge behind a curtain. Fallen sobbing; fallen retching.

There were eleven photographs in all. Every one was different – rooms large and small, victims naked and dressed. But each also the same: all pictures of a madness performed, taken with the actor already departed.

God almighty, was *he* that man?

Not having an answer for himself, he asked the question of the Rock, speaking without looking up from the shining cards.

'Did I do this?' he said.

He heard Decker sigh, but there was no answer forthcoming, so he chanced a glance at his accuser. As the photographs had been laid out before him he'd felt the man's scrutiny like a crawling ache in his scalp. But now he once more found that gaze averted.

'Please tell me,' he said. 'Did I do this?'

Decker wiped the moist purses of skin beneath his grey eyes. He was not trembling any longer.

'I hope not,' he said.

The response seemed ludicrously mild. This was not some minor infringement of the law they were debating. It was death times eleven; and how many more might there be; out of sight, out of mind?

'Tell me what I talked about,' he said. 'Tell me the words – '

'It was ramblings mostly.'

'So what makes you think I'm responsible? You must have reasons.'

'It took time,' Decker said, 'for me to piece the whole thing together.' He looked down at the mortuary on the table, aligning a photograph that was a little askew with his middle finger.

'I have to make a quarterly report on our progress. You know that. So I play all the tapes of our previous sessions sequentially, to get some sense of how we're doing . . .' He spoke slowly; wearily. '. . . and I noticed the same phrases coming up in your responses. Buried most of the time, in other material, but *there*. It was as if you were confessing to something; but something so abhorrent to you even in a trance state you couldn't quite bring yourself to say it. Instead it was coming out in this . . . *code*.'

Boone knew codes. He'd heard them everywhere during the bad times. Messages from the imagined enemy in the noise between stations on the radio; or in the murmur of traffic before dawn. That he might have learned the art himself came as no surprise.

'I made a few casual enquiries,' Decker continued, 'amongst police officers I've treated. Nothing specific. And they told me about the killings. I'd heard some of the details, of course, from the press. Seems they've been going on for two and a half years. Several here in Calgary; the rest within an hour's drive. The work of one man.'

'Me.'

'I don't know,' Decker said, finally looking up at Boone. 'If I was certain, I'd have reported it all – '

'But you're not.'

'I don't want to believe this anymore than you do. It doesn't cover me in glory if this turns out to be true.' There was anger in him, not well concealed. 'That's why I waited. Hoping you'd be with me when the next one happened.'

'You mean some of these people died while you knew?'

'Yes,' Decker said flatly.

'Jesus!'

The thought propelled Boone from the chair, his leg catching the table. The murder scenes flew.

'Keep your voice down,' Decker demanded.

'People died, and you *waited*?'

'I took that risk for *you*, Boone. You'll respect that.'

Boone turned from the man. There was a chill of sweat on his spine.

'Sit down,' said Decker. 'Please sit down and tell me what these photographs mean to you.'

Involuntarily Boone had put his hand over the lower half of his face. He knew from Decker's instruction what that particular piece of body language signified. His mind was using his body to muffle some disclosure; or silence it completely.

'Boone. I need answers.'

'They mean nothing,' Boone said, not turning.

'At all?'

'At all.'

'Look at them again.'

'No,' Boone insisted. 'I can't.'

He heard the doctor inhale, and half expected a demand that he face the horrors afresh. But instead Decker's tone was placatory.

'It's all right, Aaron,' he said. 'It's all right. I'll put them away.'

Boone pressed the heels of his hands against his closed eyes. His sockets were hot, and wet.

'They're gone, Aaron,' Decker said.

'No, they're not.'

They were with him still, perfectly remembered. Eleven rooms and eleven bodies, fixed in his mind's eye, beyond exorcism. The wall Decker had taken five years to build had been brought down in as many minutes, and by its architect. Boone was at the mercy of his madness again. He heard it whine in his head, coming from eleven slit windpipes from eleven punctured bellies. Breath and bowel gas, singing the old mad songs.

Why had his defences tumbled so easily, after so much labour? His eyes knew the answer, spilling tears to admit what his tongue couldn't. He was guilty. Why else? Hands he was even now wiping dry on his trousers had tortured and slaughtered. If he pretended otherwise he'd only tempt them to further crime. Better that he confessed, though he remembered nothing, than offer them another unguarded moment.

He turned and faced Decker. The photographs had been gathered up and laid face down on the table.

'You remember something?' the doctor said, reading the change on Boone's face.

'Yes,' he replied.

'What?'

'I did it,' Boone said simply. 'I did it all.'

II

Academy

1

Decker was the most benign prosecutor any accused man could ask for. The hours he spent with Boone after that first day were filled with carefully plied questions as – murder by murder – they examined together the evidence for Boone's secret life. Despite the patient's insistence that the crimes were his, Decker counselled caution. Admissions of culpability were not hard evidence. They had to be certain that confession wasn't simply Boone's self-destructive tendencies at work, admitting to the crime out of hunger for the punishment.

Boone was in no position to argue. Decker knew him better than he knew himself. Nor had he forgotten Decker's observation that if the worst was proved true, the doctor's reputation as a healer would be thrown to the dogs: they could neither of them afford to be wrong. The only way to be sure was to run through the details of the killings – dates, names and locations – in the hope that Boone would be prompted into remembering. Or else that they'd discover a killing that had occurred when he was indisputably in the company of others.

The only part of the process Boone balked at was re-examining the photographs. He resisted Decker's gentle pressure for forty-eight hours, only conceding when the gentility faltered and Decker rounded on him, accusing him of cowardice and deceit. Was all this just a game, Decker demanded; an exercise in self-mortification that would end with them both none the wiser? If so, Boone could get the hell out of his office now and bleed on somebody else's time.

Boone agreed to study the photographs.

There was nothing in them that jogged his memory. Much of the detail of the rooms had been washed out by the flash of the camera; what remained was commonplace. The only sight that might have won a response from him – the faces of the victims – had been erased by the killer, hacked beyond recognition; the most expert of morticians would not be able to piece those shattered façades together again. So it was all down to the petty details of where Boone had been on this night or that; with whom; doing what. He had never kept a diary so verifying the facts was difficult, but most of the time – barring the hours he spent with Lori or Decker, none of which seemed to coincide with murder nights – he was alone, and without alibi. By the end of the fourth day the case against him began to look very persuasive.

'Enough,' he told Decker. 'We've done enough.'

'I'd like to go over it all one more time.'

'What's the use?' Boone said. 'I want to get it all finished with.'

In the past days – and nights – many of the old symptoms, the signs of the sickness he thought he'd been so close to throwing off forever, had returned. He could sleep for no more than minutes at a time before appalling visions threw him into befuddled wakefulness; he couldn't eat properly; he was trembling from his gut outwards, every minute of the day. He wanted an end to this; wanted to spill the story and be punished.

'Give me a little more time,' Decker said. 'If we go to the police now they'll take you out of my hands. They probably won't even allow me access to you. You'll be alone.'

'I already am,' Boone replied. Since he'd first seen

26

the photographs he'd cut himself off from every contact, even with Lori, fearing his capacity to do harm.

'I'm a monster,' he said. 'We both of us know that.
We've got all the evidence we need.'

'It's not just a question of evidence.'

'What then?'

Decker leaned against the window frame, his bulk a
burden to him of late.

'I don't understand you, Boone,' he said.

Boone's gaze moved off from man to sky. There was
a wind from the south-east today; scraps of cloud
hurried before it. A good life, Boone thought, to be up
there, lighter than air. Here everything was heavy;
flesh and guilt cracking your spine.

'I've spent four years trying to understand your
illness, hoping I could cure it. And I thought I was
succeeding. Thought there was a chance it would all
come clear . . .'

He fell silent, in the pit of his failure. Boone was not
so immersed in his own agonies he couldn't see how
profoundly the man suffered. But he could do nothing
to mitigate that hurt. He just watched the clouds pass,
up there in the light, and knew there were only dark
times ahead.

'When the police take you . . .' Decker murmured, 'it
won't just be you who's alone, Boone. I'll be alone too.
You'll be somebody else's patient: some criminal psy-
chologist. I won't have access to you any longer. That's
why I'm asking . . . Give me a little more time. Let me
understand as much as I can before it's over between
us.'

He's talking like a lover, Boone vaguely thought;
like what's between us is his life.

'I know you're in pain;' Decker went on. 'So I've got
medication for you. Pills, to keep the worst of it at bay.
Just till we've finished – '

'I don't trust myself,' Boone said. 'I could hurt
somebody.'

27

'You won't,' Decker replied, with welcome certainty. 'The drugs'll keep you subdued through the night. The rest of the time you'll be with me. You'll be safe with me.'

'How much longer do you want?'

'A few days, at the most. That's not so much to ask, is it? I need to know why we failed.'

The thought of re-treading that bloodied ground was abhorrent, but there was a debt here to be paid. With Decker's help he'd had a glimpse of new possibilities; he owed the doctor the chance to snatch something from the ruins of that vision.

'Make it quick,' he said.

'Thank you,' Decker said. 'This means a lot to me.'

'And I'll need the pills.'

2

The pills he had. Decker made sure of that. Pills so strong he wasn't sure he could have named himself correctly once he'd taken them. Pills that made sleep easy, and waking a visit to a half-life he was happy to escape from again. Pills that, within twenty-four hours, he was addicted to.

Decker's word was good. When he asked for more they were supplied, and under their soporific influence they went back to the business of the evidence, as the doctor went over, and over again, the details of Boone's crimes, in the hope of comprehending them. But nothing came clear. All Boone's increasingly passive mind could recover from these sessions were slurred images of doors he'd slipped through and stairs he'd climbed in the performance of murder. He was less and less aware of Decker, still fighting to salvage something of worth from his patient's closed mind. All Boone knew now was sleep, and guilt, and the hope, increasingly cherished, of an end to both.

Only Lori, or rather memories of her, pricked the drugs' regime. He could hear her voice sometimes, in his inner ear, clear as a bell, repeating words she'd spoken to him in some casual conversation, which he was dredging up from the past. There was nothing of consequence in these phrases; they were perhaps associated with a look he'd treasured, or a touch. Now he could remember neither look nor touch – the drugs had removed so much of his capacity to *imagine*. All he was left with were these dislocated lines, distressing him not simply because they were spoken as if by somebody at his shoulder, but because they had no context that he could recall. And worse than either, their sound reminded him of the woman he'd loved and would not see again, unless across a courtroom. A woman to whom he had made a promise he'd broken within weeks of his making it. In his wretchedness, his thoughts barely cogent, that broken promise was as monstrous as the crimes in the photographs. It fitted him for Hell.

Or death. Better death. He was not entirely sure how long had passed since he'd done the deal with Decker exchanging this stupor for a few more days of investigation, but he was certain he had kept his side of the bargain. He was talked out. There was nothing left to say, nor hear. All that remained was to take himself to the law, and confess his crimes, or to do what the state no longer had the power to do, and kill the monster.

He didn't dare alert Decker to this plan; he knew the doctor would do all in his power to prevent his patient's suicide. So he went on playing the quiescent subject one day more. Then, promising Decker he'd be at the office the following morning, he returned home and prepared to kill himself.

There was another letter from Lori awaiting him, the fourth since he'd absented himself, demanding to know what was wrong. He read it as best his befuddled thoughts would allow, and attempted a reply, but couldn't make sense of the words he was trying to write. Instead, pocketing the appeal she'd sent to him, he went out into the dusk to look for death.

3

The truck he threw himself in front of was unkind. It knocked the breath from him but not the life. Bruised, and bleeding from scrapes and cuts, he was scooped up and taken to hospital. Later, he'd come to understand how all of this was in the scheme of things, and that he'd been denied his death beneath the truck wheels for a purpose. But sitting in the hospital, waiting in a white room till people worse off than he had been attended to, all he could do was curse his bad fortune. Other lives he could take with terrible ease; his own resisted him. Even in this he was divided against himself.

But that room – though he didn't know it when he was ushered in – held a promise its plain walls belied. In it he'd hear a name that would with time make a new man of him. At its call he'd go like the monster he was, by night, and meet with the miraculous.

That name was Midian.

It and he had much in common, not least that they shared the power to make promises. But while his avowals of eternal love had proved hollow in a matter of weeks, Midian made promises – midnight, like his own, deepest midnight – that even death could not break.

III

The Rhapsodist

In the years of his illness, in and out of mental wards and hospices, Boone had met very few fellow sufferers who didn't cleave to some talisman, some sign or keepsake to stand guard at the gates of their heads and hearts. He'd learned quickly not to despise such charms. *Whatever gets you through the night* was an axiom he understood from hard experience. Most of these safeguards against chaos were personal to those that wielded them. Trinkets, keys, books and photographs: mementoes of good times treasured as defence against the bad. But some belonged to the collective mind. They were words he would hear more than once: nonsense rhymes whose rhythm kept the pain at bay; names of Gods.

Amongst them, Midian.

He'd heard the name of that place spoken maybe half a dozen times by people he'd met on the way through, usually those whose strength was all burned up. When they called on Midian it was as a place of refuge; a place to be carried away to. And more: a place where whatever sins they'd committed – real or imagined – would be forgiven them. Boone didn't know the origins of this mythology; nor had he ever been interested enough to enquire. He had not been in need of forgiveness, or so he thought. Now he knew better. He had plenty to seek cleansing of; obscenities his mind had kept from him until Decker had brought them to light, which no agency he knew could lift from him. He had joined another class of creature.

Midian called.

Locked up in his misery, he'd not been aware that someone else now shared the white room with him until he heard the rasping voice.

'Midian . . .'

He thought at first it was another voice from the past, like Lori's. But when it came again it was not at his shoulder, as hers had been, but from across the room. He opened his eyes, the left lid gummy with blood from a cut on his temple, and looked towards the speaker. Another of the night's walking wounded, apparently, brought in for mending and left to fend for himself until some patchwork could be done. He was sitting in the corner of the room furthest from the door, on which his wild eyes were fixed as though at any moment his saviour would step into view. It was virtually impossible to guess anything of his age or true appearance: dirt and caked blood concealed both. I must look as bad or worse, Boone thought. He didn't much mind; people were always staring at him. In their present state he and the man in the corner were the kind folks crossed the street to avoid.

But whereas he, in his jeans and his scuffed boots and black teeshirt, was just another nobody, there were some signs about the other man that marked him out. The long coat he wore had a monkish severity to it; his grey hair pulled back tight on his scalp, hung to the middle of his back in a plaited pony tail. There was jewellery at his neck, almost hidden by his high collar, and on his thumbs two artificial nails that looked to be silver, curled into hooks.

Finally, there was that name, rising from the man again.

'. . . Will you take me?' he asked softly. 'Take me to Midian?'

His eyes had not left the door for an instant. It seemed he was oblivious of Boone, until without warning, he turned his wounded head and spat across the room. The blood-marbled phlegm hit the floor at Boone's feet.

'Get the fuck out of here!' he said. 'You're keeping them from me. They won't come while you're here.'

Boone was too weary to argue, and too bruised to get up. He let the man rant.

'Get out!' he said again. 'They won't show themselves to the likes of you. Don't you see that?'

Boone put his head back and tried to keep the man's pain from invading him.

'Shit!' the other said. 'I've missed them. *I've missed them!*'

He stood up and crossed to the window. Outside there was solid darkness.

'They passed by,' he murmured, suddenly plaintive. The next moment he was a yard from Boone, grinning through the dirt.

'Got anything for the pain?' he wanted to know.

'The nurse gave me something,' Boone replied.

The man spat again; not at Boone this time, but at the floor.

'*Drink*, man . . .' he said. 'Have you got a drink?'

'No.'

The grin evaporated instantly, and the face began to crumple up as tears overtook him. He turned away from Boone, sobbing, his litany beginning again.

'Why won't they take me? Why won't they come for me?'

'Maybe they'll come later,' Boone said. 'When I've gone.'

The man looked back at him.

'What do you know?' he said.

Very little was the answer; but Boone kept that fact to himself. There were enough fragments of Midian's mythology in his head to have him eager for more. Wasn't it a place where those who had run out of refuges could find a home? And wasn't that *his* condition now? He had no source of comfort left. Not

33

Decker, not Lori, not even Death. Even though Midian was just another talisman, he wanted to hear its story recited.

'Tell me,' he said.

'I asked you what you know,' the other man replied, catching the flesh beneath his unshaven chin with the hook of his left hand.

'I know it takes away the pain,' Boone replied.

'And?'

'I know it turns nobody away.'

'Not true,' came the response.

'No?'

'If it turned nobody away you think I wouldn't be there already? You think it wouldn't be the biggest city on earth? Of course it turns people away . . .'

The man's tear-brightened eyes were fixed on Boone. Does he realize I know nothing? Boone wondered. It seemed not. The man talked on, content to debate the secret. Or more particularly, his fear of it.

'I don't go because I may not be worthy,' he said. 'And they don't forgive that easily. They don't forgive at all. You know what they do . . . to those who aren't worthy?'

Boone was less interested in Midian's rites of passage than in the man's certainty that it existed at all. He didn't speak of Midian as a lunatic's Shangri-la, but as a place to be found, and entered, and made peace with.

'Do you know how to get there?' he asked.

The man looked away. As he broke eye-contact a surge of panic rose in Boone: fearing that the bastard was going to keep the rest of the story to himself.

'I need to know,' Boone said.

The other man looked up again.

'I can see that,' he said, and there was a twist in his voice that suggested the spectacle of Boone's despair entertained him.

'It's north-west of Athabasca,' the man replied.

'Yes?'

34

'That's what I heard.'

'That's empty country,' Boone replied. 'You could wander forever, less you've got a map.'

'Midian's on no map,' the man said. 'You look east of Peace River; near Shere Neck; north of Dwyer.'

There was no taint of doubt in this recitation of directions. He believed in Midian's existence as much as, perhaps more than, the four walls he was bound by.

'What's your name?' Boone asked.

The question seemed to flummox him. It had been a long time since anyone had cared to ask him his name.

'Narcisse,' he said finally. 'You?'

'Aaron Boone. Nobody ever calls me Aaron. Only Boone.'

'Aaron,' said the other. 'Where d'you hear about Midian?'

'Same place you did,' Boone said. 'Same place anyone hears. From others. People in pain.'

'Monsters,' said Narcisse.

Boone hadn't thought of them as such, but perhaps to dispassionate eyes they were; the ranters and the weepers, unable to keep their nightmares under lock and key.

'They're the only ones welcome in Midian,' Narcisse explained. 'If you're not a beast, you're a victim. That's true, isn't it? You can only be one or the other. That's why I don't dare go unescorted. I wait for friends to come for me.'

'People who went already?'

'That's right,' Narcisse said. 'Some of them alive. Some of them who died, and went after.'

Boone wasn't certain he was hearing this story correctly.

'Went *after*?' he said.

'Don't you have anything for the pain, man?' Narcisse said, his tone veering again, this time to the wheedling.

'I've got some pills,' Boone said, remembering the dregs of Decker's supply. 'Do you want those?'

'Anything you got.'

Boone was content to be relieved of them. They'd kept his head in chains, driving him to the point where he didn't care if he lived or died. Now he did. He had a place to go, where he might find someone at last who understood the horrors he was enduring. He would not need the pills to get to Midian. He'd need strength, and the will to be forgiven. The latter he had. The former his wounded body would have to find.

'Where are they?' said Narcisse, appetite igniting his features.

Boone's leather jacket had been peeled from his back when he'd first been admitted, for a cursory examination of the damage he'd done himself. It hung on the back of a chair, a twice discarded skin. He plunged his hand into the inside pocket but found to his shock that the familiar bottle was not there.

'Someone's been through my jacket.'

He rummaged through the rest of the pockets. All of them were empty. Lori's notes, his wallet, the pills: all gone. It took him seconds only to realize why they'd want evidence of who he was and the consequence of that. He'd attempted suicide; no doubt they thought him prepared to do the same again. In his wallet was Decker's address. The doctor was probably already on his way, to collect his erring patient and deliver him to the police. Once in the hands of the law he'd never see Midian.

'You said there were *pills*!' Narcisse yelled.

'They've been taken!'

Narcisse snatched the jacket from Boone's hands, and began to tear at it.

'*Where*?' he yelled. '*Where*?'

His face was once more crumpling up as he realized he was not going to get a fix of peace. He dropped the

36

jacket and backed away from Boone, his tears beginning again, but sliding down his face to meet a broad smile.

'I know what you're doing,' he said, pointing at Boone. Laughter and sobs were coming in equal measure. 'Midian sent you. To see if I'm worthy. You came to see if I was one of you or not!'

He offered Boone no chance to contradict, his elation spiralling into hysteria.

'I'm sitting here praying for someone to come; *begging*; and you're here all the time, watching me shit myself. Watching me *shit*!'

He laughed hard. Then, deadly serious:

'I never doubted. Never once. I always knew somebody'd come. But I was expecting a face I recognized. Marvin maybe. I should have known they'd send someone new. Stands to reason. And you *saw*, right? You *heard*. I'm not ashamed. They never made me ashamed. You ask anyone. They tried. Over and over. They got in my fucking head and tried to take me apart, tried to take the Wild Ones out of me. But I held on. I knew you'd come sooner or later, and I wanted to be ready. That's why I wear these.'

He thrust his thumbs up in front of his face. 'So I could show you.'

He turned his head to right and left.

'Want to see?' he said.

He needed no reply. His hands were already up to either side of his face, the hooks touching the skin at the base of each ear. Boone watched, words of denial or appeal redundant. This was a moment Narcisse had rehearsed countless times; he was not about to be denied it. There was no sound as the hooks, razor sharp, slit his skin, but blood began to flow instantly, down his neck and arms. The expression on his face didn't change, it merely intensified: a mask in which comic muse and tragic were united. Then, fingers spread to either side of his face, he steadily drew the razor hooks down the line of his jaw. He had a surgeon's precision. The wounds opened with perfect symmetry, until the twin hooks met at his chin.

Only then did he drop one hand to his side, blood dripping from hook and wrist, the other moving across his face to seek the flap of skin his work had opened.

'You want to see?' he said again.

Boone murmured:

'Don't.'

It went unheard. With a sharp, upward jerk Narcisse detached the mask of skin from the muscle beneath, and began to tear, uncovering his true face.

From behind him, Boone heard somebody scream. The door had been opened, and one of the nursing staff stood on the threshold. He saw from the corner of his eye: her face whiter than her uniform, her mouth open wide; and beyond her the corridor, and freedom. But he couldn't bring himself to look away from Narcisse; not while the blood filling the air between them kept the revelation from view. He wanted to see the man's secret face: the Wild One beneath the skin that made him fit for Midian's ease. The red rain was dispersing. The air began to clear. He saw the face now, a little, but couldn't make sense of its complexity. Was that a beast's anatomy that knotted up and snarled in front of him, or human tissue agonized by self-mutilation? A moment more, and he'd know —

Then, someone had hold of him, seizing his arms and dragging him towards the door. He glimpsed Narcisse raising the weapons of his hands to keep his saviours at bay, then the uniforms were upon him, and he was eclipsed. In the rush of the moment Boone took his chance. He pushed the nurse from him, snatched up his leather jacket, and ran for the unguarded door. His bruised body was not prepared for violent action. He stumbled, nausea and darting pains in his bruised limbs vying for the honour of bringing him to his knees, but the sight of Narcisse surrounded and tethered was enough to give him strength. He was away down the hall before anyone had a chance to come after him.

As he headed for the door to the night he heard Narcisse's voice raised in protest; a howl of rage that was pitifully human.

IV

Necropolis

1

Though the distance from Calgary to Athabasca was little more than three hundred miles the journey took a traveller to the borders of another world. North of here the highways were few, and the inhabitants fewer still, as the rich prairie lands of the province steadily gave way to forest, marshland and wilderness. It also marked the limits of Boone's experience. A short stint as a truck driver, in his early twenties, had taken him as far as Bonnyville to the south-east, Barrhead to the south-west and Athabasca itself. But the territory beyond was unknown to him except as names on a map. Or more correctly, as an absence of names. There were great stretches of land here that were dotted only with small farming settlements; one of which bore the name Narcisse had used: Shere Neck.

The map which carried this information he found, along with enough change to buy himself a bottle of brandy, in five minutes of theft on the outskirts of Calgary. He rifled three vehicles left in an underground parking facility and was away, mapped and monied, before the source of the car alarms had been traced by security.

The rain washed his face; his bloodied tee-shirt he dumped, happy to have his beloved jacket next to his skin. Then he found himself a ride to Edmonton, and another which took him through Athabasca to High Prairie. It was easy.

2

Easy? To go in search of a place he'd only heard rumour of amongst lunatics? Perhaps not easy. But it was necessary; even inevitable. From the moment the truck he'd chosen to die beneath had cast him aside this journey had been beckoning. Perhaps from long before that, only he'd never seen the invitation. The sense he had of its *rightness* might almost have made a fatalist of him. If Midian existed, and was willing to embrace him, then he was travelling to a place where he would finally find some self-comprehension and peace. If not – if it existed only as a talisman for the frightened and the lost – then that too was *right*, and he would meet whatever extinction awaited him searching for a nowhere. Better that than the pills, better that than Decker's fruitless pursuit of rhymes and reasons.

The doctor's quest to root out the monster in Boone had been bound to fail. That much was clear as the skies overhead. Boone the man and Boone the monster could not be divided. They were one; they travelled the same road in the same mind and body. And whatever lay at the end of that road, death or glory, would be the fate of both.

3

East of Peace River, Narcisse had said, near the town of Shere Neck; north of Dwyer.

He had to sleep rough in High Prairie, until the following morning when he found a ride to Peace River. The driver was a woman in her late fifties, proud of the region she'd known since childhood and happy to give him a quick geography lesson. He made no mention of Midian, but Dwyer and Shere Neck she knew – the latter a town of five thousand souls away to the east of Highway 67. He'd have saved himself a good two hundred miles if he'd not travelled as far as High Prairie, he was told, but taken himself north earlier. No matter, she said; she knew a place in Peace River where the farmers stopped off to eat before heading back to their homesteads. He'd find a ride there, to take him where he wanted to go.

Got people there? she asked. He said he had.

It was close to dusk by the time the last of his rides dropped him a mile or so shy of Dwyer. He watched the truck take a gravel road off into the deepening blue, then began to walk the short distance to the town. A night of sleeping rough, and travelling in farm vehicles on roads that had seen better days, had taken its toll on his already battered system. It took him an hour to come within sight of the outskirts of Dwyer, by which time night had fallen completely. Fate was once again on his side. Without the darkness he might not have seen the lights flashing ahead; not in welcome but in warning.

The police were here before him; three or four cars he judged. It was possible they were in pursuit of someone else entirely but he doubted it. More likely Narcisse, lost to himself, had told the law what he'd told Boone. In which case this was a reception committee. They were probably already searching for him, house to house. And if here, in Shere Neck too. He was expected.

Thankful for the cover of the night, he made his way off the road and into the middle of a rape seed field, where he could lie and think through his next move. There was certainly no wisdom in trying to go into

Dwyer. Better he set off for Midian now, putting his hunger and weariness aside and trusting to the stars and his instinct to give him directions.

He got up, smelling of earth, and headed off in what he judged to be a northerly direction. He knew very well he might miss his destination by miles with such rough bearings to travel by, or just as easily fail to see it in the darkness. No matter; he had no other choice, which was a kind of comfort to him.

In his five minute spree as thief he'd not found a watch to steal, so the only sense he had of time passing was the slow progression of the constellations overhead. The air became cold, then bitter, but he kept up his painful pace, avoiding the roads wherever possible, though they would have been easier to walk than the ploughed and seeded ground. This caution proved well founded at one point when two police vehicles, bookending a black limousine, slid all but silently down a road he had a minute ago crossed. He had no evidence whatsoever for the feeling that seized him as the cars passed by, but he sensed more than strongly that the limo's passenger was Decker, the good doctor, still in pursuit of *understanding*.

4

Then, Midian.

Out of nowhere, Midian. One moment the night ahead was featureless darkness, the next there was a cluster of buildings on the horizon, their painted walls glimmering grey blue in the starlight. Boone stood for several minutes and studied the scene. There was no light burning in any window, or on any porch. By now it was surely well after midnight, and the men and women of the town, with work to rise to the following morning, would be in bed. But not one single light? That struck him as strange. Small Midian might be –

forgotten by map-makers and signpost writers alike – but did it not lay claim to one insomniac?; or a child who needed the comfort of a lamp burning through the night hours? More probably they were in wait for him – Decker and the law – concealed in the shadows until he was foolish enough to step into the trap. The simplest solution would be to turn tail and leave them to their vigil, but he had little enough energy left. If he retreated now how long would he have to wait before attempting a return, every hour making recognition and a rest more likely?

He decided to skirt the edge of the town and get some sense of the lie of the land. If he could find no evidence of a police presence then he'd enter, and take the consequences. He hadn't come all this way to turn back.

Midian revealed nothing of itself as he moved around its south eastern flank, except perhaps its emptiness. Not only could he see no sign of police vehicles in the streets, or secreted between the houses, he could see no automobile of any kind: no truck, no farm vehicle. He began to wonder if the town was one of those religious communities he'd read of, whose dogmas denied them electricity or the combustion engine.

But as he climbed toward the spine of a small hill on the summit of which Midian stood, a second and plainer explanation occurred. There was nobody *in* Midian. The thought stopped him in his tracks. He stared across at the houses, searching for some evidence of decay, but he could see none. The roofs were intact, as far as he could make out, there were no buildings that appeared on the verge of collapse. Yet, with the night so quiet he could hear the whoosh of falling stars overhead, he could hear *nothing* from the town. If somebody in Midian had moaned in their sleep the night would have brought the sound his way, but there was only silence.

Midian was a ghost town.

Never in his life had he felt such desolation. He stood like a dog returned home to find its masters gone, not knowing what his life now meant or would ever mean again.

It took him several minutes to uproot himself and continue his circuit of the town. Twenty yards on from where he'd stood, however, the height of the hill gave him sight of a scene more mysterious even than the vacant Midian.

On the far side of the town lay a cemetery. His vantage point gave him an uninterrupted view of it, despite the high walls that bounded the place. Presumably it had been built to serve the entire region, for it was massively larger than a town Midian's size could ever have required. Many of the mausoleums were of impressive scale, that much was clear even from a distance, the layout of avenues, trees and tombs lending the cemetery the appearance of a small city.

Boone began down the slope of the hill towards it, his route still taking him well clear of the town itself. After the adrenalin rush of finding and approaching Midian he felt his reserves of strength failing fast; the pain and exhaustion that expectation had numbed now returned with a vengeance. It could not be long, he knew, before his muscles gave out completely and he collapsed. Perhaps behind the cemetery's walls he'd be able to find a niche to conceal himself from his pursuers and rest his bones.

There were two means of access. A small gate in the side wall, and large double gates that faced towards the town. He chose the former. It was latched but not locked. He gently pushed it open, and stepped inside. The impression he'd had from the hill, of the cemetery as city, was here confirmed, the mausoleums rising house-high around him. Their scale, and, now that he could study them close up, their elaboration, puzzled him. What great families had occupied the town or its surrounds, moneyed enough to bury their dead in such

46

splendour? The small communities of the prairie clung to the land as their sustenance, but it seldom made them rich; and on the few occasions when it did, with oil or gold, never in such numbers. Yet here were magnificent tombs, avenue upon avenue of them, built in all manner of styles from the classical to the baroque, and marked – though he was not certain his fatigued senses were telling him the truth – with motifs from warring theologies.

It was beyond him. He needed sleep. The tombs had been standing a century or more; the puzzle would still be there at dawn.

He found himself a bed out of sight between two graves and laid his head down. The spring growth of grass smelt sweet. He'd slept on far worse pillows, and would again.

V

A Different Ape

The sound of an animal woke him, its growls finding their way into floating dreams and calling him down to earth. He opened his eyes, and sat up. He couldn't see the dog, but he heard it still. Was it behind him?; the proximity of the tombs threw echoes back and forth. Very slowly, he turned to look over his shoulder. The darkness was deep, but did not quite conceal a large beast, its species impossible to read. There was no misinterpreting the threat from its throat however. It didn't like his scrutiny, to judge by the tenor of its growls.

'Hey, boy . . .' he said softly, 'it's OK.'

Ligaments creaking, he started to stand up, knowing that if he stayed on the ground the animal had easy access to his throat. His limbs had stiffened lying on the cold ground; he moved like a geriatric. Perhaps it was this that kept the animal from attacking, for it simply watched him, the crescents of the whites of its eyes – the only detail he could make out – widening as its gaze followed him into a standing position. Once on his feet he turned to face the creature, which began to move towards him. There was something in its advance that made him think it was wounded. He could hear it dragging one of its limbs behind it; its head low, its stride ragged.

He had words of comfort on his lips when an arm hooked about his neck, taking breath and words away.

'*Move and I gut you.*'

With the threat a second arm slid around his body,

49

the fingers digging into his belly with such force he had no doubt the man would make the threat good with his bare hand.

Boone took a shallow breath. Even that minor motion brought a tightening of the death grip at neck and abdomen. He felt blood run down his belly and into his jeans.

'Who the fuck are you?' the voice demanded.

He was a bad liar; the truth was safer.

'My name's Boone. I came here . . . I came to find Midian.'

Did the hold on his belly relax a little when he named his purpose?

'Why?' a second voice now demanded. It took Boone no more than a heart beat to realize that the voice had come from the shadows ahead of him, where the wounded beast stood. Indeed *from* the beast.

'My friend asked you a question,' said the voice at his ear. 'Answer him.'

Boone, disoriented by the attack, fixed his gaze again on whatever occupied the shadows and found himself doubting his eyes. The head of his questioner was not *solid*; it seemed almost to be *inhaling* its redundant features, their substance darkening and flowing through socket and nostrils and mouth back into itself.

All thought of his jeopardy disappeared; what seized him now was elation. *Narcisse had not lied*. Here was the transforming truth of that.

'I came to be amongst you – ' he said, answering the miracle's question. 'I came because I belong here.'

A question emerged from the soft laughter behind him.

'What does he look like, Peloquin?'

The thing had drunk its beast-face down. There were human features beneath, set on a body more reptile than mammal. That limb he dragged behind him was a tail; his wounded lope the gait of a low slung lizard.

That too was under review, as the tremor of change moved down its jutting spine.

'He looks like a Natural,' Peloquin replied. 'Not that that means much.'

Why could his attacker not see for himself, Boone wondered.

He glanced down at the hand on his belly. It had six fingers, tipped not with nails but with claws, now buried half an inch in his muscle.

'Don't kill me,' he said. 'I've come a long way to be here.'

'Hear that, Jackie?' said Peloquin, thrusting from the ground with its four legs to stand upright in front of Boone. His eyes, now level with Boone's, were bright blue. His breath was as hot as the blast from an open furnace.

'What kind of beast are you, then?' he wanted to know. The transformation was all but finished. The man beneath the monster was nothing remarkable. Forty, lean and sallow skinned.

'We should take him below,' said Jackie. 'Lylesburg will want to see him.'

'Probably,' said Peloquin. 'But I think we'd be wasting his time. This is a Natural, Jackie. I can smell 'em.'

'I've spilled blood . . .' Boone murmured. 'Killed eleven people.'

The blue eyes perused him. There was humour in them.

'I don't think so,' Peloquin said.

'It's not up to us,' Jackie put in. 'You can't judge him.'

'I've got eyes in my head, haven't I?' said Peloquin. 'I know a clean man when I see one.' He wagged his finger at Boone. 'You're not Nightbreed,' he said. 'You're meat. That's what you are. Meat for the beast.'

The humour drained from his expression as he spoke, and *hunger* replaced it.

'We can't do this,' the other creature protested.

'Who'll know?' said Peloquin. 'Who'll *ever* know?'

'We're breaking the law.'

Peloquin seemed indifferent to that. He bared his teeth, dark smoke oozing from the gaps and rising up over his face. Boone knew what was coming next. The man was breathing *out* what he'd moments ago inhaled: his lizard self. The proportions of his head were already altering subtly, as though his skull were dismantling and re-organizing himself beneath the hood of his flesh.

'You can't kill me!' he said. 'I belong with you.'

Was there a denial out of the smoke in front of him? If so it was lost in translation. There was to be no further debate. The beast intended to eat him –

He felt a sharp pain in his belly, and glanced down to see the clawed hand detach itself from his flesh. The hold at his neck slipped, and the creature behind him said:

'*Go.*'

He needed no persuasion. Before Peloquin could complete his reconstruction Boone slid from Jackie's embrace and ran. Any sense of direction he might have had was forfeited in the desperation of the moment, a desperation fuelled by a roar of fury from the hungry beast, and the sound – almost instant, it seemed – of pursuit.

The necropolis was a maze. He ran blindly, ducking to right and left wherever an opening offered itself, but he didn't need to look over his shoulder to know that the devourer was closing on him. He heard its accusation in his head as he ran:

You're not Nightbreed. You're meat. Meat for the beast.

The words were an agony profounder than the ache in his legs or his lungs. Even here, amongst the monsters of Midian he *did not belong.* And if not here, where? He was running, as prey had always run when the hungry were on their heels, but it was a race he couldn't win.

He stopped. He turned.

Peloquin was five or six yards behind him, his body still human, naked and vulnerable, but the head entirely bestial, the mouth wide and ringed with teeth like thorns. He too stopped running, perhaps expecting Boone to draw a weapon. When none was forthcoming, he raised his arms towards his victim. Behind him, Jackie stumbled into view, and Boone had his first glimpse of the man. Or was it *men*? There were two faces on his lumpen head, the features of both utterly distorted; eyes dislodged so they looked everywhere but ahead, mouths collided into a single gash, noses slits without bones. It was the face of a freak show foetus.

Jackie tried one last appeal, but Peloquin's outstretched arms were already transforming from fingertip to elbow, their delicacy giving way to formidable power.

Before the muscle was fixed he came at Boone, leaping to bring his victim down. Boone fell before him. It was too late now to regret his passivity. He felt the claws tear at his jacket to bare the good flesh of his chest. Peloquin raised his head and *grinned*, an expression this mouth was not made for; then he bit. The teeth were not long, but many. They hurt less than Boone had expected until Peloquin pulled back, tearing away a mouthful of muscle, taking skin and nipple with it.

The pain shocked Boone from resignation; he began to thrash beneath Peloquin's weight. But the beast spat the morsel from its maw and came back for better, exhaling the smell of blood in its prey's face. There was reason for the exhalation; on its next breath it would suck Boone's heart and lungs from his chest. He cried out for help, and it came. Before the fatal breath could be drawn Jackie seized hold of Peloquin and dragged him from his sustenance. Boone felt the weight of the creature lifted, and through the blur of agony

53

saw his champion wrestling with Peloquin, their thrashing limbs intertwined. He didn't wait to cheer the victor. Pressing his palm to the wound on his chest, he got to his feet.

There was no safety for him here; Peloquin was surely not the only occupant with a taste for human meat. He could feel others watching him as he staggered through the necropolis, waiting for him to falter and fall so they could take him with impunity.

Yet his system, traumatized as it was, didn't fail. There was a vigour in his muscles he'd not felt since he'd done violence to himself, a thought that repulsed him now as it had never before. Even the wound, throbbing beneath his hand, had its *life*, and was celebrating it. The pain had gone, replaced not by numbness but by a sensitivity that was almost erotic, tempting Boone to reach into his chest and stroke his heart. Entertained by such nonsenses he let instinct guide his feet and it brought him to the double gates. The latch defeated his blood-slicked hands so he climbed, scaling the gates with an ease that brought laughter to his throat. Then he was off up towards Midian, running not for fear of pursuit but for the pleasure his limbs took in usage, and his senses in speed.

VI

Feet of Clay

The town was indeed empty, as he'd known it must be. Though the houses had seemed in good shape at half a mile's distance, closer scrutiny showed them to be much the worse for being left unoccupied for the cycle of seasons. Though the feeling of well being still suffused him, he feared that loss of blood would undo him in time. He needed something to bind his wound, however primitive. In search of a length of curtaining, or a piece of forsaken bedlinen, he opened the door of one of the houses and plunged into the darkness within.

He hadn't been aware, until he was inside, how strangely attenuated his senses had become. His eyes pierced the gloom readily, discovering the pitiful debris the sometime tenants had left behind, all dusted by the dry earth years of prairie had borne in through broken window and the ill-fitting door. There was cloth to be found; a length of damp stained linen that he tore between teeth and right hand into strips while keeping his left upon the wound.

He was in that process when he heard the creak of boards on the stoop. He let the bandaging drop from his teeth. The door stood open. On the threshold a silhouetted man, whose name Boone knew though the face was all darkness. It was Decker's cologne he smelt; Decker's heartbeat he heard; Decker's sweat he tasted on the air between them.

'So,' said the doctor. 'Here you are.'

There were forces mustering in the starlit street.

With ears preternaturally sharp Boone caught the sound of nervous whispers, and of wind passed by churning bowels, and of weapons cocked ready to bring the lunatic down should he try to slip them.

'How did you find me?' he said.

'Narcisse, was it?' Decker said. 'Your friend at the hospital?'

'Is he dead?'

'I'm afraid so. He died fighting.'

Decker took a step into the house.

'You're hurt,' he said. 'What did you do to yourself?'

Something prevented Boone from replying. Was it that the mysteries of Midian were so bizarre he'd not be believed? Or that their nature was not Decker's business? Not the latter surely. Decker's commitment to comprehending the monstrous could not be in doubt. Who better then to share the revelation with? Yet he hesitated.

'Tell me,' Decker said again. 'How did you get the wound?'

'Later,' said Boone.

'There'll be no later. I think you know that.'

'I'll survive,' Boone said. 'This isn't as bad as it looks. At least it doesn't feel bad.'

'I don't mean the wound. I mean the police. They're waiting for you.'

'I know.'

'And you're not going to come quietly, are you?'

Boone was no longer sure. Decker's voice reminded him so much of being safe, he almost believed it would be possible again, if the doctor wanted to make it so.

But there was no talk of safety from Decker now. Only of death.

'You're a multiple murderer, Boone. Desperate. Dangerous. It was tough persuading them to let me near you.'

'I'm glad you did.'

'I'm glad too,' Decker replied. 'I wanted a chance to say goodbye.'

'Why does it have to be this way?'

'You know why.'

He didn't; not really. What he did know, more and more certainly, was that Peloquin had told the truth.

You're not Nightbreed, he'd said.

Nor was he; he was innocent.

'I killed nobody,' he murmured.

'*I* know that,' Decker replied.

'That's why I couldn't remember any of the rooms. I was never *there.*'

'But you remember now,' Decker said.

'Only because – ' Boone stopped, and stared at the man in the charcoal suit. ' – because you showed me.'

'*Taught* you,' Decker corrected him.

Boone kept staring, waiting for an explanation that wasn't the one in his head. It couldn't be Decker. Decker was Reason, Decker was Calm.

'There are two children dead in Westlock tonight,' the doctor was saying. 'They're blaming you.'

'I've never been to Westlock,' Boone protested.

'But I have,' Decker replied. 'I made sure they saw the pictures; the men out there. Child murderers are the worst. It'd be better you died here than be turned over to them.'

'You?' Boone said. 'You did it?'

'Yes.'

'All of them?'

'And more.'

'Why?'

Decker pondered on this a moment.

'Because I like it,' he said flatly.

He still looked so sane, in his well cut suit. Even his face, which Boone could see clearly now, bore no visible clue to the lunacy beneath. Who would have doubted, seeing the bloodied man and the clean, which was the lunatic and which his healer? But appearances deceived. It was only the monster, the child of Midian, who actually altered its flesh to parade its true self. The rest hid behind their calm, and plotted the deaths of children.

Decker drew a gun from the inside of his jacket.

'They armed me,' he said. 'In case you lost control.'

His hand trembled, but at such a distance he could scarcely miss. In moments it would all be over. The bullet would fly and he'd be dead, with so many mysteries unsolved. The wound; Midian; Decker. So many questions that he'd never answer.

There was no other moment but now. Flinging the cloth he still held at Decker, he threw himself aside behind it. Decker fired, the shot filling the room with sound and light. By the time the cloth hit the ground Boone was at the door. As he came within a yard of it the gun's light came again. And an instant after, the sound. And with the sound a blow to Boone's back that threw him forward, out through the door and onto the stoop.

Decker's shout came with him.

'He's armed!'

Boone heard the shadows prepare to bring him down. He raised his arms in sign of surrender; opened his mouth to protest his innocence.

The men gathered behind their cars saw only his bloodied hands; guilt enough. They fired.

Boone heard the bullets coming his way – two from the left, three from the right, and one from straight ahead, aimed at his heart. He had time to wonder at how slow they were, and how musical. Then they struck him: upper thigh, groin, spleen, shoulder, cheek and heart. He stood upright for several seconds; then somebody fired again, and nervous trigger fingers unleashed a second volley. Two of these shots went wide. The rest hit home: abdomen, knee, two to the chest, one to the temple. This time he fell.

As he hit the ground he felt the wound Peloquin had

given him convulse like a second heart, its presence curiously comforting in his dwindling moments.

Somewhere nearby he heard Decker's voice, and his footsteps approaching as he emerged from the house to peruse the body.

'Got the bastard,' somebody said.

'He's dead,' Decker said.

'No I'm not,' Boone thought.

Then thought no more.

PART TWO

DEATH'S A BITCH

'The miraculous too is born, has its season,
and dies . . .'

Carmel Sands
Orthodoxies

VII

Rough Roads

1

Knowing Boone was gone from her was bad enough, but what came after was so much worse. First, of course, there'd been that telephone call. She'd met Philip Decker only once, and didn't recognize his voice until he identified himself.

'I've got some bad news I'm afraid.'

'You've found Boone.'

'Yes.'

'He's hurt?'

There was a pause. She knew before the silence was broken what came next.

'I'm afraid he's dead, Lori.'

There it was, the news she'd half known was coming, because she'd been too happy, and it couldn't last. Boone had changed her life out of all recognition. His death would do the same.

She thanked the doctor for the kindness of telling her himself, rather than leaving the duty to the police. Then she put the phone down, and waited to believe it.

There were those amongst her peers who said she'd never have been courted by a man like Boone if he'd been sane, meaning not that his illness made him choose blindly but that a face like his, which inspired such fawning in those susceptible to faces, would have been in the company of like beauty had the mind behind it not been unbalanced. These remarks bit deep, because in her heart of hearts she thought them true. Boone had little by way of possessions, but his face was his glory, demanding a devotion to its study that embarrassed and discomfited him. It gave him no pleasure to be stared at. Indeed Lori had more than once feared he'd scar himself in the hope of spoiling whatever drew attention to him, an urge rehearsed in his total lack of interest in his appearance. She'd known him go days without showering, weeks without shaving, half a year without a hair cut. It did little to dissuade the devotees. He haunted them because *he* in his turn was haunted; simple as that.

She didn't waste time trying to persuade her friends of the fact. Indeed she kept conversation about him to the minimum, particularly when talk turned to sex. She'd slept with Boone three times only, each occasion a disaster. She knew what the gossips would make of that. But his tender, eager way with her suggested his overtures were more than dutiful. He simply couldn't carry them through, which fact made him rage, and fall into such depression she'd come to hold herself back, cooling their exchanges so as not to invite further failure.

She dreamt of him often though; scenarios that were unequivocally sexual. No symbolism here. Just she and Boone in bare rooms, fucking. Sometimes there were people beating on the doors to get in and see, but they never did. He belonged to her completely; in all his beauty and his wretchedness.

But only in dreams. Now more than ever, only in dreams.

Their story together was over. There'd be no more dark days, when his conversation was a circle of defeat, no moments of sudden sunshine because she'd chanced upon some phrase that gave him hope. She'd not been unprepared for an abrupt end. But nothing like this.

Not Boone unmasked as a killer and shot down in a town she'd never heard of. This was the wrong ending.

But bad as it was, there was worse to follow.

After the telephone call there'd been the inevitable cross questioning by the police: had she ever suspected him of criminal activities? had he ever been violent in his dealings with her? She told them a dozen times he'd never touched her except in love, and then only with coaxing. They seemed to find an unspoken confirmation in her account of his tentativeness, exchanging knowing looks as she made a blushing account of their lovemaking. When they'd finished with their questions they asked her if she would identify the body. She agreed to the duty. Though she'd been warned it would be unpleasant, she wanted a goodbye.

It was then that the times, which had got strange of late, got stranger still.

Boone's body had disappeared.

At first nobody would tell her why the identification process was being delayed; she was fobbed off with excuses that didn't quite ring true. Finally, however, they had no option but to tell her the truth. The corpse, which had been left in the police mortuary overnight, had simply vanished. Nobody knew how it had been stolen – the mortuary had been locked up, and there was no sign of forced entry – or indeed why. A search was under way but to judge by the harassed faces that delivered this news there didn't seem to be much hope held out of finding the body snatchers. The inquest on Aaron Boone would have to proceed without a corpse.

2

That he might never now be laid to rest tormented her. The thought of his body as some pervert's plaything, or worse some terrible icon, haunted her night and day. She shocked herself with her power to imagine what uses his poor flesh might be put to, her mind set on a downward spiral of morbidity which made her fearful – for the first time in her life – of her own mental processes.

Boone had been a mystery in life, his affection a miracle which gave her a sense of herself she'd never had. Now, in death, that mystery deepened. It seemed she'd not known him at all, even in those moments of traumatic lucidity between them, when he'd been ready to break his skull open till she coaxed the distress from him; even then he'd been hiding a secret life of murder from her.

It scarcely seemed possible. When she pictured him now, making idiot faces at her, or weeping in her lap, the thought that she'd never known him properly was like a physical hurt. Somehow, she had to heal that hurt, or be prepared to bear the wound of his betrayal for ever. She had to know *why* his other life had taken him off to the back of beyond. Maybe the best solution was to go looking where he'd been found: in Midian. Perhaps there she'd find the mystery answered.

The police had instructed her not to leave Calgary until after the inquest, but she was a creature of impulse like her mother. She'd woken at three in the morning with the idea of going to Midian. She was packing by five, and was heading north on Highway 2 an hour after dawn.

3

Things went well at first. It was good to be away from the office – where she'd be missed, but what the hell? – and the apartment, with all its reminders of her time with Boone. She wasn't quite driving blind, but as near as damn it; no map she'd been able to lay hands on marked any town called Midian. She'd heard mention of other towns, however, in exchanges between the police. Shere Neck was one, she remembered – and that *was* marked on the maps. She made that her target.

She knew little or nothing about the landscape she was crossing. Her family had come from Toronto – the civilized east as her mother had called it to the day she died, resenting her husband for the move that had taken them into the hinterland. The prejudice had rubbed off. The sight of wheat fields stretching as far as the eye could see had never done much for Lori's imagination and nothing she saw as she drove changed her mind. The grain was being left to grow, its planters and reapers about other business. The sheer monotony of it wearied her more than she'd anticipated. She broke her journey at McLennan, an hour's drive short of Peace River, and slept a full night undisturbed on a motel bed, to be up good and early the next morning, and off again. She'd make Shere Neck by noon, she estimated.

Things didn't quite work out that way, however. Somewhere east of Peace River she lost her bearings, and had to drive forty miles in what she suspected was the wrong direction till she found a gas station, and someone to help her on her way.

There were twin boys playing with plastic armies in the dirt of the station office step. Their father, whose blond hair they shared, ground a cigarette out amongst the battalions and crossed to the car.

'What can I get you?'

'Gas, please. And some information?'

'It'll cost you,' he said, not smiling.

'I'm looking for a town called Shere Neck. Do you know it?'

The war games had escalated behind him. He turned on the children.

'Will you shut up?' he said.

The boys threw each other sideways glances, and fell silent, until he turned back to Lori. Too many years of working outdoors in the summer sun had aged him prematurely.

'What do you want Shere Neck for?' he said.

'I'm trying . . . to track somebody.'

'That so?' he replied, plainly intrigued. He offered her a grin designed for better teeth. 'Anyone I know?' he said. 'We don't get too many strangers through here.'

There was no harm in asking, she supposed. She reached back into the car and fetched a photograph from her bag.

'You didn't ever see this man I suppose?'

Armageddon was looming at the step. Before looking at Boone's photograph he turned on the children.

'I told you to *shut the fuck up!*' he said, then turned back to study the picture. His response was immediate. 'You know who this guy is?'

Lori hesitated. The raw face before her was scowling. It was too late to claim ignorance, however.

'Yes,' she said, trying not to sound offensive. 'I know who it is.'

'And you know what he did?' The man's lip curled as he spoke. 'There were pictures of him. I saw them.' Again, he turned on the children. 'Will you *shut up*?'

'It wasn't me,' one of the pair protested.

'I don't give a fuck who it was!' came the reply.

He moved towards them, arm raised. They were out from his shadow in seconds, forsaking the armies in fear of him. His rage at the children and his disgust at the picture were welded into one revulsion now.

'A fucking animal,' he said, turning to Lori. 'That's what he was. A fucking animal.'

He thrust the tainted photograph back at her.

'Damn good thing they took him out. What you wanna do, go bless the spot?'

She claimed the photograph from his oily fingers without replying, but he read her expression well enough. Unbowed he continued his tirade.

'Man like that should be put down like a *dog*, lady. Like a fucking dog.'

She retreated before his vehemence, her hands trembling so much she could barely open the car door.

'Don't you want no gas?' he suddenly said.

'Go to hell,' she replied.

He looked bewildered.

'What's your problem?' he spat back.

She turned the ignition, muttering a prayer that the car would not play dead. She was in luck. Driving away at speed she glanced in her mirror to see the man shouting after her through the dust she'd kicked up.

She didn't know where his anger had come from, but she knew where it would go: to the children. No use to fret about it. The world was full of brutal fathers and tyrannical mothers; and come to that, cruel and uncaring children. It was the way of things. She couldn't police the species.

Relief at her escape kept any other response at bay for ten minutes, but then it ran out, and a trembling overtook her, so violent she had to stop at the first sign of civilization and find somewhere to calm herself down. There was a small diner amongst the dozen or so stores, where she ordered coffee and a sugar fix of pie, then retired to the rest room to splash some cold water on her flushed cheeks. Solitude, albeit snatched, was the only cue her tears needed. Staring at her blotchy, agitated features in the cracked mirror she began to sob so insistently, nothing – not even the entrance of another customer – could shame her into stopping.

The newcomer didn't do as Lori would have done in such circumstances, and withdraw. Instead, catching Lori's eye in the mirror, she said:

'What is it? Men or money?'

Lori wiped the tears away with her fingers.

'I'm sorry?' she said.

'When I cry – ' the girl said, putting a comb through her hennaed hair. ' – it's only ever men or money.'

'Oh.' The girl's unabashed curiosity helped hold fresh tears at bay. 'A man,' Lori said.

'Leave you, did he?'

'Not exactly.'

'Jesus,' said the girl. 'Did he come back? That's even worse.'

The remark earned a tiny smile from Lori.

'It's usually the ones you don't want, right?' the girl went on. 'You tell 'em to piss off, they just keep coming back, like dogs – '

Mention of dogs reminded Lori of the scene at the garage, and she felt tears mustering again.

'Oh shut up, Sheryl,' the newcomer chided herself, 'you're making it worse.'

'No,' said Lori. 'No really. I need to talk.'

Sheryl smiled.

'As badly as I need coffee?'

Sheryl Margaret Clark was her name, and she could have coaxed gossip from angels. By their second hour of conversation and their fifth coffee, Lori had told her the whole sorry story, from her first meeting with Boone to the moment she and Sheryl had exchanged looks in the mirror. Sheryl herself had a story to tell – more comedy than tragedy – about her lover's passion for cars and hers for his brother, which had ended in hard words and parting. She was on the road to clear her head.

'I've not done this since I was a kid,' she said, 'just going where the fancy takes me. I've forgotten how good it feels. Maybe we could go on together. To Shere Neck. I've always wanted to see the place.'

'Is that right?'

Sheryl laughed.

'No. But it's as good a destination as any. All directions being equal to the fancy-free.'

70

VIII

Where He Fell

S o they travelled on together, having taken directions from the owner of the diner, who claimed he
had a better than vague idea of Midian's whereabouts. The instructions were good. Their route took
them through Shere Neck, which was bigger than Lori
had expected, and on down an unmarked road that in
theory led to Midian.

'Why d'you wanna go there?' the diner owner had
wanted to know. 'Nobody goes there anymore. It's
empty.'

'I'm writing an article on the gold rush,' Sheryl had
replied, an enthusiastic liar. '*She's* sightseeing.'

'Some sight,' came the response.

The remark had been made ironically, but it was
truer than its speaker had known. It was late afternoon,
the light golden on the gravel road, when the town
came into view, and until they were in the streets
themselves they were certain this could not be the
right place, because what ghost town ever looked so
welcoming? Once out of the sun, however, that impression changed. There was something forlornly romantic
about the deserted houses, but finally the sight was
dispiriting and not a little eerie. Seeing the place, Lori's
first thought was:

'Why would Boone come here?'

Her second:

'He didn't come of his own volition. He was chased.
It was an accident that he was here at all.'

They parked the car in the middle of the main street, which was, give or take an alleyway, the only street.

'No need to lock it,' Sheryl said. 'Ain't anybody coming to steal it.'

Now that they were here, Lori was gladder than ever of Sheryl's company. Her verve and good humour were an affront to this sombre place; they kept whatever haunted it at bay.

Ghosts could be laid with laughter; misery was made of sterner stuff. For the first time since Decker's telephone call she felt something approximating bereavement. It was so easy to imagine Boone here, alone and confused, knowing his pursuers were closing on him. It was easier still to find the place where they'd shot him down. The holes the stray bullets had made were ringed with chalk marks; smears and splashes of blood had soaked into the planks of the porch. She stood off from the spot for several minutes, unable to approach it yet equally unable to retreat. Sheryl had tactfully taken herself off exploring: there was nobody to break the hypnotic hold the sight of his death-bed had upon her.

She would miss him forever. Yet there were no tears. Perhaps she'd sobbed them out back in the diner washroom. What she felt instead, fuelling her loss, was the mystery of how a man she'd known and loved – or loved and thought she'd known – could have died here for crimes she'd never have suspected him of. Perhaps it was the anger she felt towards him that prevented tears, knowing that despite his professions of love he'd hidden so much from her, and was now beyond the reach of her demands for explanation. Could he not at least have left a sign? She found herself staring at the blood stains wondering if eyes more acute than hers might have found some meaning in them. If prophecies could be read from the dregs in a coffee cup surely the last mark Boone had made on the world carried some significance. But she was no interpreter. The signs

72

were just of many unsolved mysteries, chief amongst them the feeling she voiced aloud as she stared at the stairs:

'I still love you Boone.'

Now *there* was a puzzle, that despite her anger and her bewilderment she'd have traded the life that was left in her just to have him walk out through that door now and embrace her.

But there was no reply to her declaration, however oblique. No wraith breath against her cheek; no sigh against her inner ear. If Boone was still here in some phantom form he was mute, and breathless; not released by death, but its prisoner.

Somebody spoke her name. She looked up.

' – don't you think?' Sheryl was saying.

'I'm sorry?'

'Time we went,' Sheryl repeated. 'Don't you think it's time we went?'

'Oh.'

'You don't mind me saying, you look like shit.'

'Thanks.'

Lori put her hand out, in need of steadying. Sheryl grasped it.

'You've seen all you need to, honey,' she said.

'Yes . . .'

'Let it go.'

'You know it still doesn't seem quite *real*,' Lori said. 'Even standing here. Even seeing the place. I can't quite believe it. How can he be so . . . *irretrievable*? There should be some way we could *reach*, don't you think, some way to reach and touch them.'

'Who?'

'The dead. Otherwise it's all nonsense, isn't it? It's all sadistic nonsense.' She broke her hold with Sheryl; put her hand to her brow and rubbed it with her fingertips.

'I'm sorry,' she said, 'I'm not making much sense, am I?'

'Honestly? No.'

Lori proffered an apologetic look.

'Listen,' Sheryl said, 'the old town's not what it used to be. I think we should get out of here and leave it to fall apart. Whadda you say?'

'I'd vote for that.'

'I keep thinking . . .' Sheryl stopped.

'What?'

'I just don't like the company very much,' she said. 'I don't mean you,' she added hurriedly.

'Who then?'

'All these dead folk,' she said.

'What dead folk?'

'Over the hill. There's a bloody cemetery.'

'Really?'

'It's not ideal viewing in your state of mind,' Sheryl said hurriedly. But she could tell by the expression on Lori's face she shouldn't have volunteered the information.

'You don't want to see,' she said. 'Really you don't.'

'Just a minute or two.' Lori said.

'If we stay much longer, we'll be driving back in the dark.'

'I'll never come here again.'

'Oh sure. You should see the sights. Great sights. Dead people's houses.'

Lori made a small smile.

'I'll be quick,' she said, starting down the street in the direction of the cemetery. Sheryl hesitated. She'd left her sweater in the car, and was getting chilly. But all the time she'd been here she hadn't been able to dislodge the suspicion that they were being watched. With dusk close she didn't want to be alone in the street.

'Wait for me,' she said, and caught up with Lori who was already in sight of the graveyard wall.

'Why's it so big?' Lori wondered aloud.

'Lord knows. Maybe they all died out at once.'

'So many? It's just a little town.'

'True.'

'And look at the size of the tombs.'

'I should be impressed?'

'Did you go in?'

'No. And I don't much want to.'

'Just a little way.'

'Where have I heard that before?'

There was no reply from Lori. She was at the cemetery gates now, reaching through the ironwork to operate the latch. She succeeded. Pushing one of the gates open far enough to slip through, she entered. Reluctantly, Sheryl followed.

'Why so many?' Lori said again. It wasn't simply curiosity that had her voice the question; it was that this strange spectacle made her wonder again if Boone had simply been cornered here by accident or whether Midian had been his *destination*. Was somebody buried here he'd come hoping to find alive?; or at whose grave he'd wanted to confess his crimes? Though it was all conjecture, the avenues of tombs seemed to offer some faint hope of comprehension the blood he'd shed would not have supplied had she studied it till the sky fell.

'It's late,' Sheryl reminded her.

'Yes.'

'And I'm cold.'

'Are you?'

'I'd like to *go*, Lori.'

'Oh ... I'm sorry. Yes. Of course. It's getting too dark to see much anyhow.'

'You noticed.'

They started back up the hill towards the town, Sheryl making the pace.

What little light remained was almost gone by the time they reached the outskirts of the town. Letting Sheryl march on to the car Lori stopped to take one final look at the cemetery. From this vantage point it resembled a fortress. Perhaps the high walls kept animals out, though it seemed an unnecessary precaution. The dead were surely secure, beneath their memorial stones. More likely the walls were the mourners' way to keep the dead from having power over them. Within those gates the ground was sacred to the departed, tended in their name. Outside, the world belonged to the living, who had nothing left to learn from those they'd lost.

She was not so arrogant. There was much she wanted to say to the dead tonight; and much to hear. That was the pity of it.

She returned to the car oddly exhilarated. It was only once the doors were locked and the engine running that Sheryl said:

'There's been somebody watching us.'

'You sure?'

'I swear. I saw him just as I got to the car.'

She was rubbing her breasts vigorously. 'Jesus, my nipples get numb when I'm cold.'

'What did he look like?' Lori said.

Sheryl shrugged. 'Too dark to see,' she said. 'Doesn't matter now. Like you said, we won't be coming back here again.'

True, Lori thought. They could drive away down a straight road and never look back. Maybe the deceased citizens of Midian envied them that, behind their fortress walls.

IX

Touched

1

It wasn't difficult to choose their accommodation in Shere Neck; there were only two places available, and one was already full to brimming with buyers and sellers for a farm machinery sale that had just taken place, some of the spillage occupying the rooms at the other establishment: the Sweetgrass Inn. Had it not been for Sheryl's way with a smile they might have been turned away from there too; but after some debate a twin-bedded room was found that they could share. It was plain, but comfortable.

'You know what my mother used to tell me?' said Sheryl, as she unpacked her toiletries in the bathroom.

'What?'

'She used to say: there's a man out there for you, Sheryl; he's walking around with your name on. Mind you this is from a woman who's been looking for her particular man for thirty years and never found him. But she was always stuck on this romantic notion. You know, the man of your dreams is just around the next corner. And she stuck me on it too, damn her.'

'Still?'

'Oh yeah. I'm still looking. You'd think I'd know better, after what I've been through. You want to shower first?'

'No. You go ahead.'

A party had started up in the next room, the walls too thin to muffle much of the noise. While Sheryl took her shower Lori lay on the bed and turned the events of the day over in her head. The exercise didn't last long. The next thing she knew she was being stirred from sleep by Sheryl, who'd showered and was ready for a night on the town.

'You coming?' she wanted to know.

'I'm too tired,' Lori said. 'You go have a good time.'

'If there's a good time to be had – ' said Sheryl ruefully.

'You'll find it,' Lori said. 'Give 'em something to talk about.'

Sheryl promised she would, and left Lori to rest, but the edge had been taken off her fatigue. She could do no more than doze, and even that was interrupted at intervals by loud bursts of drunken hilarity from the adjacent room.

She got up to go in search of a soda machine and ice, returning with her calorie-free nightcap to a less than peaceful bed. She'd take a leisurely bathe, she decided, until drink or fatigue quieted the neighbours. Immersed to her neck in hot water she felt her muscles unknotting themselves, and by the time she emerged she felt a good deal mellower. The bathroom had no extractor, so both the mirrors had steamed up. She was grateful for their discretion. The catalogue of her frailties was quite long enough without another round of self-scrutiny to swell it. Her neck was too thick, her face too thin, her eyes too large, her nose too small. In essence she was one excess upon another, and any attempt on her part to undo the damage merely exacerbated it. Her hair, which she grew long to cover the sins of her neck, was so luxuriant and so dark her face looked sickly in its frame. Her mouth, which was her mother's mouth to the last flute, was naturally, even indecently, red, but taming its colour with a pale lipstick merely made her eyes look vaster and more vulnerable than ever.

It wasn't that the sum of her features was unattractive. She'd had more than her share of men at her feet. No, the trouble was she didn't look the way she felt. It was a *sweet* face, and she wasn't sweet; didn't want to *be* sweet, or *thought of* as sweet. Perhaps the powerful feelings that had touched her in the last few hours – seeing the blood, seeing the tombs – would make their mark in time. She hoped so. The memory of them moved in her still, and she was richer for them, however painful they'd been.

Still naked, she wandered back into the bedroom. As she'd hoped the celebrants next door had quietened down. The music was no longer rock 'n' roll, but something smoochy. She sat on the edge of the bed and ran her palms back and forth over her breasts, enjoying their smoothness. Her breath had taken on the slow rhythm of the music through the wall; music for dancing groin to groin, mouth to mouth. She lay back on the bed, her right hand sliding down her body. She could smell several months' accrual of cigarette smoke in the coverlet she lay on. It made the room seem almost a public place, with its nightly comings and goings. The thought of her nakedness in such a room, and the smell of her skin's cleanliness on this stale bed, was acutely arousing.

She eased her first and middle fingers into her cunt, raising her hips a little to meet the exploration. This was a joy she offered herself all too seldom; her Catholic upbringing had put guilt between her instinct and her fingertips. But tonight she was a different woman. She found the gasping places quickly, putting her feet on the edge of the bed and spreading her legs wide to give both hands a chance to play.

It wasn't Boone she pictured as the first waves of gooseflesh came. Dead men were bad lovers. Better she forgot him. His face had been pretty, but she'd never kiss it again. His cock had been pretty too, but she'd never stroke it, or have it in her again. All she had was

79

herself, and pleasure for pleasure's sake. That was what she pictured now: the very act she was performing. A clean body naked on a stale bed. A woman in a strange room enjoying her own strange self.

The rhythm of the music no longer moved her. She had her own rhythm, rising and falling, rising and falling, each time climbing higher. There was no peak. Just height after height, till she was running with sweat and gorged on sensation. She lay still for several minutes. Then, knowing sleep was quickly overtaking her and that she could scarcely pass the night in her present position, she threw off all the covers but a single sheet, put her head on the pillow, and fell into the space behind her closed eyes.

2

The sweat on her body cooled beneath the thin sheet. In sleep, she was at Midian's necropolis, the wind coming to meet her down its avenues from all directions at once – north, south, east and west – chilling her as it whipped her hair above her head, and ran up inside her blouse. The wind was not invisible. It had a texture, as though it carried a weight of dust, the motes steadily gumming up her eyes and sealing her nose, finding its way into her underwear and up into her body by those routes too.

It was only as the dust blinded her completely that she realized what it was – the remains of the dead, the ancient dead, blown on contrary winds from pyramids and mausoleums, from vaults and dolmen, charnel houses and crematoria. Coffin-dust, and human ash, and bone pounded to bits, all blown to Midian, and catching her at the crossroads.

She felt the dead inside her. Behind her lids; in her throat; carried up towards her womb. And despite the chill, and the fury of the four storms, she had no fear of them, nor desire to expel them. They sought her warmth and her womanliness. She would not reject them.

'Where's Boone?' she asked in her dream, assuming the dead would know. He was one of their number after all.

She knew he was not far from her, but the wind was getting stronger, buffeting her from all directions, howling around her head.

'Boone?' she said again. 'I want Boone. Bring him to me.'

The wind heard her. Its howling grew louder.

But somebody else was nearby, distracting her from hearing its reply.

'He's dead, Lori,' the voice said.

She tried to ignore the idiot voice, and concentrate on interpreting the wind. But she'd lost her place in the conversation, and had to begin again.

'It's Boone I want,' she said. 'Bring me – '

'*No!*'

Again, that damn voice.

She tried a third time, but the violence of the wind had become another violence; she was being shaken.

'Lori! Wake up!'

She clung to sleep; to the dream of wind. It might yet tell her what she needed to know if she could resist the assault of consciousness a moment longer.

'Boone!' she called again, but the winds were receding from her, and taking the dead with them. She felt the itch of their exit from her veins and senses. What knowledge they had to impart was going with them. She was powerless to hold them.

'*Lori.*'

Gone now; all of them gone. Carried away on the storm.

She had no choice but to open her eyes knowing they

would find Sheryl, mere flesh and blood, sitting at the end of the bed and smiling at her.

'Nightmare?' she said.

'No. Not really.'

'You were calling his name.'

'I know.'

'You should have come out with me,' Sheryl said. 'Get him out of your system.'

'Maybe.'

Sheryl was beaming; she clearly had news to tell.

'You met somebody?' Lori guessed.

Sheryl's smile became a grin.

'Who'd have thought it?' she said. 'Mother may have been right after all.'

'That good?'

'That good.'

'Tell all.'

'There's not much to tell. I just went out to find a bar, and I met this great guy. Who'd have thought it?' she said again. 'In the middle of the damn prairies? Love comes looking for me.'

Her excitement was a joy to behold; she could barely contain her enthusiasm, as she gave Lori a complete account of the night's romance. The man's name was Curtis; a banker, born in Vancouver, divorced and recently moved to Edmonton. They were perfect complimentaries she said; star signs, tastes in food and drink, family background. And better still, though they'd talked for hours he'd not once tried to persuade her out of her underwear. He was a gentleman: articulate, intelligent and yearning for the sophisticated life of the West Coast, to which he'd intimated he'd return if he could find the right companion. Maybe she was it.

'I'm going to see him again tomorrow night,' Sheryl said. 'Maybe even stay over a few weeks if things go well.'

'They will,' Lori replied. 'You deserve some good times.'

'Are you going back to Calgary tomorrow?' Sheryl asked.

'Yes' was the reply her mind was readying. But the dream was there before her, answering quite differently.

'I think I'll go back to Midian first,' it said. 'I want to see the place one more time.'

Sheryl pulled a face.

'Please don't ask me to go.' she said. 'I'm not up for another visit.'

'No problem,' Lori replied. 'I'm happy to go alone.'

X

Sun and Shade

The sky was cloudless over Midian, the air effervescent. All the fretfulness she'd felt during her first visit here had disappeared. Though this was still the town where Boone had died, she could not hate it for that. Rather the reverse: she and it were allies, both marked by the man's passing.

It was not the town itself she'd come to visit however, it was the graveyard, and it did not disappoint her. The sun gleamed on the mausoleums, the sharp shadows flattering their elaboration. Even the grass that sprouted between the tombs was a more brilliant green today. There was no wind, from any quarter; no breath of the dream-storms, bringing the dead. Within the high walls there was an extraordinary stillness, as if the outside world no longer existed. Here was a place sacred to the dead, who were *not* the living ceased, but almost another species, requiring rites and prayers that belonged uniquely to them. She was surrounded on every side by such signs: epitaphs in English, French, Polish and Russian; images of veiled women and shattered urns, saints whose martyrdom she could only guess at, stone dogs sleeping upon their masters' tombs – all the symbolism that accompanied this other people. And the more she explored, the more she found herself asking the question she'd posed the day before: why was the cemetery so big? And why, as became apparent the more tombs she studied, were there so many nationalities laid here? She thought of her dream; of the wind that had come from all quarters of the earth. It was as if there'd been something prophetic in it. The thought didn't worry her. If that was the way the world worked – by omens and prophecies – then it was at least a *system*, and she had lived too long without one. Love had failed her; perhaps this would not.

It took her an hour, wandering down the hushed avenues to reach the back wall of the cemetery against which she found a row of animals' graves – cats interred beside birds, dogs beside cats; at peace with each other as common clay. It was an odd sight. Though she knew of other animal cemeteries she'd never heard of pets being laid in the same consecrated ground as their owners. But then should she be surprised at anything here? The place was a law unto itself, built far from any who would care or condemn.

Turning from the back wall, she could see no sign of the front gate, nor could she remember which of the avenues led back there. It didn't matter. She felt secure in the emptiness of the place, and there was a good deal she wanted to see: sepulchres whose architecture, towering over its fellows, invited admiration. Choosing a route that would take in half a dozen of the most promising, she began an idling return journey. The sun was warmer by the minute now, as it climbed towards noon. Though her pace was slow she broke out into a sweat, and her throat became steadily drier. It would be no short drive to find somewhere to quench her thirst. But parched throat or no, she didn't hurry. She knew she'd never come here again. She intended to leave with her memories well stocked.

Along the way were several tombs which had been virtually overtaken by saplings planted in front of them. Evergreens mostly, reminders of the life eternal, the trees flourished in the seclusion of the walls, fed well on rich soil. In some cases their spreading roots had cracked the very memorials they'd been planted to offer shade and protection. These scenes of verdancy and ruin she found particularly poignant. She was lingering at one when the perfect silence was broken.

Hidden in the foliage somebody, or some*thing*, was panting. She automatically stepped back, out of the tree's shadow and into the hot sun. Shock made her heart beat furiously, its thump deafening her to the sound that had excited it. She had to wait a few moments, and listen hard, to be sure she'd not imagined the sound. There was no error. Something was in hiding beneath the branches of the tree, which were so weighed by their burden of leaves they almost touched the ground. The sound, now that she listened more carefully, was not human; nor was it healthy. Its roughness and raggedness suggested a dying animal.

She stood in the heat of the sun for a minute or more, just staring into the mass of foliage and shadow, trying to catch some sight of the creature. Occasionally there was a movement: a body vainly trying to right itself, a desperate pawing at the ground as the creature tried to rise. Its helplessness touched her. If she failed to do what she could for it the animal would certainly perish, knowing – this was the thought that moved her to action – that someone had heard its agony and passed it by.

She stepped back into the shadow. For a space the panting stopped completely. Perhaps the creature was fearful of her, and – reading her approach as aggression – was preparing some final act of defence. Readying herself to retreat before claws and teeth, she parted the outer twigs and peered through the mesh of branches. Her first impression was not one of sight or sound but of *smell*: a bitter-sweet scent that was not unpleasant, its source the pale flanked creature she now made out in the murk, gazing at her wide-eyed. It was a young animal, she guessed, but of no species she could name.

A wild cat of some kind, perhaps, but that the skin resembled deer hide rather than fur. It watched her warily, its neck barely able to support the weight of its delicately marked head. Even as she returned its gaze it seemed to give up on life. Its eyes closed and its head sank to the ground.

The resilience of the branches defied any further approach. Rather than attempting to bend them aside she began to break them in order to get to the failing creature. They were living wood, and fought back. Halfway through the thicket a particularly truculent branch snapped back in her face with such stinging force it brought a shout of pain from her. She put her hand to her cheek. The skin to the right of her mouth was broken. Dabbing the blood away she attacked the branch with fresh vigour, at last coming within reach of the animal. It was almost beyond responding to her touch, its eyes momentarily fluttering open as she stroked its flank, then closing again. There was no sign that she could see of a wound, but the body beneath her hand was feverish and full of tremors.

As she struggled to pick the animal up it began to urinate, wetting her hands and blouse, but she drew it to her nevertheless, a dead weight in her arms. Beyond the spasms that ran through its nervous system there was no power left in its muscles. Its limbs hung limply, its head the same. Only the smell she'd first encountered had any strength, intensifying as the creature's final moments approached.

Something like a sob reached her ears. She froze.

Again, the sound. Off to her left, some way, and barely suppressed. She stepped back, out of the shadow of the evergreen, bringing the dying animal with her. As the sunlight fell on the creature it responded with a violence utterly belied by its apparent frailty, its limbs jerking madly. She stepped back into the shade, instinct rather than analysis telling her the brightness was responsible. Only then did she look again in the direction from which the sob had come.

The door of one of the mausoleums further down the avenue – a massive structure of cracked marble – stood ajar, and in the column of darkness beyond she could vaguely make out a human figure. Vaguely, because it was dressed in black, and seemed to be veiled.

She could make no sense of this scenario. The dying animal, tormented by light; the sobbing woman – surely a woman – in the doorway, dressed for mourning. What was the association?

'Who are you?' she called out.

The mourner seemed to shrink back into the shadows as she was addressed, then regretted the move and approached the open door again, but so very tentatively the connection between animal and woman became clear.

She's afraid of the sun *too*, Lori thought. They belonged together, animal and mourner, the woman sobbing for the creature Lori had in her arms.

She looked at the pavement that lay between where she stood and the mausoleum. Could she get to the door of the tomb without having to step back into the sun, and so hasten the creature's demise? Perhaps, with care. Planning her route before she moved, she started to cross towards the mausoleum, using the shadows like stepping stones. She didn't look up at the door – her attention was wholly focused on keeping the animal from the light – but she could feel the mourner's presence, willing her on. Once the woman gave voice; not with a word but with a soft sound, a cradle-side sound, addressed not to Lori but to the dying animal.

With the mausoleum door three or four yards from her, Lori dared to look up. The woman in the door could be patient no longer. She reached out from her refuge, her arms bared as the garment she wore rode back, her flesh exposed to the sunlight. The skin was white – as ice, as paper – but only for an instant. As the fingers stretched to relieve Lori of her burden they darkened and swelled as though instantly bruised. The mourner made a cry of pain, and almost fell back into the tomb as she withdrew her arms, but not before the skin broke and trails of dust – yellowish, like pollen – burst from her fingers and fell through the sunlight on to the patio.

Seconds later, Lori was at the door; then through it into the safety of the darkness beyond. The room was no more than an antechamber. Two doors led out of it: one into a chapel of some sort, the other below ground. The woman in mourning was standing at this second door, which was open, as far from the wounding light as she could get. In her haste, her veil had fallen. The face beneath was fine-boned, and thin almost to the point of being wasted, which lent additional force to her eyes, which caught, even in the darkest corner of the room, some trace of light from through the open door, so that they seemed almost to glow.

Lori felt no trace of fear. It was the other woman who trembled as she nursed her sunstruck hands, her gaze moving from Lori's bewildered face to the animal.

'I'm afraid it's dead,' Lori said, not knowing what disease afflicted this woman, but recognizing her grief from all too recent memory.

'No,' the woman said with quiet conviction. 'She can't die.'

Her words were statement not entreaty, but the stillness in Lori's arms contradicted such certainty. If the creature wasn't yet dead it was surely beyond recall.

'Will you bring her to me?' the woman asked.

Lori hesitated. Though the weight of the body was making her arms ache, and she wanted the duty done, she didn't want to cross the chamber.

'Please,' the woman said, reaching out with wounded hands.

Relenting, Lori left the comfort of the door and the sunlit patio beyond. She'd taken two or three steps, however, when she heard the sound of whispering.

There could only be one source: the stairs. There were people in the crypt. She stopped walking, childhood superstitions rising up in her. Fear of tombs; fear of stairs *descending*; fear of the Underworld.

'It's nobody,' the woman said, her face pained. 'Please, bring me Babette.'

As if to further reassure Lori she took a step away from the stairs, murmuring to the animal she'd called Babette. Either the words, or the woman's proximity, or perhaps the cool darkness of the chamber, won a response from the creature: a tremor that ran down its spine like an electric charge, so strong Lori almost lost hold of it. The woman's murmurs grew louder, as if she were chiding the dying thing, her anxiety to claim it suddenly urgent. But there was an impasse. Lori was no more willing to approach the entrance to the crypt than the woman to come another step towards the outer door, and in the seconds of stasis the animal found new life. One of its claws seized Lori's breast as it began to writhe in her embrace.

The chiding became a shout –

'*Babette!*'

– but if the creature heard, it didn't care to listen. Its motion became more violent: a mingling of fit and sensuality. One moment it shuddered as though tortured; the next it moved like a snake sloughing off its skin.

'*Don't look, don't look!*' she heard the woman say, but Lori wasn't about to take her eyes off this horrendous dance. Nor could she give the creature over to the woman's charge, while the claw gripped her so tightly any attempt to separate them would draw blood.

But that *Don't Look*! had purpose. Now it was Lori's turn to raise her voice in panic, as she realized that what was taking place in her arms defied all reason.

'*Jesus God!*'

The animal was changing before her eyes. In the luxury of slough and spasm it was losing its bestiality, not by re-ordering its anatomy but by liquefying its whole self – through to the bone – until what had been solid was a tumble of matter. Here was the origin of the bitter-sweet scent she'd met beneath the tree: the stuff of the beast's dissolution. In the moment it lost its coherence the matter was ready to be out of her grasp, but somehow the essence of the thing – its will, perhaps; perhaps its *soul* – drew it back for the business of re-making. The last part of the beast to melt was the claw, its disintegration sending a throb of pleasure through Lori's body. It did not distract her from the fact that she was released. Horrified, she couldn't get what she held from her embrace fast enough, tipping it into the mourner's outstretched arms like so much excrement.

'*Jesus*,' she said, backing away. '*Jesus. Jesus.*'

There was no horror on the woman's face however; only joy. Tears of welcome rolled down her pale cheeks, and fell into the melting pot she held. Lori looked away towards the sunlight. After the gloom of the interior it was blinding. She was momentarily disoriented, and closed her eyes to allow herself a reprieve from both tomb and light.

It was sobbing that made her open her eyes. Not the woman this time, but a child, a girl of four or five, lying naked where the muck of transformation had been.

'Babette,' the woman said.

Impossible, reason replied. This thin white child could not be the animal she'd rescued from beneath the tree. It was sleight of hand, or some idiot delusion she'd foisted upon herself. Impossible; all impossible.

'She likes to play outside,' the woman was saying, looking up from the child at Lori. 'And I tell her: never, never in the sun. Never play in the sun. But she's a child. She doesn't understand.'

Impossible, reason repeated. But somewhere in her gut Lori had already given up trying to deny. The animal had been real. The transformation had been real. Now here was a living child, weeping in her mother's arms. She too was real. Every moment she wasted saying No to what she *knew*, was a moment lost to comprehension. That her world-view couldn't contain such a mystery without shattering was its liability, and a problem for another day. For now she simply wanted to be away; into the sunlight where she knew these shape-shifters feared to follow. Not daring to take her eyes off them until she was in the sun, she reached out to the wall to guide her tentative backward steps. But Babette's mother wanted to hold her a while longer.

'I owe you something . . .' she said.

'No,' Lori replied. 'I don't . . . want anything . . . from you.'

She felt the urge to express her revulsion, but the scene of reunion before her – the child reaching up to touch her mother's chin, its sobs passing – were so tender. Disgust became bewilderment; fear, confusion.

'Let me help you,' the woman said. 'I know why you came here.'

'I doubt it,' Lori said.

'Don't waste your time here.' the woman replied. 'There's nothing for you here, Midian's a home for the Nightbreed. Only the Nightbreed.'

Her voice had dropped in volume; it was barely a whisper.

'The Nightbreed?' Lori said, more loudly.

The woman looked pained.

'Shh . . .' she said. 'I shouldn't be telling you this. But I owe you, this much at least.'

Lori had stopped her retreat to the door. Her instinct was telling her to wait.

'Do you know a man called Boone?' she said.

The woman opened her mouth to reply, her face a mass of contrary feelings. She wanted to answer, that much was clear; but fear prevented her from speaking.

It didn't matter. Her hesitation was answer enough. She *did* know Boone; or had.

'Rachel.'

A voice rose from the door that led down into the earth. A man's voice.

'Come away,' it demanded. 'You've nothing to tell.'

The woman looked towards the stairs.

'Mister Lylesburg,' she said, her tone formal. 'She saved Babette.'

'We know,' came the reply from the darkness, 'We saw. Still, you must come away.'

We, Lori thought. How many others were there below ground; how many more of the *Nightbreed*?

Taking confidence from the proximity of the open door she challenged the voice that was attempting to silence her informant.

'I saved the child,' she said. 'I think I deserve something for that.'

There was a silence from the darkness; then a point of heated ash brightened in its midst and Lori realized that Mister Lylesburg was standing almost at the top of the stairs, where the light from outside should have illuminated him, albeit poorly, but that somehow the shadows were clotted about him, leaving him invisible but for his cigarette.

'The child has no life to save,' he said to Lori, 'but what she has is yours, if you want it.' He paused. 'Do you want it? If you do, take her. She belongs to you.'

The notion of this exchange horrified her.

'What do you take me for?' she said.

'I don't know,' Lylesburg replied. 'You were the one demanded recompense.'

'I just want some questions answered,' Lori protested. 'I don't want the child. I'm not a savage.'

'No,' the voice said softly. 'No, you're not. So go. You've no business here.'

He drew on the cigarette and by its tiny light Lori glimpsed the speaker's features. She sensed that he willingly revealed himself in this moment, dropping the veil of shadow for a handful of instants to meet her gaze face to face. He, like Rachel, was wasted, his gauntness more acute because his bones were large, and made for solid cladding. Now, with his eyes sunk into their sockets, and the muscles of his face all too plain beneath papery skin, it was the sweep of his brow that dominated, furrowed and sickly.

'This was never intended,' he said. 'You weren't meant to see.'

'I know that,' Lori replied.

'Then you also know that to speak of this will bring dire consequences.'

'Don't threaten me.'

'Not for you,' Lylesburg said. 'For *us*.'

She felt a twinge of shame at her misunderstanding. She wasn't the vulnerable one; she who could walk in the sunlight.

'I won't say anything,' she told him.

'I thank you,' he said.

He drew on his cigarette again, and the dark smoke took his face from view.

'What's below . . .' he said from behind the veil, '. . . remains below.'

Rachel sighed softly at this, gazing down at the child as she rocked it gently.

'Come away,' Lylesburg told her, and the shadows that concealed him moved off down the stairs.

'I have to go,' Rachel said, and turned to follow. 'Forget you were ever here. There's nothing you can do. You heard Mister Lylesburg. What's below – '

' – remains below. Yes, I heard.'

'Midian's for the Breed. There's no-one here who needs you – '

'Just tell me,' Lori requested. 'Is Boone here?'

Rachel was already at the top of the stairs, and now began to descend.

'He is, isn't he?' Lori said, forsaking the safety of the

open door and crossing the chamber towards Rachel. 'You people stole the body!'

It made some terrible, macabre sense. These tomb-dwellers, this Nightbreed, keeping Boone from being laid to rest.

'You *did! You stole him*!'

Rachel paused and looked back up at Lori, her face barely visible in the blackness of the stairs.

'We stole nothing,' she said, her reply without rancour.

'*So where is he?*' Lori demanded.

Rachel turned away, and the shadows took her completely from view.

'*Tell me! Please God!*' Lori yelled down after her. Suddenly she was crying: in a turmoil of rage and fear and frustration. '*Tell me, please!*'

Desperation carried her down the stairs after Rachel, her shouts becoming appeals.

'Wait . . . talk to me . . .'

She took three steps, then a fourth. On the fifth she stopped, or rather her body stopped, the muscles of her legs becoming rigid without her instruction, refusing to carry her another step into the darkness of the crypt. Her skin was suddenly crawling with gooseflesh; her pulse thumping in her ears. No force of will could overrule the animal imperative forbidding her to descend; all she could do was stand rooted to the spot, and stare into the depths. Even her tears had suddenly dried, and the spit gone from her mouth, so she could no more speak than walk. Not that she wanted to call down into the darkness now, for fear the forces there answered her summons. Though she could see nothing of them her gut knew they were more terrible by far than Rachel and her beast-child. Shape-shifting was almost a natural act beside the skills these others had to hand. She felt their perversity as a quality of the air. She breathed it in and out. It scoured her lungs and hurried her heart.

If they had Boone's corpse as a plaything it was beyond reclamation. She would have to take comfort from the hope that his spirit was somewhere brighter.

Defeated, she took a step backwards. The shadows seemed unwilling to relinquish her, however. She felt them weave themselves into her blouse and hook themselves on her eyelashes, a thousand tiny holds upon her, slowing her retreat.

'I won't tell anyone,' she murmured. 'Please let me go.'

But the shadows held on, their power a promise of retribution if she defied them.

'I promise,' she said. 'What more can I do?'

And suddenly, they capitulated. She hadn't realized how strong their claim was until it was withdrawn. She stumbled backwards, falling up the stairs into the light of the antechamber. Turning her back on the crypt she fled for the door, and out into the sun.

It was too bright. She covered her eyes, holding herself upright by gripping the stone portico, so that she could accustom herself to its violence. It took several minutes, standing against the mausoleum, shaking and rigid by turn. Only when she felt able to see through half-closed eyes did she attempt to walk, her route back to the main gate a farrago of cul-de-sacs and missed turnings.

By the time she reached it, however, she'd more or less accustomed herself to the brutality of light and sky. Her body was still not back at her mind's disposal however. Her legs refused to carry her more than a few paces up the hill to Midian without threatening to drop her to the ground. Her system, overdosed on adrenalin, was cavorting. But at least she was alive. For a short while there on the stairs it had been touch and go. The shadows that had held her by lash and thread could have taken her, she had no doubt of that. Claimed her for the Underworld and snuffed her out. Why had they released her? Perhaps because she'd saved the child;

perhaps because she'd sworn silence and they'd trusted her. Neither, however, seemed the motives of monsters; and she had to believe that what lived beneath Midian's cemetery deserved that name. Who other than monsters made their nests amongst the dead? They might call themselves the Nightbreed, but neither words nor gestures of good faith could disguise their true nature.

She had escaped demons – things of rot and wickedness – and she would have offered up a prayer of thanks for her deliverance if the sky had not been so wide and bright, and so plainly devoid of deities to hear.

PART THREE

DARK AGES

'. . . out on the town, with two skins. The leather and the flesh. Three if you count the fore. All out to be touched tonight, yessir. All ready to be rubbed and nuzzled and loved tonight, yessir.'

Charles Kyd
Hanging by a thread

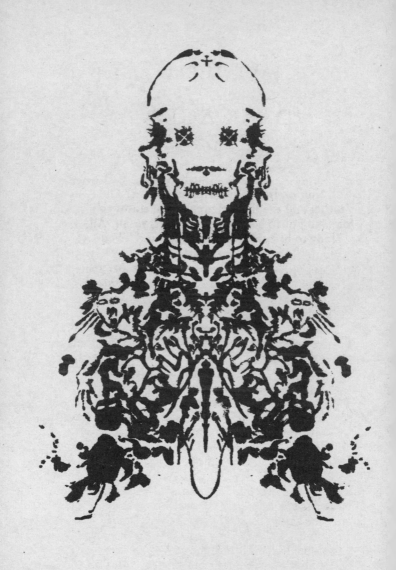

XI

The Stalking Ground

1

Driving back to Shere Neck, the radio turned up to a deafening level both to confirm her existence and keep it from straying, she became more certain by the mile that promises not withstanding she'd not be able to conceal the experience from Sheryl. How could it not be obvious, in her face, in her voice? Such fears proved groundless. Either she was better at concealment than she'd thought, or Sheryl was more insensitive. Either way, Sheryl asked only the most perfunctory questions about Lori's return visit to Midian, before moving on to talk of Curtis.

'I want you to meet him,' she said, 'just to be sure I'm not dreaming.'

'I'm going to go home, Sheryl,' Lori said.

'Not tonight, surely. It's too late.'

She was right; the day was too advanced for Lori to contemplate a homeward trip. Nor could she fabricate a reason for denying Sheryl's request without offending.

'You won't feel like a lemon, I promise,' Sheryl said. 'He said he wanted to meet you. I've told him all about you. Well ... not *all*. But enough, you know, about how we met.' She made a forlorn face. 'Say you'll come,' she said.

'I'll come.'

'Fabulous! I'll call him right now.'

While Sheryl went about making her call Lori took a

shower. There was news of the night's arrangements within two minutes.

'He'll meet us at this restaurant he knows, around eight,' Sheryl hollered. 'He'll even find a friend for you – '

'No, Sheryl – '

'I think he was just kidding,' came the reply. Sheryl appeared at the bathroom door. 'He's got a funny sense of humour,' she said. 'You know, when you're not sure if someone's making a joke or not? He's like that.'

Great, Lori thought, a failed comedian. But there was something undeniably comforting about coming back to Sheryl and this girlish passion. Her endless talk of Curtis – none of which gave Lori more than a street artist's portrait of the man: all surface and no insight – was the perfect distraction from thoughts of Midian and its revelations. The early evening was so filled with good humour, and the rituals of preparing for a night on the town, that on occasion Lori found herself wondering if all that had happened in the necropolis had not been a hallucination. But she had evidence that confirmed the memory: the cut beside her mouth from that wayward branch. It was little enough sign, but the sharp hurt of it kept her from doubting her sanity. She *had* been to Midian. She *had* held the shape-shifter in her arms, and stood on the crypt stairs gazing into a miasma so profound it could have rotted the faith of a saint.

Though the unholy world beneath the cemetery was as far from Sheryl and her whirlwind romances as night from day, it was no less real for that. In time she would have to address that reality; find a place for it, though it defied all sense, all logic. For now, she would keep it in mind, with the cut as its guardian, and enjoy the pleasures of the evening ahead.

'It's a joke,' said Sheryl, as they stood outside the Hudson Bay Sunset. 'Didn't I tell you he had this weird sense of humour?'

The restaurant he'd named had been completely gutted by fire, several weeks ago to judge by the state of the timbers.

'Are you sure you got the right address?' Lori asked.

Sheryl laughed.

'I tell you it's one of his jokes,' she said.

'So we've laughed,' said Lori. 'When do we get to eat?'

'He's probably watching us,' Sheryl said, her good humour slightly forced.

Lori looked around for some sign of the voyeur. Though there was nothing to fear on the streets of a town like this, even on a Saturday night, the neigh-bourhood was far from welcoming. Every other shop along the block was closed up – several of them permanently – and the sidewalks completely deserted in both directions. It was no place they wanted to linger.

'I don't see him,' she said.

'Neither do I.'

'So what do we do now?' Lori asked, doing her best to keep any trace of irritation from her voice. If this was Curtis the Beau's idea of a good time Sheryl's taste had to be in doubt; but then who was she to judge, who'd loved and lost a psycho in her time?

'He's got to be here somewhere,' Sheryl said hope-fully. 'Curtis?' she called out, pushing open the heat-blistered door.

'Why don't we wait for him out here, Sheryl?'

'He's probably inside.'

'The place could be dangerous.'

Her appeal was ignored.

'*Sheryl.*'

'I hear you. I'm OK.' She was already immersed in the darkness of the interior. The smell of burned wood and fabric stung Lori's nostrils.

'Curtis?' she heard Sheryl call.

A car went past, its engine badly tuned. The passenger, a youth, prematurely balding, leaned out of the window.

'Need any help?'

'No thanks,' Lori yelled back, not certain if the question was small town courtesy or a come-on. Probably the latter, she decided, as the car picked up speed and disappeared; people were the same all over. Her mood, which had improved by leaps and bounds since she'd been back in Sheryl's company, was rapidly souring. She didn't like being on this empty street, with what little was left of the day sliding towards extinction. The night, which had always been a place of promise, belonged too much to the Breed, who had taken its name for themselves. And why not? All darkness was one darkness in the end. Of heart or heavens; one darkness. Even now, in Midian, they'd be dragging back the doors of the mausoleums, knowing the starlight would not wither them. She shuddered at the thought.

Off down one of the streets she heard the car engine rev up, and roar, then a squeal of brakes. Were the Good Samaritans coming round for a second look?

'Sheryl?' she called out. 'Where are you?'

The joke, if joke it had been and not Sheryl's error – had long since lost what questionable humour it had. She wanted to get back into the car and *drive*, back to the hotel if necessary.

'Sheryl? Are you there?'

There was laughter from the interior of the building;

Sheryl's gurgling laughter. Suspecting now her compliance in this fiasco, Lori stepped through the door in search of the tricksters.

The laughter came again, then broke off as Sheryl said:

'*Curtis*,' in a tone of mock indignation that decayed into further inane laughter. So the great lover *was* here. Lori half contemplated returning to the street, getting back into the car and leaving them to their damn fool games. But the thought of the evening alone in the hotel room, listening to more partying, spurred her on through an assault course of burnt furniture.

Had it not been for the brightness of the floor tiles, throwing the street light up towards the cage of ceiling beams, she might not have risked advancing far. But ahead she could dimly see the archways through which Sheryl's laughter had floated. She made her way towards it. All sound had ceased. They were watching her every tentative step. She felt their scrutiny.

'Come on, guys,' she said. 'Joke's over. I'm hungry.'

There was no reply. Behind her, on the street, she heard the Samaritans yelling. Retreat was not advisable. She advanced, stepping through the archway.

Her first thought was: he only told half a lie; this *was* a restaurant. The exploration had taken her into a kitchen, where probably the fire had started. It too was tiled in white, surfaces smoke-stained but still bright enough to lend the whole interior, which was large, an odd luminescence. She stood in the doorway, and scanned the room. The largest of the cookers was placed in the centre, racks of shining utensils still hanging above it, truncating her view. The jokers had to be in hiding on the other side of the range; it was the only refuge the room offered.

Despite her anxieties, she felt an echo here of remembered games of hide-and-seek. The first game, because the simplest. How she'd loved to be terrorized by her father; chased and caught. If only he were here in hiding now, she found herself thinking, waiting to embrace her. But cancer had caught him long since, by the throat.

'Sheryl?' she said. 'I give up. Where are you?'

Even as she spoke her advance brought her within sight of one of the players, and the game ended.

Sheryl was not in hiding, unless death was hiding. She was crouched against the cooker, the darkness around her too wet for shadow, her head thrown back, her face slashed open.

'Jesus God.'

Behind Lori, a sound. Somebody coming to find her. Too late to h de. She'd be caught. And not by loving arms; not by her father, playing the monster. This was the monster itself.

She turned to see its face before it took her, but running at her was a sewing-box doll: zipper for mouth, buttons for eyes, all sewn on white linen and tied around the monster's face so tightly his saliva darkened a patch around his mouth. She was denied the face but not the teeth. He held them above his head, gleaming knives, their blades fine as grass-stalks, sweeping down to stab out her eyes. She threw herself out of their reach but he was after her in an instant, the mouth behind the zipper calling her name.

'Better get it over with, Lori.'

The blades were coming at her again, but she was quicker. The Mask didn't seem too hurried; he closed on her with a steady step, his confidence obscene.

'Sheryl had the right idea,' he said. 'She just stood there and let it happen.'

'Fuck you.'

'Later maybe.'

He ran one of the blades along the row of hanging pots, striking squeals and sparks.

'Later, when you're a little colder.'

He laughed, the zipper gaping.

'There's something to look forward to.'

She let him talk, while trying to get some sense of what escape routes lay open to her. The news was not good. The fire door was blocked by burnt timbers; her only exit was the arch through which she'd entered, and the Mask stood between her and it, sharpening his teeth on each other.

He started towards her again. No jibes from him now; the time for talk was over. As he closed on her she thought of Midian. Surely she'd not survived its terrors to be hacked to death by some lone psycho?

Fuck him!

As the knives slid towards her she snatched a pot from the rack above the range and brought it up to meet his face. It connected squarely. Her strength shocked her. The Mask reeled, dropping one of his blades. There was no sound from behind the linen, however. He merely transferred the remaining blade from right hand to left, shook his head as if to stop it singing, and came at her again, at a rush. She barely had time to raise the pan in defence. The blade slid down it and met her hand. For a moment there was no pain, nor even blood. Then both came in profusion, the pan falling from her hand at her feet. Now he made a sound, a cooing sound, the tilt of his head suggesting that it was the blood he was staring at, as it ran from the wound he'd fathered.

She looked towards the door, calculating the time it would take to get there against his speed of pursuit. But before she could act the Mask began his last advance. The knife was not raised. Nor was his voice, when he spoke.

'Lori,' he said. 'We must talk, you and me.'

'Keep the fuck away.'

To her amazement he obeyed the instruction. She seized what little time this offered to claim his other blade from the floor. She was less competent with her unwounded hand, but he was a large target. She could do him damage; preferably through the heart.

'That's what I killed Sheryl with,' he said. 'I'd put it down if I were you.'

The steel was sticky in her palm.

'Yes, that slit little Sheryl, ear to ear,' he went on. 'And now you've got your prints all over it. You should have worn gloves, like me.'

The thought of what the blade had done appalled her, but she wasn't about to drop it, and stand unarmed.

'Of course, you could always blame Boone,' the Mask was saying. 'Tell the police he did it.'

'How do you know about Boone?' she said. Hadn't Sheryl sworn she'd told her paramour nothing?

'You know where he is?' the Mask asked.

'He's dead,' she replied.

The sewing-box face denied it with a shake.

'No, I'm afraid not. He got up and walked. God knows how. But he got up and walked. Can you imagine that? The man was pumped full of bullets. You saw the blood he shed – '

He was watching us all the time, she thought. *He followed us to Midian, that first day.* But why? That was what she couldn't make sense of; *why*?

' – all that blood, all those bullets, and still he wouldn't lie down dead.'

'Somebody stole the body,' she said.

'No,' came the reply, 'that's not the way it was.'

'Who the hell *are* you?'

'Good question. No reason why you shouldn't have an answer.'

His hand went up to his face and he pulled off the mask. Beneath was Decker, sweaty and smiling.

'I wish I'd brought my camera,' he said. 'The look on your face.'

She couldn't wipe it off, though she hated to amuse him. The shock made her gape like a fish. Decker was Curtis, Sheryl's Mister Right.

'Why?' she demanded.

'Why what?'

'Why did you kill Sheryl?'

'For the same reason I killed all the others,' he said lightly, as though the question hadn't much vexed him. Then, deadly serious: 'For the fun of it, of course. For the pleasure. We used to talk a lot about *why*, Boone and me. Digging deep, you know; trying to understand. But when it really comes down to it, I do it because I like it.'

'Boone was innocent.'

'*Is* innocent, wherever he's hiding. Which is a problem, because he knows the real facts, and one of these days he might find someone to convince of the truth.'

'So you want to stop him?'

'Wouldn't you? All the trouble I went to so he could die a guilty man. I even put a bullet in him myself and he still gets up and walks away.'

'They told me he was dead. They were certain.'

'The mortuary was unlocked from the *inside*. Did they tell you that? His fingerprints were on the handle; his footprints on the floor: did they tell you *that*? No, of course not. But I'm telling you. I know. *Boone is alive*. And your death is going to bring him out of hiding, I'll bet on it. He'll have to show himself.'

Slowly, as he spoke, he was raising the knife.

'If it's only to mourn.'

Suddenly, he was at her. She put the blade that had killed Sheryl between her and his approach. It slowed him, but he didn't stop coming.

'Could you really do it?' he said to her. 'I don't think so. And I speak from experience. People are *squeamish* even when their lives are at stake. And that knife, of course, it's already been blunted on poor Sheryl. You'll have to really dig to make some impression on me.'

He spoke almost playfully, still advancing.

'I'd like to see you try though,' he said. 'I really would. Like to see you try.'

Out of the corner of her eye she was aware that she'd

come abreast of piled plates mere inches from her elbow. Might they offer her time enough to get to the door, she wondered? In knife to knife combat with this maniac she'd lose, no doubt of it. But she might yet outwit him.

'Come on. Try me. Kill me if you can. For Boone. For poor, mad Boone – '

As the words became laughter she threw her wounded hand out towards the plates, hooked them round, and flung them onto the floor in front of Decker. A second pile followed, and a third, china shards flying up in all directions. He took a step back, his hands going up to his face to protect himself, and she took the chance while she had it, bolting for the archway. She got through it and into the restaurant itself before she heard his pursuit. By that time she had sufficient lead to reach the outer door and fling herself through it, onto the street. Once on the sidewalk she immediately turned and faced the door through which he would come. But he had no intention of following her into the light.

'Clever bitch,' he said, from the darkness. 'I'll get you. When I've got Boone I'll come back for you; you just count the breaths till then.'

Eyes still fixed on the door she backed off down the sidewalk towards the car. Only now did she realize that she still carried the murder weapon, her grip so strong she felt almost glued to it. She had no choice but to take it with her, and give it, and her evidence, to the police. Back to the car, she opened the door and got in, only looking away from the burnt out building when the locks were on. Then she threw the knife onto the floor in front of the passenger seat, started the engine, and drove.

3

The choice before her came down to this: the police, or Midian. A night of interrogation or a return to the necropolis. If she chose the former she would not be able to warn Boone of Decker's pursuit. But then suppose Decker had been lying, and Boone had not survived the bullets? She'd not only be fleeing from the scene of a murder but putting herself within reach of the Nightbreed, and uselessly.

Yesterday she would have chosen to go to the law. She would have trusted that its procedures would make all these mysteries come clear; that they would believe her story, and bring Decker to justice. But yesterday she'd thought beasts were beasts, and children, children; she'd thought that only the dead lived in the earth, and that they were peaceful there. She'd thought doctors healed; and that when the madman's mask was raised she would say: 'But of course, that's a madman's face.'

All wrong; all so wrong. Yesterday's assumptions were gone to the wind. Anything might be true.

Boone might be alive.

She drove to Midian.

XII

Above and Below

1

Visions came to meet her down the highway, brought on by the after-effects of shock, and the loss of blood from her bound but wounded hand. They began like snow blown towards the windscreen, flakes of brightness that defied the glass and flew past her, whining as they went. As her dreamy state worsened, she seemed to see faces flying at her, and commas of life like foetuses, which whispered as they tumbled past. The spectacle did not distress her; quite the reverse. It seemed to confirm a scenario her hallucinating mind had created: that she, like Boone, was living a charmed life. Nothing could harm her, not tonight. Though her cut hand was now so numb it could no longer grip the wheel, leaving her to navigate an unlit road one-handed and at speed, fate had not let her survive Decker's attack only to kill her on the highway.

There was a reunion in the air. That was why the visions came, racing into the headlamps, and skipping over the car to burst above her in showers of white lights. They were welcoming her.

To Midian.

Once she looked in the mirror and thought she glimpsed a car behind her, its lights turned off. But when she looked again it had gone. Perhaps it had never been there. Ahead lay the town, its houses blinded by her headlights. She drove down the main street, all the way to the graveyard gates.

The mingled intoxications of blood loss and exhaustion had dulled all fear of this place. If she could survive the malice of the living she could surely survive the dead, or their companions. And Boone was here; that hope had hardened into certainty as she drove. Boone was here, and finally she'd be able to take him into her arms.

She stumbled out of the car, and almost fell flat on her face.

'Get up . . .' she told herself.

The lights were still coming at her, though she was no longer moving, but now all trace of detail in them had vanished. There was only the brightness, its ferocity threatening to wash the whole world away. Knowing total collapse was imminent she crossed to the gates, calling Boone's name. She had an answer immediately, though not the one she sought.

'He's here?' somebody said. 'Boone is *here*?'

Clinging to the gate she turned her leaden head, and through the surf of light saw Decker, standing a few yards from her. Behind him, his light-less car. Even in her dizzied state she understood how she'd been manipulated. Decker had allowed her to escape, knowing she'd seek out his enemy.

'Stupid!' she told herself.

'Well yes. But then, what were you to do? No doubt you thought you might save him.'

She had neither the strength nor the wit left to resist the man. Relinquishing the support of the gates, she staggered into the cemetery.

'*Boone!*' she yelled. '*Boone!*'

Decker didn't come after her quickly; he had no need. She was a wounded animal going in search of another wounded animal. Glancing behind her she saw him checking his gun by the light of his headlamps. Then he pushed the gate wider, and came in pursuit.

She could barely see the avenues in front of her for the bursts of light in her head. She was like a blind woman, sobbing as she stumbled; no longer even certain if Decker was behind her or in front. Any moment he would despatch her. One bullet, and her charmed life would end.

3

In the ground below, the Breed heard her arrival, their senses attuned to panic and despair. They knew the hunter's tread too; they'd heard it behind them all too often. Now they waited, pitying the woman in her last moments but too covetous of their refuge to put it at risk. There were few enough hiding places left where the monstrous might find peace. They'd not endanger their hermitage for a human life.

Still it pained them, hearing her pleas and her calls. And for one of their number the sound was almost beyond endurance.

'*Let me go to her.*'

'*You can't. You know you can't.*'

'*I can kill him. Who's to know he was ever here?*'

'*He won't be alone. There'll be others waiting outside the walls. Remember how they came for you.*'

'*I can't let her die.*'

'Boone! Please God – '

It was worse than anything he'd suffered, hearing her calling him, and knowing Midian's law wouldn't let him answer.

'*Listen to her, for god's sake!*' he said. '*Listen.*'

'*You made promises when we took you in,*' Lylesburg reminded him.

'*I know. I understand.*'

'*I wonder if you do. They weren't demanded lightly, Boone. Break them and you belong nowhere. Not with us. Not with them.*'

'*You're asking me to listen to her die.*'

'*So block your ears. It'll soon be over.*'

4

She could no longer find the breath to call his name. No matter. He wasn't here. Or if he was, he was dead in the earth, and corrupted. Beyond help, in the giving or the taking.

She was alone, and the man with the gun was closing on her.

Decker took the mask from his pocket; the button mask he felt so safe behind. Oh, the number of times, in those tiresome days with Boone, teaching him the dates and the places of the murders he was inheriting, when Decker's pride had almost brimmed over and he'd itched to claim the crimes back. But he needed the scapegoat more than the quick thrill of confession, to keep suspicion at bay. Boone's admitting to the crimes wouldn't have been an end to it all of course. In time the Mask would start speaking to its owner again, demanding to be bloodied, and the killings would have to begin afresh. But not until Decker had found himself another name, and another city to set up his store in. Boone had spoiled those well-laid plans, but he'd get no chance to tell what he knew. Ol' Button Face would see to that.

Decker pulled the mask on. It smelt of his excitement. As soon as he breathed in he got a hard. Not the little sex-hard, but the death-hard; the murder-hard. It sniffed the air for him, even through the thickness of his trousers and underwear. It smelt the victim that ran ahead of him. The Mask didn't care that his prey was female; he got the murder-hard for anyone. In his time he'd had a heat for old men, pissing their pants as they went down in front of him; for girls, sometimes; sometimes women; even children. Ol' Button Face looked with the same cross-threaded eyes on the whole of humanity.

This one, this woman in the dark up ahead, meant no more to the Mask than any of the others. Once they started to panic and bleed, they were all the same. He followed her with steady step; that was one of Button Head's trade marks, the executioner's tread. And she fled before him, her pleas deteriorating into snot and gasps. Though she hadn't got breath to call for her hero, no doubt she prayed he'd still come for her. Poor bitch. Didn't she know they never showed? He'd heard them all called upon in his time, begged for, bargained with, the Holy Fathers and Mothers, the champions, the interceders; none of them ever showed.

But her agony would be over soon. A shot through the back of the head to bring her down, and then he'd take the big knife, the heavy knife, to her face, the way he did with all of them. Criss cross, criss cross, like the threads in his eye, till there was nothing left to look at but meat.

Ah! She was falling. Too tired to run any further.

He opened Ol' Button Head's steel mouth, and spoke to the fallen girl —

'Be still,' he said.

'It's quicker that way.'

* * *

117

She tried to get up one final time, but her legs had given out completely, and the wash of whiteness was practically all consuming. Giddily, she turned her head in the direction of Decker's voice, and in a trough between the white waves, she saw that he'd put his mask back on. Its face was a death's head.

He raised the gun –

In the ground beneath her, she felt tremors. Was it the sound of a shot, perhaps? She couldn't see the gun any longer, or even Decker. One final wave had washed him from sight. But her body felt the earth rock, and through the whine in her head she heard somebody calling the name of the man she'd hoped to find here.

Boone!

She didn't hear an answer – perhaps there wasn't one – but the call came again, as if summoning him back into the earth.

Before she could muster the last of her power to counter the call her good arm gave out beneath her and she was face down on the ground.

Button Head walked towards his quarry, disappointed that the woman would not be conscious to hear his final benediction. He liked to offer a few words of insight at the penultimate moment; words he never planned but that came like poetry from the zipper mouth. On occasion they'd laughed at his sermon, and that had made him cruel. But if they cried, and they often did, then he took it in good part, and made certain the last moment, the *very* last, was swift and painless.

He kicked the woman over onto her back, to see if he could raise her from her sleep. And yes, her eyes flickered open slightly.

'Good,' he said, pointing the gun at her face.

As he felt wisdom coming to his lips he heard the growl. It drew his gaze off the woman for a moment. A soundless wind had risen from somewhere, and was shaking the trees. There was complaint in the ground beneath his feet.

The Mask was untouched. Wandering in tomb yards didn't raise a hair on his neck. He was the New Death, tomorrow's face today: what harm could dust do him?

He laughed at the melodrama of it. Threw back his head and laughed.

At his feet the woman started moaning. Time to shut her up. He took aim at her open mouth.

As he recognized the word she was shaping the dark ahead of him divided, and that word stepped out of hiding.

'Boone,' she'd said.

It was.

He emerged from the shadow of the shaking trees, dressed just as the Mask remembered, in dirty tee shirt and jeans. But there was a brightness in his eyes the Mask did not remember; and he walked – despite the bullets he'd taken – like a man who'd never known an ache in his life.

Mystery enough. But there was more. Even as he stepped into view he began to *change*, breathing out a veil of smoke that took his flesh for fantasy.

This was the scapegoat; yet not. So much *not*.

The Mask looked down at the woman to confirm that they shared this vision but she had fallen into unconsciousness. He had to trust what the cross-sewn eyes told him, and they told him terrors.

The sinews of Boone's arms and neck were rippling with light and darkness; his fingers were growing larger; his face, behind the smoke he exhaled, seemed to be running with dazzling filaments that described a hidden form within his head which muscle and bone were conforming to.

And out of the confusion, a voice. It was not the voice the Mask remembered. No scapegoat's voice, hushed with guilt. It was a yell of fury.

'*You're a dead man, Decker!*' the monster cried.

The Mask hated that name; that *Decker*. The man was just some old flame he'd fucked once in a while. In a heat like this, with the murder-hard so strong, Ol' Button Head could barely remember whether Dr Decker was alive or dead.

Still the monster called him by that name.

'You hear me, *Decker*?' he said.

Bastard thing, the Mask thought. Mis-begotten, half-aborted bastard thing. He pointed a gun at its heart. It had finished breathing transformations, and stood before its enemy complete, if a thing born on a butcher's slab could ever be called complete. Mothered by a she-wolf, fathered by a clown, it was ridiculous to a fault. There'd be no benediction for this one, the Mask decided. Only phlegm on its hybrid face when it was dead on the ground.

Without further thought he fired. The bullet opened a hole in the centre of Boone's tee shirt and in the changed flesh beneath but the creature only grinned.

'You tried that already, Decker,' Boone said. 'Don't you ever learn?'

'*I'm not Decker*,' the Mask replied, and fired again. Another hole opened up beside the first but there was no blood from either.

Boone had begun to advance on the gun. No last, faltering step but a steady approach which the Mask recognized as his own executioner's tread. He could smell the filth of the beast, even through the linen across his face. It was bitter-sweet, and sickened him to the stomach.

'Be still,' the monster said.

'It's quicker that way.'

The stolen step was insult enough, but to hear the purity of his own words from that unnatural throat drove the Mask to distraction. He shrieked against the cloth, and aimed the gun at Boone's mouth. But before he could blow out the offending tongue Boone's swollen hands reached and took hold of the gun. Even as it was snatched from him the Mask pulled the trigger, firing against Boone's hand. The bullets blew off his smallest finger. The expression on his face darkened with displeasure. He dragged the gun out of the Mask's hands and flung it away. Then he reached for his mutilator and drew him close.

Faced with imminent extinction, the Mask and its wearer divided. Ol' Button Head did not believe he could ever die. Decker did. His teeth grated against the cage across his mouth, as he began to beg.

'Boone . . . you don't know what you're doing.'

He felt the mask tighten over his head in fury at this cowardice but he talked on, trying to find that even tone he remembered calming this man with, once upon a time.

'You're diseased, Boone.'

Don't beg, he heard the Mask saying: don't you *dare* beg.

'And you can heal me, can you?' the monster said.

'Oh yes,' Decker replied. 'Oh certainly. Just give me a little time.'

Boone's wounded hand stroked the mask.

'Why do you hide behind this thing?' he asked.

'It *makes* me hide. I don't want to, but it makes me.'

The Mask's fury knew no bounds. It shrieked in Decker's head, hearing him betray his master. If he survived tonight it would demand the vilest compensation for these lies. He'd pay it gladly, tomorrow. But he had to outwit the beast to live that long.

'You must feel the same as me,' he said. 'Behind that skin you have to wear.'

'The same?' said Boone.

'Trapped. Made to spill blood. You don't want to spill blood any more than I do.'

'You don't understand,' Boone said. 'I'm not *behind* this face. I *am* this face.'

Decker shook his head.

121

'I don't think so. I think that somewhere you're still Boone.'

'Boone is dead. Boone was shot down in front of you. Remember? You put bullets in him yourself.'

'But you survived.'

'Not alive.'

Decker's bulk had been trembling. Now it stopped. Every muscle in his body became rigid, as the explanation for these mysteries came clear.

'You drove me into the hands of monsters, Decker. And I became one. Not your kind of monster. Not the soulless kind.' He drew Decker very close, his face inches from the mask. 'I'm dead, Decker. Your bullets mean nothing to me. I've got Midian in my veins. That means I'll heal myself over and over. But you – '

The hand stroking the mask now gripped the fabric.

' – you, Decker . . . when you die, you die. And I want to see your face when it happens.'

Boone pulled at the mask. It was tied on securely and wouldn't come. He had to get his claws into the warp and weft to tear it open and uncover the sweaty facts beneath. How many hours had he spent watching this face, hanging on its every flicker of approbation? So much wasted time. This was the healer's true condition: lost and weak and weeping.

'I was afraid,' Decker said. 'You understand that, don't you? They were going to find me, punish me. I needed someone to blame.'

'You chose the wrong man.'

'*Man?*' said a soft voice from the darkness. 'You call yourself a man?'

Boone stood corrected.

'Monster,' he said.

Laughter followed. Then:

'Well are you going to kill him or not?'

Boone looked away from Decker to the speaker squatting on the tomb. His face was a mass of scar tissue.

'Does he remember me?' the man asked Boone.

'I don't know. Do you?' Boone demanded of Decker. 'His name's Narcisse.'

Decker just stared.

'Another of Midian's tribe,' Boone said.

'I was never quite certain I belonged,' Narcisse mused. 'Not till I was picking the bullets from my face. Kept thinking I was dreaming it all.'

'Afraid,' said Boone.

'I was. You know what they do to natural men.'

Boone nodded.

'So kill him,' Narcisse said. 'Eat out his eyes or I'll do it for you.'

'Not till I get a confession from him.'

'Confession – ' said Decker, his eyes widening at the thought of reprieve. 'If that's what you want, say the word.'

He began rummaging in his jacket, as if looking for a pen.

'What the fuck's the use of a confession?' Narcisse said. 'You think anybody's ever gonna forgive you now? Look at yourself!'

He jumped down off the tomb.

'Look,' he whispered, 'if Lylesburg knows I came up here he'll have me out. Just give me his eyes, for old times' sake. Then the rest's yours.'

'Don't let him touch me,' Decker begged Boone. 'Anything you want . . . full confession . . . anything. But keep him off me!'

Too late; Narcisse was already reaching for him, with or without Boone's permission. Boone attempted to keep him at bay with his free hand, but the man was too eager for revenge to be blocked. He forced himself between Boone and his prey.

'Look your last,' he grinned, raising his hooked thumbs.

But Decker's rummaging hadn't been all panic. As the hooks came at his eyes he drew the big knife out of

123

hiding in his jacket and thrust it into his attacker's belly. He'd made long and sober study of his craft. The cut he gave Narcisse was a disembowelling manoeuvre learnt from the Japanese: deep into the intestines and up towards the navel, drawing the blade two-handed against the weight of meat. Narcisse cried out – more in memory of pain than in pain itself.

In one smooth motion Decker pulled the big knife out, knowing from researches in the field that the well packed contents were bound to follow. He wasn't wrong. Narcisse's gut uncoiled, falling like a flesh apron to its owner's knees. The wounding – which would have dropped a living man to the ground on the spot – merely made a clown of Narcisse. Howling in disgust at the sight of his innards, he clutched at Boone.

'Help me,' he hollered, 'I'm coming undone.'

Decker took the moment. While Boone was held fast he fled towards the gates. There wasn't much ground to cover. By the time Boone had struggled free of Narcisse the enemy was within sight of unconsecrated earth. Boone gave chase, but before he was even half-way to the gates he heard Decker's car door slam and the engine rev. The doctor was away. Damn it, *away*!

'What the fuck do I do with *this*?' Boone heard Narcisse sob. He turned from the gates. The man had his guts looped between his hands like so much knitting.

'Go below,' Boone said flatly. It was useless to curse Narcisse for his interference. 'Somebody'll help you,' he said.

'I can't. They'll know I was up here.'

'You think they don't know already?' Boone replied. 'They know everything.'

He was no longer concerned about Narcisse. It was the body sprawled on the walkway that had claimed his attentions. In his hunger to terrorize Decker he'd forgotten Lori entirely.

'They'll throw us both out,' Narcisse was saying.

'Maybe,' said Boone.

124

'What will we do?'

'Just go below,' Boone said wearily. 'Tell Mister Lylesburg I led you astray.'

'You did?' said Narcisse. Then, warming to the idea, 'Yes, I think you did.'

Carrying his guts, he limped away.

Boone knelt beside Lori. Her scent made him dizzy; the softness of her skin beneath his palms was almost overpowering. She was still alive; her pulse strong despite the traumas she must have endured at Decker's hand. Gazing on her gentle face the thought that she might wake and see him in the shape he'd inherited from Peloquin's bite distressed him beyond measure. In Decker's presence he'd been proud to call himself a *monster*: to parade his Nightbreed self. But now, looking at the woman he had loved, and had been loved by in return for his frailty and his humanity, he was ashamed.

He inhaled, his will making flesh smoke, which his lungs drew back into his body. It was a process as strange in its ease as its nature. How quickly he'd become accustomed to what he'd once have called miraculous.

But he was no wonder; not compared with this woman. The fact that she'd enough faith to come looking for him with death on her heels was more than any natural man could hope for; and, for one such as himself, the true miracle.

Her humanity made him proud: of what he'd been, and could still pretend to be.

So it was in human form he picked her up, and tenderly carried her underground.

XIII

The Prophetic Child

Lori listened to the fury of the voices.

'You cheated us!'

The first was Lylesburg.

'I had no choice!'

The second, Boone.

'So Midian's put at risk for your finer feelings?'

'Decker won't tell anyone,' Boone responded. *'What's he going to say? That he tried to kill a girl and a dead man stopped him? Talk sense.'*

'So suddenly you're the expert. A few days here and you're re-writing the law. Well do it somewhere else, Boone. Take the woman and leave.'

Lori wanted to open her eyes and go to Boone; calm him before his anger made him say or do something stupid. But her body was numb. Even the muscles of her face wouldn't respond to instruction. All she could do was lie still, and listen as the argument raged.

'I belong here,' Boone said. *'I'm Nightbreed now.'*

'Not any longer.'

'I can't live out there.'

'We did. For generations we took our chances in the natural world, and it nearly extinguished us. Now you come along and damn near destroy our one hope of surviving. If Midian's unearthed, you and the woman will be responsible. Think of that on your travels.'

There was a long silence. Then Boone said:

'Let me make amends.'

'Too late. The law makes no exceptions. The other one goes too.'

'*Narcisse? No. You'll break his heart. He spent half his life waiting to come here.*'

'*The decision's made.*'

'*Who by? You? Or Baphomet?*'

At the sound of that name Lori felt a chill. The word meant nothing to her, but clearly it did to others nearby. She heard whispers echoing around her; repeated phrases like words of worship.

'*I demand to speak with it,*' Boone said.

'*Out of the question.*'

'*What are you afraid of? Losing your grip on your tribe? I want to see Baphomet. If you want to try and stop me, do it now.*'

As Boone threw the challenge down, Lori's eyes opened. There was a vaulted roof above her, where last there'd been sky. It was painted with stars; however, more fireworks than celestial bodies; catherine wheels, throwing off sparks as they rolled across the stone heavens.

She inclined her head a little. She was in a crypt. There were sealed coffins on every side of her, up-ended against the walls. To her left a profusion of squat candles, their wax grimy, their flame as weak as she. To her right, Babette, sitting cross-legged on the floor, watching her intently. The child was dressed completely in black, her eyes catching the candlelight and steadying its flicker. She was not pretty. Her face was too solemn for prettiness. Even in the smile she offered Lori, seeing her wake, couldn't mellow the sadness in her features. Lori did her best to return the welcoming look, but wasn't certain her muscles were yet obeying her.

'It was a bad hurt he did us,' Babette said.

Lori assumed she meant Boone. But the child's next words put her right.

'Rachel made it clean. Now it doesn't sting.'

She raised her right hand. It was bandaged with dark linen, around thumb and forefinger.

'Nor you either.'

Mustering her will, Lori raised her own right hand from her side. It was bandaged identically.

'Where ... is Rachel?' Lori asked, her voice barely audible to herself. Babette heard the question clearly however.

'Somewhere near,' she said.

'Could you get her for me?'

Babette's perpetual frown deepened.

'Are you here forever?' she asked.

'No,' came the reply, not from Lori but from Rachel, who had appeared at the door, 'no she's not. She's going to be away very soon.'

'Why?' said Babette.

'I heard Lylesburg,' Lori murmured.

'*Mister* Lylesburg,' Rachel said, crossing to where Lori lay. 'Boone broke his word going overground to fetch you. He's put us all in danger.'

Lori understood only a fraction of Midian's story, but enough to know that the maxim she'd first heard from Lylesburg's lips – '*what's below remains below*' was not some idle catchphrase. It was a law the inhabitants of Midian had sworn to live by or else forfeit their place here.

'Can you help me?' she asked. She felt vulnerable lying on the floor.

It wasn't Rachel who came to her aid, however, but Babette, by laying her small, bandaged hand on Lori's stomach. Her system responded instantly to the child's touch, all trace of numbness leaving her body at once. She remembered the same sensation, or its like, from her last encounter with the girl: that feeling of transferred power that had moved through her when the beast had dissolved in her arms.

'She's formed quite a bond with you,' Rachel said.

'So it seems.' Lori sat up. 'Is she hurt?'

'Why don't you ask *me*?' Babette said. 'I'm here too.'

129

'I'm sorry,' Lori said, chastened. 'Did you get cut too?'

'No. But I felt your hurt.'

'She's empathic,' Rachel said. 'She feels what others feel; particularly if she has some emotional connection with them.'

'I knew you were coming here,' Babette said. 'I saw through your eyes. And you can see through mine.'

'Is that true?' Lori asked Rachel.

'Believe her,' came the reply.

Lori wasn't quite certain she was ready to get to her feet yet, but she decided to put her body to the test. It was easier than she'd expected. She stood up readily, her limbs strong, her head clear.

'Will you take me to Boone?' she requested.

'If that's what you want.'

'He was here all along, wasn't he?' she said.

'Yes.'

'Who brought him?'

'Brought him?'

'To Midian.'

'Nobody.'

'He was almost dead,' Lori said. 'Somebody must have got him out of the mortuary.'

'You still don't understand, do you?' said Rachel grimly.

'About Midian? No; not really.'

'Not just Midian. About Boone, and why he is here.'

'He thinks he's Nightbreed,' Lori said.

'He *was*, until he broke his word.'

'So we'll go,' Lori replied. 'That's what Lylesburg wants, isn't it? And I've got no wish to stay.'

'Where will you go?' Rachel asked.

'I don't know. Maybe back to Calgary. It shouldn't be so hard to prove Decker's the guilty man. Then we can start over.'

Rachel shook her head.

'That won't be possible,' she said.

'Why not? Have you got some prior claim on him?'

'He came here because he's one of us.'

'*Us*. Meaning what?' Lori replied sharply. She was tired of evasion and innuendo. 'Who are you? Sick people living in the dark. Boone isn't sick. He's a sane man. A sane, healthy man.'

'I suggest you ask him how healthy he feels,' was Rachel's retort.

'Oh I will, when the time comes.'

Babette was not untouched by this exchange of contempt.

'You mustn't go,' she said to Lori.

'I have to.'

'Not into the light.' She took fierce hold of Lori's sleeve. 'I can't come with you there.'

'She has to go,' Rachel said, reaching over to prise her child loose. 'She doesn't belong with us.'

Babette held fast.

'You *can*,' she said, looking up at Lori. 'It's easy.'

'She doesn't want to,' Rachel said.

Babette looked up at Lori.

'Is that true?' she asked.

'Tell her,' Rachel said, taking plain satisfaction in Lori's discomfort. 'Tell her she's one of the sick people.'

'But we live forever,' Babette said. She glanced at her mother, 'Don't we?'

'Some of us.'

'*All* of us. If we want to live for ever and ever. And one day, when the sun goes out – '

'*Enough!*' said Rachel.

But Babette had more to say.

' – when the sun goes out and there's only night, we'll live on the earth. It'll be ours.'

Now it was Rachel's turn to be ill at ease.

'She doesn't know what she's saying,' the woman muttered.

'I think she knows very well,' Lori replied.

131

The proximity of Babette, and the thought that she had some bond with the child, suddenly chilled her. What little peace her rational mind had made with Midian was rapidly crumbling. She wanted more than anything to be away from here, from children who talked of the end of the world, from candles and coffins and the life of the tomb.

'Where's Boone?' she said to Rachel.

'Gone to the Tabernacle. To Baphomet.'

'Who or what is Baphomet?'

Rachel made a ritualistic gesture at mention of Baphomet, touching her forefinger to tongue and heart. It was so familiar to her, and so often performed, Lori doubted she even knew she'd done it.

'Baphomet is the Baptiser,' she said. 'Who Made Midian. Who called us here.'

Finger touched tongue and heart again.

'Will you take me to the Tabernacle?' Lori asked.

Rachel's reply was a plain and simple: 'No.'

'Direct me at least.'

'I'll take you,' Babette volunteered.

'No you won't,' Rachel said, this time snatching the child's hand from Lori's sleeve with such speed Babette had no chance to resist.

'I've paid my debt to you,' Rachel said, 'healing the wound. We've no more business together.'

She took hold of Babette, and lifted the child up into her arms. Babette squirmed in her mother's embrace so as to look back at Lori.

'I want you to see beautiful things for me.'

'Be quiet,' Rachel chided.

'What *you* see *I'll* see.'

Lori nodded.

'Yes?' Babette said.

'Yes.'

Before her child could utter another mournful word Rachel had carried her out of the room, leaving Lori to the company of the coffins.

She threw her head back and exhaled slowly. Calm, she thought; be calm. It'll be over soon.

The painted stars cavorted overhead, seeming to turn as she watched. Was their riot just the artist's fancy, she wondered, or was this the way the sky looked to the Breed, when they stepped out of their mausoleums at night to take the air?

Better not to know. It was bad enough that these creatures had children and art; that they might also have *vision* was too dangerous a thought to entertain.

When first she'd encountered them, halfway down the stairs into this underworld, she'd feared for her life. She still did, in some hushed corner of herself. Not that it would be taken away, but that it would be *changed*; that somehow they'd taint her with their rites and visions, so she'd not be able to scrub them from her mind.

The sooner she was out of here, with Boone beside her, the sooner she'd be back in Calgary. The street lights were bright there. They tamed the stars.

Reassured by the thought, she went in search of the Baptiser.

XIV

Tabernacle

This was the true Midian. Not the empty town on the hill; not even the necropolis above her; but this network of tunnels and chambers which presumably spread beneath the entire cemetery. Some of the tombs were occupied only by the undisturbed dead; their caskets laid on shelves to moulder. Were these the first occupants of the cemetery, laid to rest here before the Nightbreed had taken possession? Or were they Breed who had died from their half-life, caught in the sun, perhaps, or withered by longing? Whichever, they were in the minority. Most of the chambers were tenanted by more vital souls, their quarters lit by lamps or candles, or on occasion by the occupant itself: a being that burned with its own light.

Only once did she glimpse such an entity, supine on a mattress in the corner of its boudoir. It was naked, corpulent and sexless, its sagging body a motley of dark oily skin and larval eruptions which seeped phosphorescence, soaking its simple bed. It seemed every other doorway let on to some fragment as mysterious, her response to them problematic as the tableaux that inspired it. Was it simply disgust that made her stomach flip, seeing the stigmatic in full flood, with sharp-toothed adherents sucking noisily at her wounds; or excitement, confronting the legend of the vampire in the flesh? And what was she to make of the man whose body broke into birds when he saw her watching, or the dog-headed painter who turned from his fresco and beckoned her to join his apprentice mixing paint? Or the machine beasts running up the walls on caliper legs? After a dozen corridors she no longer knew horror from fascination. Perhaps she'd never known.

She might have spent days lost and seeing the sights, but luck or instinct brought her close enough to Boone that further progress was blocked. It was Lylesburg's shadow that appeared before her, seeming to step from the solid wall.

'You may go no further.'

'I intend to find Boone,' she told him.

'You're not to blame in this,' Lylesburg said. 'That's completely understood. But you must in turn understand: what Boone did has put us all in danger – '

'Then let me speak to it. We'll get out of here together.'

'That might have been possible, a little while ago,' Lylesburg said, the voice emerging from his shadow-coat as measured and authoritative as ever.

'And now?'

'He's beyond my recall. And yours too. He's made appeal to another force entirely.'

Even as he spoke there was noise from further down the catacomb; a din the like of which Lori had never heard. For an instant she felt certain an earthquake was at its source, the sound seemed to be *in* and *of* the earth around them. But as the second wave began she heard something animal in it: a moan of pain, perhaps; or of ecstasy . . . Surely this was Baphomet – *Who Made Midian*, Rachel had said. What other voice could shake the very fabric of the place?

Lylesburg confirmed the belief.

'*That* is what Boone has gone to parley with,' he said. 'Or so he thinks.'

'Let me go to him.'

'It's already devoured him,' Lylesburg said. 'Taken him into the flame.'

'I want to see for myself,' Lori demanded.

Unwilling to delay a moment longer she pushed past Lylesburg, expecting resistance. But her hands sank into the darkness he wore and touched the wall behind him. He had no substance. He couldn't keep her from going anywhere.

'It will kill you too,' she heard him warn, as she ran in pursuit of the sound. Though it was all around her, she sensed its source. Every step she took it got louder, and more complex, layers of raw sound each of which touched a different part of her: head, heart, groin.

A quick backward glance confirmed what she'd already guessed: that Lylesburg had made no attempt to follow. She turned a corner, and another, the under-currents in the voice still multiplying, until she was walking against them as if in a high wind, head down, shoulders hunched.

There were no chambers now along the passageway, and consequently no lights. There was a glow up ahead however – fitful and cold, but bright enough to illumi-nate both the ground she stumbled over, which was bare earth, and the silvery frost on the walls.

'Boone?' she shouted. 'Are you there? Boone?'

After what Lylesburg had said she didn't hope too hard for an answer, but she got one. His voice came to meet her from the core of light and sound ahead. But all she heard through the din was:

'*Don't –* '

Don't *what*? she wondered.

Don't come any further? Don't leave me here?

She slowed her pace, and called again, but the noise the Baptiser was making virtually drowned out the sound of her own voice, never mind a reply. Having come so far, she had to go forward, not knowing if his call had been a warning or not.

Ahead, the passageway became a slope – a steep

slope. She halted at the top, and squinted into the brightness. This was Baphomet's hole, no doubt of that. The din it was making eroded the walls of the slope and carried the dust up into her face. Tears began to fill her eyes to wash the grit away, but it kept coming. Deafened by voice, blinded by dust, she teetered on the lip of the slope, unable to go forward or back.

Suddenly, the Baptiser fell silent, the layers of sound all dying at once, and completely.

The hush that followed was more alarming than the din that had preceded it. Had it shut its mouth because it knew it had a trespasser in its midst? She held her breath, afraid to utter a sound.

At the bottom of the slope was a sacred place, she had not the slightest doubt of that. Standing in the great cathedrals of Europe with her mother, years before, gazing at the windows and the altars, she'd felt nothing approaching the surge of recognition she felt now. Nor, in all her life – dreaming or awake – had such contradictory impulses run in her. She wanted to flee the place with a passion – wanted to forsake it and forget it; and yet it *summoned*. It was not Boone's presence there that called her, but the pull of the holy, or the unholy, or the two in one; and it wouldn't be resisted.

Her tears had cleared the dust from her eyes now. She had no excuse but cowardice to remain where she stood. She began down the slope. It was a descent of thirty yards, but she'd covered no more than a third of it when a familiar figure staggered into view at the bottom.

The last time she'd seen Boone had been overground, as he emerged to confront Decker. In the seconds before she'd passed out she'd seen him as never before: like a man who'd forgotten pain and defeat entirely. Not so now. He could barely hold himself upright.

She whispered his name, the word gathering weight as it tumbled towards him.

He heard, and raised his head towards her. Even in his worst times, when she'd rocked him and held him to keep the terrors at bay, she'd not seen such grief on his face as she saw now. Tears coming and coming, his features so crumpled with sorrow they were like a baby's.

She began the descent again, every sound her feet made, every tiny breath she took, multiplied by the acoustics of the slope.

Seeing her approach he left off holding himself up to wave her away, but in doing so lost his only means of support and fell heavily. She picked up her pace, careless now of the noise she was making. Whatever power occupied the pit at the bottom it knew she was there. Most likely it knew her history. In a way she hoped it did. She wasn't afraid of its judgement. She had loving reason for her trespass; she came weaponless, and alone. If Baphomet was indeed the architect of Midian then it understood vulnerability, and would not act against her. She was within five yards of Boone by now. He was attempting to roll himself onto his back.

'Wait!' she said, distressed by his desperation.

He didn't look her way, however. It was Baphomet his eyes went to, once he got onto his back. Her gaze went with his, into a room with walls of frozen earth, and a floor the same, the latter split from corner to corner, and a fissure opened in it from which a flame column rose four or five times the size of a man. There was bitter cold off it rather than heat, and no reassuring flicker in its heart. Instead its innards churned upon themselves, turning over and over some freight of stuff which she failed to recognize at first, but her appalled stare rapidly interpreted.

There was a *body* in the fire, hacked limb from limb, human enough that she recognized it as flesh, but no more than that. Baphomet's doing presumably; some torment visited on a transgressor.

Boone said the Baptiser's name even now, and she readied herself for sight of its face. She had it too, but from *inside* the flame, as the creature there – not dead, but alive; not Midian's subject, but its creator – rolled its head over in the turmoil of flame and looked her way.

This was *Baphomet*. This diced and divided thing. Seeing its face, she screamed. No story or movie screen, no desolation, no bliss had prepared her for the maker of Midian. Sacred it must be, as anything so extreme must be sacred. A thing beyond things. Beyond love or hatred, or their sum; beyond the beautiful or the monstrous, or *their* sum. Beyond, finally, her mind's power to comprehend or catalogue. In the instant she looked away from it she had already blanked every fraction of the sight from conscious memory and locked it where no torment or entreaty would ever make her look again.

She hadn't known her own strength till the frenzy to be out of its presence had her hauling Boone to his feet and dragging him up the slope. He could do little to help her. The time he'd spent in the Baptiser's presence had driven all but the rags of power from his muscles. It seemed to Lori that it took an age staggering up to the head of the slope, the flame's icy light throwing their shadows before them like prophecies.

The passageway above was deserted. She had half expected Lylesburg to be in wait somewhere with more solid cohorts, but the silence of the chamber below had spread throughout the tunnel. Once she'd hauled Boone a few yards from the summit of the slope she halted, her lungs burning with the effort of bearing him up. He was emerging from the daze of grief or terror she'd found him in.

'Do you know a way out of here?' she asked him.

'I think so,' he said.

'You're going to have to give me some help. I can't support you much longer.'

He nodded, then looked back at the entrance to Baphomet's pit.

'What did you see?' he asked.

'Nothing.'

'Good.'

He covered his face with his hands. One of his fingers was missing, she saw, the wound fresh. He seemed indifferent to it, however, so she asked no questions but concentrated on encouraging him to move. He was reluctant, almost sullen in the aftermath of high emotion, but she chivvied him along, until they reached a steep stairway which took them up through one of the mausoleums and into the night.

The air smelt of *distance* after the confinement of the earth, but rather than linger to enjoy it, she insisted they get out of the cemetery, threading their way through the maze of tombs to the gate. There Boone halted.

'The car's just outside,' she said.

He was shuddering, though the night was quite warm.

'I can't . . .' he said.

'Can't what?'

'I belong here.'

'No you don't,' she said. 'You belong with me. We belong with each other.'

She stood close to him, but his head was turned towards the shadow. She took hold of his face in her hands and pulled his gaze round upon her.

'We belong to each other, Boone. That's why you're alive. Don't you see? After all this. After all we've been through. We've survived.'

'It's not that easy.'

'I know that. We've both had terrible times. I understand things can't be the same. I wouldn't want them to be.'

141

'You don't know . . .' he began.

'Then you'll tell me,' she said. 'When the time's right. You have to forget Midian, Boone. It's already forgotten you.'

The shudders were not cold, but the precursors of tears, which broke now.

'I can't go,' he said, 'I can't go.'

'We've got no choice,' she reminded him. 'All we've got is each other.'

The pain of his hurt was almost bending him double.

'Stand up, Boone,' she said. 'Put your arms around me. The Breed don't want you; they don't need you. I do. Boone. Please.'

Slowly he drew himself upright, and embraced her.

'Tight,' she told him. 'Hold me tight, Boone.'

His grip tightened. When she dropped her hands from his face to reciprocate, his gaze did not now return to the necropolis. He looked at her.

'We're going to go back to the Inn and pick up all my belongings, yes? We have to do that. There are letters, photographs – lots of stuff we don't want anyone finding.'

'Then?' he said.

'Then we find somewhere to go where no-one will look for us, and work out a way to prove you innocent.'

'I don't like the light,' he said.

'Then we'll stay out of it,' she replied. 'Till you've got this damn place in perspective.'

She couldn't find anything in his face resembling an echo of her optimism. His eyes shone, but that was only the dregs of his tears. The rest of him was so *cold*; so much still a part of Midian's darkness. She didn't wonder at that. After all this night (and the days that had preceded it) had brought, she was surprised to find such capacity for hope in herself. But it was there, strong as a heart-beat, and she wouldn't let the fears she'd learned from the Breed undercut it.

'I love you, Boone,' she said, not expecting an answer.

Maybe in time he'd speak up. If not words of love, at least of explanation. And if he didn't, or *couldn't*, it was not so bad. She had better than explanations. She had the fact of him, the flesh of him. His body was solid in her arms. Whatever claim Midian had upon his memories Lylesburg had been perfectly explicit: he would never be allowed to return there. Instead he would be beside her again at night, his simple presence more precious than any display of passion.

And as time went by she'd persuade him from the torments of Midian, as she had from the self-inflicted torments of his lunacy. She hadn't failed in that, as Decker's deceits had convinced her she had. Boone had not concealed a secret life from her; he was innocent. As was she. Innocents both, which fact had brought them alive through this precarious night and into the safety of the day.

PART FOUR

SAINTS AND SINNERS

'You want my advice? Kiss the Devil, eat the worm'

Jan de Mooy
Another matter; or, Man remade

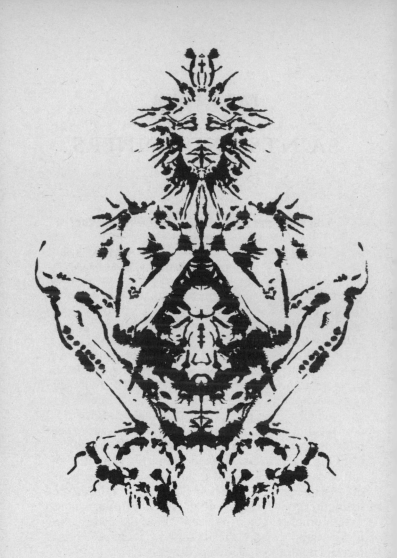

XV

The Toll

1

The sun rose like a stripper, keeping its glory well covered by cloud till it seemed there'd be no show at all, then casting its rags off one by one. As the light grew so did Boone's discomfort. Rummaging in the glove compartment Lori rooted out a pair of sunglasses, which Boone put on to keep the worst of the light from his sensitized eyes. Even then he had to keep his head down, his face averted from the brightening East.

They spoke scarcely at all. Lori was too concerned to keep her weary mind on the task of driving, and Boone made no attempt to break the silence. He had thoughts of his own, but none that he could have articulated to the woman at his side. In the past Lori had meant a great deal to him, he knew, but making contact with those feelings now was beyond him. He felt utterly removed from his life with her; indeed from life at all. Through the years of his sickness he'd clung always to the threads of consequence he saw in living: how one action resulted in another; this feeling in that. He'd got through, albeit with stumbling steps, by seeing how the path behind him became the one ahead. Now he could see neither forward nor backward, except dimly.

Clearest in his head, Baphomet, the Divided One. Of all Midian's occupants it was the most powerful and the most vulnerable, taken apart by ancient enemies

147

but preserved, suffering and suffering, in the flame Lylesburg had called the Trial Fire. Boone had gone into Baphomet's pit hoping to argue his case; but it was the Baptiser that had spoken, oracles from a severed head. He could not now remember its pronouncements but he knew the news had been grim.

Amongst his memories of the whole and the human, sharpest was that of Decker. He could piece together several fragments of their shared history, and knew it should enrage him, but he could not find it in himself to hate the man who'd led him to Midian's deeps, anymore than he could love the woman who'd brought him out of them. They were part of some other biography; not quite *his*.

What Lori understood of his condition he didn't know, but he suspected she remained for the most part ignorant. Whatever she guessed, she seemed content to accept him as he was, and in a simple, animal way he needed her presence too much to risk telling her the truth, assuming that he could have found the words. He was as much and as little as he was. Man. Monster. Dead. Alive. In Midian he'd seen all these states in a single creature: they were, most likely, all true of him. The only people who might have helped him understand how such contraries could co-exist were behind him, in the necropolis. They'd only begun the long, long process of educating him in Midian's history when he'd defied them. Now he was exiled from their presence forever, and he'd never know.

There was a paradox. Lylesburg had warned him clearly enough as they'd stood together in the tunnels and listened to Lori's cries for help; told him unequivocally that if he broke cover he broke his covenant with the Breed.

'*Remember what you are now,*' he'd said. '*You can't save her, and keep our refuge. So you have to let her die.*'

Yet he couldn't. Though Lori belonged in another

148

life, a life he'd lost forever, he couldn't leave her to the
fiend. What that meant, if anything, was beyond his
capacity to grasp right now. These few circling
thoughts aside he was sealed in the moment he was
living, and the next moment, and the moment after
that; moving second by second through his life as the
car moved over the road, ignorant of the place it had
been and blind to where it was headed.

2

They were almost within sight of the Sweetgrass Inn
when it occurred to Lori that if Sheryl's body had been
found at the Hudson Bay Sunset there was a chance
their destination would already be crawling with
police.

She stopped the car.

'What's wrong?' Boone asked.

She told him.

'Perhaps it'd be safer if I went there alone,' she said.
'If it's safe I'll get my things and come back for you.'

'No,' he said. 'That's not so good.'

She couldn't see his eyes behind the sunglasses, but
his voice carried fear in it.

'I'll be quick,' she said.

'No.'

'Why not?'

'It's better we stay together,' he replied. He put his
hands over his face, as he had at Midian's gates. 'Don't
leave me alone,' he said, his voice hushed. 'I don't
know where I am, Lori. I don't even know *who* I am.
Stay with me.'

She leaned over to him, and kissed the back of his
hand. He let both fall from his face. She kissed his
cheek, then his mouth. They drove on together to the
Inn.

In fact her fears proved groundless. If Sheryl's body had indeed been located overnight – which was perhaps unlikely given its location – no connection had been made with the Inn. Indeed not only were there no police to bar their way there was little sign of life at all. Only a dog yapping in one of the upper rooms, and a baby crying somewhere. Even the lobby was deserted, the desk clerk too occupied with the Morning Show to keep his post. The sound of laughter and music followed them through the hall and up the stairs to the first floor. Despite the ease of it, by the time they'd reached the room Lori's hands were trembling so much she could scarcely align the key with the lock. She turned to Boone for assistance, only to discover that he was no longer close behind her but lingering at the top of the stairs, looking back and forth along the corridor. Again, she cursed the sunglasses, which prevented her reading his feelings with any certainty. At least until he backed against the wall, his fingers seeking some purchase though there was none to be had.

'What's the problem, Boone?'

'There's nobody here,' he returned.

'Well that's good for us, isn't it?'

'But I can smell . . .'

'What can you smell?'

He shook his head.

'*Tell me.*'

'I smell *blood*.'

'Boone?'

'I smell so much *blood*.'

'Where? Where from?'

He made no answer, nor did he look her way, but stared off down the corridor.

'I'll be quick,' she told him. 'Just stay where you are, and I'll be back with you.'

Going down on her haunches she clumsily fitted key to lock, then stood up and opened the door. There was no scent of blood from the room, only the stale perfume of the previous night. It reminded her instantly of Sheryl, and of the good times they'd had together, even in the midst of such bad. Less than twenty-four hours ago she'd been laughing in this very room, and talking of her killer as the man of her dreams.

Thinking of which, Lori looked back towards Boone. He was still pressed against the wall, as if it was the only way to be certain the world wasn't toppling. Leaving him to it, she stepped into the room, and went about her packing. First into the bathroom, to collect up her toiletries, and then back into the bedroom to gather her strewn clothes. It was only as she put her bag on the bed to pack it that she saw the crack in the wall. It was as if something had hit it from the other side, very hard. The plaster had come away in clods, and littered the floor between the twin beds. She stared at the crack a moment. Had the party got so riotous they'd started throwing the furniture around?

Curious, she crossed to the wall. It was little more than a plasterboard partition, and the impact from the far side had actually opened a hole in it. She pulled a piece of loose plaster away and put her eye to the aperture.

The curtains were still drawn in the room beyond, but the sun was strong enough to penetrate, lending the air an ochre gloom. Last night's party must have been even more debauched than the one the night before, she thought. Wine stains on the walls, and the celebrants still asleep on the floor.

But the smell: it wasn't wine.

She stepped back from the wall, her stomach turning.

Fruit spilled no such juice –

Another step.

– flesh did. And if it was blood she smelt then it was blood she saw, and if it was blood she saw then the sleepers were not sleeping, because who lies down in an abattoir? Only the dead.

She went quickly to the door. Down the corridor

Boone was no long standing, but crouched against the wall, hugging his knees. His face, as he turned to her, was full of distressing tics.

'Get up,' she told him.

'I smell blood,' he said softly.

'You're right. So get up. Quickly. Help me.'

But he was rigid; rooted to the floor. She knew this posture of old: hunched in a corner, shivering like a beaten dog. In the past she'd had comforting words to offer, but there was no time for such solace now. Perhaps someone had survived the blood-bath in the next room. If so, she had to help, with Boone or without. She turned the handle of the slaughterhouse door, and opened it.

As the smell of death came out to meet her Boone started to moan.

'. . . blood . . .' she heard him say.

Everywhere, blood. She stood and stared for a full minute before forcing herself over the threshold to search for some sign of life. But even the most cursory glance at each of the corpses confirmed that the same nightmare had claimed all six. She knew his name too. He'd left his mark; wiping their features out with his knives the way he had Sheryl's. Three of the six he'd caught in *flagrante delicto*. Two men and a woman, partially undressed and slumped over each other on the bed, their entanglements fatal. The others had died lying in spirit sodden comas around the room, most likely without even waking. Hand over her mouth to keep the smell out and the sobs in, she retreated from the room, the taste of her stomach in her throat. As she stepped out into the corridor her peripheral vision caught sight of Boone. He wasn't sitting any longer, but moving purposefully down the passageway towards her.

'We have . . . to get . . . out,' she said.

He made no sign that he'd even heard her voice, but moved past her towards the open door.

'Decker . . .' she said, '. . . it was Decker.'

He still offered no reply.

'Talk to me, Boone.'

He murmured something –

'He could still be here,' she said. 'We have to hurry.'

– but he was already stepping inside to view the carnage at closer quarters. She had no desire to look again. Instead she returned to the adjacent room to finish her hurried packing. As she went about it she heard Boone moving around the room next door, his breathing almost pained. Afraid of leaving him on his own for any time she gave up on trying to collect all but the most telling items – the photographs and an address book chief amongst them – and that done went out into the corridor.

The din of police sirens was there to meet her, their panic fuelling hers. Though the cars were still some way off she couldn't doubt their destination. Louder with every whoop, they were coming to the Sweetgrass, hot for the guilty.

She called for Boone.

'I'm finished!' she said. 'Let's get going!'

There was no reply from the room.

'Boone?'

She went to the door trying to keep her eyes off the bodies. Boone was on the far side of the room, silhouetted against the curtains. His breath was no longer audible.

'Do you hear me?' she said.

He didn't move a muscle. She could read no expression on his face – it was too dark – but she could see that he'd taken the sunglasses off.

'We haven't got much time,' she said. 'Will you come on?'

As she spoke, he exhaled. It was no normal breath; she knew that even before the smoke started from his throat. As it came he raised his hands to his mouth as if to stop it, but at his chin they halted and began to convulse.

'*Get out,*' he said, on the same breath that brought the smoke.

She couldn't move, or even take her eyes off him. The murk was not so thick she couldn't see the change coming, his face re-ordering itself behind the veil, light burning in his arms and climbing his neck in waves to melt the bones of his head.

'*I don't want you to see,*' he begged her, his voice deteriorating.

Too late. She'd seen the man with fire in his flesh at Midian; and the dog-headed painter, and more besides: Boone had all their diseases in his system, undoing his humanity before her eyes. He was the stuff of nightmares. No wonder he howled, head thrown back as his face was forfeited.

The sound was almost cancelled by the sirens, however. They could be no more than a minute from the door. If she went now she might still outpace them.

In front of her, Boone was done, or undone, entirely. He lowered his head, remnants of smoke evaporating around him. Then he began to move, his new sinews bearing him lightly, like an athlete.

Even now she hoped he understood his jeopardy and was coming to the door to be saved. But no. It was to the dead he moved, where the *ménage à trois* still lay, and before she had the wit to look away one of his clawed hands was reaching down and claiming a body from the heap, drawing it up towards his mouth.

'No, Boone!' she shrieked. '*No!*'

Her voice found him, or a part that was still Boone, lost in the chaos of this monster. He let the meat drop a little and looked up at her. He still had his blue eyes, and they were full of tears.

She started towards him.

'Don't,' she begged.

For an instant he seemed to weigh up love and

154

appetite. Then he forgot her, and lifted the human meat to his lips. She didn't watch his jaws close on it, but the sound reached her, and it was all she could do to stay conscious, hearing him tear and chew.

From below, brakes screeching, doors slamming. In moments they'd have the building surrounded, blocking any hope of escape; moments later they'd be coming up the stairs. She had no choice but to leave the beast to its hunger. Boone was lost to her.

She elected not to return the way they'd come, but to take the back stairs. The decision was well made; even as she turned the corner of the upper corridor she heard the police at the other end, rapping on doors. Almost immediately afterwards she heard the sound of forced entry from above, and exclamations of disgust. This couldn't be on finding Boone; he wasn't behind a locked door. Clearly they'd discovered something *else* on the upper corridor. She didn't need to hear the morning news to know what. Her instinct told her loud and strong how thorough Decker had been the night before. There *was* a dog alive somewhere in the building, and he'd overlooked a baby in his heat, but the rest he'd taken. He'd just come straight back from his failure at Midian and killed every living soul in the place.

Above and below the investigating officers were discovering that very fact, and the shock of it made them incompetent. She had no difficulty slipping out of the building and away into the scrub at the back. Only as she reached the cover of the trees did one of the cops appear round the corner of the building, but even he had other business than the search. Once out of sight of his colleagues he threw up his breakfast in the dirt, then scrupulously wiped his mouth with his handkerchief and went back to the job in hand.

Secure that they wouldn't start a search of the exterior until they'd finished inside, she waited. What would they do to Boone when they found him? Shoot him down, most likely. There was nothing she could think of to prevent it. But the minutes passed, and though there were shouts from within, there was no sound of gunfire. They must have found him by now. Maybe she'd get a better grasp of what had happened from the front of the building.

The Inn was shielded on three sides by shrubbery and trees. It wasn't difficult to make her way through the undergrowth to the flank, her movement countered by an influx of rifle-bearing cops from the front, to take up stations at the rear exit. Two more patrol cars were arriving at the scene. The first contained further armed troopers; the second a selection of interested parties. Two ambulance vans followed.

They'll need more, she thought grimly. *A lot more.*

Though the congregation of so many cars and armed men had attracted an audience of passers by, the scene at the front was subdued, even casual. There were as many men standing and staring at the building as moving to enter and explore it. They grasped the point now. The place was a two storey coffin. More people had probably been murdered here in one night than had died by violence in Shere Neck over its entire life. Anyone here this bright morning was part of history. The knowledge hushed them.

Her attention went from the witnesses to a knot of people standing around the lead car. A break in the circle of debaters allowed for a glimpse of the man at its centre. Sober-suited, polished spectacles glinting in the sun. Decker held court. What was he arguing for: a chance to coax his patient out into the open air? If that was his pitch he was being overruled by the only member of the circle in uniform, Shere Neck's Police Chief presumably, who dismissed his appeal with a wave of the hand, then stepped out of the argument entirely. From a distance it was impossible to read Decker's response, but he seemed perfectly in control of himself, leaning to speak into the ear of one of the others, who nodded sagely at the whispered remark.

Last night Lori had seen Decker the madman unmasked. Now she wanted to unmask him again. Strip away this façade of civilized concern. But how? If she stepped out of hiding and challenged him – tried to begin to explain all that she'd seen and experienced in the last twenty four hours – they'd be measuring her up for a strait-jacket before she'd taken a second breath.

He was the one in the well cut suit, with the doctorate and the friends in high places; *he* was the *man*, the voice of reason and analysis, while she – a mere woman! – what credentials did she have? – lover of a lunatic and a sometime beast? Decker's midnight face was quite secure.

There was a sudden eruption of shouts from inside the building. On an order from their chief the troopers outside levelled their weapons at the front door; the rest retired a few yards. Two cops, pistols aimed at someone inside, backed out of the door. A beat later, Boone, his hands cuffed in front of him, was pushed into the light. It near blinded him. He tried to turn from its brilliance, back into the shadows, but there were two armed men following, who pressed him forward.

There was no sign remaining of the creature Lori had seen him become, but there was ample reminder of his hunger. Blood glued his tee shirt to his chest, and spattered his face and arms.

There was some applause from the audience, uniformed and otherwise, at the sight of the killer chained. Decker joined it, nodding and smiling, as Boone was led away, head averted from the sun, and put into the back of one of the cars.

Lori watched the scene with so many feelings grappling for her attention. Relief that Boone had not been shot on sight, mingled with horror at what she now knew he was; rage at Decker's performance, and disgust at those who were taken in by it.

So many masks. Was she the only one who had no secret life; no other self in marrow or mind? If not, then perhaps she had no place in this game of *appearances*; perhaps Boone and Decker were the true lovers here, swapping blows and faces but *necessary* to each other.

And she'd hugged this man, demanded he embrace her, put her lips to his face. She could never do that again, knowing what lay in wait behind his lips, behind his eyes. She could never *kiss the beast*.

So why did the thought make her heart hammer?

XVI

Now or Never

1

'What are you telling me? That there's more of these people involved? Some kind of cult?'

Decker drew breath to deliver his warning about Midian over again. The troopers called their Chief everything but his name behind his back. Five minutes in his presence and Decker knew why; ten and he was plotting the man's dismemberment. But not today. The day he needed Irwin Eigerman: and Eigerman, did he but know it, needed him. While daylight lasted Midian was vulnerable, but they had to be swift. It was already one o'clock. Nightfall might still be a good distance away, but so was Midian. To get a task force out there to uproot the place was the work of several hours; and every minute lost to argument was a minute lost to action.

'Beneath the cemetery,' Decker said, beginning again at the place he'd begun half an hour before.

Eigerman scarcely made a pretence of listening. His euphoria had increased in direct proportion to the number of bodies brought out of the Sweetgrass Inn, a count which presently stood at sixteen. He had hopes for more. The only human survivor was a year-old baby found in a tumble of blood-soaked sheets. He'd taken her out of the building himself, for the benefit of the cameras. Tomorrow the country would know his name.

None of this would have been possible without

Decker's tip off, of course, which was why he was humouring the man, though at this stage in proceedings, with interviewers and flashlights calling, he was damned if he was going to go after a few freaks who liked corpses for company, which was what Decker was suggesting he do.

He took out his comb and began to rake over his thinning crop, in the hope of fooling the cameras. He was no beauty, he knew. Should it ever slip his mind he had Annie to remind him. You look like a sow, she was fond of remarking, usually before bedtime on a Saturday night. But then people saw what they wanted to see. After today, he'd look like a hero.

'Are you listening?' Decker said.

'I hear you. There's folks grave robbing. I hear you.'

'Not grave robbing. Not *folks*.'

'Freaks,' Eigerman said. 'I seen 'em.'

'Not the likes of these.'

'You're not saying any of them were at the Sweetgrass are you?'

'No.'

'We've got the man responsible right here?'

'Yes.'

'Under lock and key.'

'Yes. But there are others in Midian.'

'Murderers?'

'Probably.'

'You're not sure?'

'Just get some of your people out there.'

'What's the hurry?'

'If I told you once I told you a dozen times.'

'So tell me again.'

'They have to be rounded up by daylight.'

'What are they? Some kind of bloodsuckers?' He chuckled to himself. 'That what they are?'

'In a manner of speaking,' Decker replied.

'Well, in a manner of speaking I gotta tell you, it's

gonna have to wait. I got people want to interview me, doctor. Can't leave them begging. It's not polite.'

'Fuck polite. You've got deputies, haven't you? Or is this a one cop town?'

Eigerman clearly bridled at this.

'I've got deputies.'

'Then may I suggest you dispatch some of them to Midian?'

'To do what?'

'Dig around.'

'That's probably consecrated ground, mister,' Eigerman replied. 'That's holy.'

'What's under it isn't,' Decker replied, with a gravity that had Eigerman silenced. 'You trusted me once, Irwin,' he said. 'And you caught a killer. Trust me again. You have to turn Midian upside down.'

2

There had been terrors, yes, but the old imperatives remained the same: the body had to eat, had to sleep. After leaving the Sweetgrass Inn Lori satisfied the first of these, wandering the streets until she found a suitably anonymous and busy store, then buying a collection of instant gratification foods: doughnuts, custard filled and dutch apple, chocolate milk, cheese. Then she sat in the sun and ate, her numbed mind unable to think much beyond the simple business of biting, chewing and swallowing. The food made her so sleepy she couldn't have denied her lids falling if she'd tried. When she woke her side of the street, which had been bathed in sunshine, was in shadow. The stone step was chilly, and her body ached. But the food and the rest, however primitive, had done her some good. Her thought processes were a little more in order.

She had little cause for optimism, that was certain,

but the situation had been bleaker when she'd first come through this town, on her way to find the spot where Boone had fallen. Then she'd believed the man she loved was dead; it had been a widow's pilgrimage. Now at least he was alive, though God alone knew what horror, contracted in the tombs of Midian, possessed him. Given that fact, it was perhaps good that he was safe in the hands of the law, the slow process of which would give her time to think their problems through. Most urgent of those, a way to unmask Decker. No-one could kill so many without leaving some trace of evidence. Perhaps back at the restaurant, where he'd murdered Sheryl. She doubted he'd lead the police there as he'd led them to the Inn. It would seem too like complicity with the accused, knowing all the murder sites. He'd wait for the other corpse to be found by accident, knowing the crime would be ascribed to Boone. Which meant – *perhaps* – the site was untouched, and she might still find some clue that would incriminate him; or at very least open a crack in that pristine face of his.

Returning to where Sheryl had died, and where she'd endured Decker's provocations, would be no picnic, but it was the only alternative to defeat she had.

She went quickly. By daylight, she had a hope of getting up the courage to step through that burnt out door. By night it would be another matter.

3

Decker watched as Eigerman briefed his deputies, four men who shared with their Chief the looks of bullies made good.

'Now I trust our source,' he said magnanimously, throwing a look back at Decker, 'and if he tells me something bad's going down in Midian, then I think that's worth listening to. I want you to dig around a little. See what you can see.'

'What exactly are we looking for?' one of the number wanted to know. His name was Pettine. A forty-year-old with the wide, empty face of a comedian's foil; and a voice too loud, and a belly too big.

'Anything weird,' Eigerman told him.

'Like people been messing with the dead?' the youngest of the four said.

'Could be, Tommy,' Eigerman said.

'It's more than that,' Decker put in. 'I believe Boone's got friends in the cemetery.'

'A fuckwit like that has friends?' Pettine said. 'Sure as shit wanna know what *they* look like.'

'Well you bring 'em back, boys.'

'And if they won't come?'

'What are you asking, Tommy?'

'Do we use force?'

'Do unto others, boy, before they do unto you.'

'They're good men,' Eigerman told Decker, when the quartet had been dispatched. 'If there's anything to find there, they'll find it.'

'Good enough.'

'I'm going to see the prisoner. You want to come?'

'I've seen as much of Boone as I ever want to see.'

'No problem,' Eigerman said, and left Decker to his calculations.

He'd almost elected to go with the troopers to Midian but there was too much work to do here preparing the ground for the revelations ahead. There would *be* revelations. Though so far Boone had declined to respond to even the simplest enquiries, he'd break his silence eventually, and when he did Decker would have questions asked of him. There was no chance any of Boone's accusations could stick – the man had been found with human meat in his mouth, bloodied from head to foot – but there were elements of recent events that confounded even Decker, and until every variable in the scenario had been pinned down and understood he would fret.

What, for instance, had happened to Boone? How had the scapegoat filled with bullets and filed as dead become the ravening monster he'd almost lost his life to the night before? Boone had even claimed he was *dead*, for Christ's sake – and in the chill of the moment Decker had almost shared the psychosis. Now he saw more clearly. Eigerman was right. They *were* freaks, albeit stranger than the usual stuff. Things in defiance of nature, to be poked from under their stones and soaked in gasoline. He'd happily strike the match himself.

'Decker?'

He turned from his thoughts to find Eigerman closing the door on the babble of journalists outside. All trace of his former confidence had fled. He was sweating profusely.

'OK. What the fuck's going on?'

'Do we have a problem, Irwin?'

'Shit alive, do we have a problem.'

'Boone?'

'Of course Boone.'

'What?'

'The doctors have just looked him over. That's procedure.'

'And?'

'How many times did you shoot him? Three, four?'

'Yeah, maybe.'

'Well the bullets are still in him.'

'I'm not that surprised,' Decker said. 'I told you we're not dealing with ordinary people here. What are the doctors saying? He should be dead?'

'He *is* dead.'

'When?'

'I don't mean lying down dead, shithead,' Eigerman

said. 'I mean sitting in my fucking cell dead. I mean his heart isn't beating.'

'That's impossible.'

'I've got two fuckers telling me the man is walking dead, and inviting me to listen for myself. You wanna tell me about that, *doctor*?'

XVII

Delirium

Lori stood across the street from the burnt out restaurant, and watched it for five minutes, to see if there was any sign of activity. There was none. Only now, in the full light of day, did she realize just how run down this neighbourhood was. Decker had chosen well. The chance of anyone having seen him enter or leave the place the night before was most likely zero. Even in the middle of the afternoon no pedestrian passed along the street in either direction, and the few vehicles that used the thoroughfare were speeding on their way to somewhere more promising.

Something about the scene – perhaps the heat of the sun, in contrast to Sheryl's unmarked grave – brought her solitary adventure in Midian back to her; or more particularly, her encounter with Babette. It wasn't just her mind's eye which conjured the girl. It seemed her whole body was reliving their first meeting. She could feel the weight of the beast she'd picked up from beneath the tree against her breast. Its laboured breathing was in her ears, its bitter sweetness pricked her nostrils.

The sensations came with such force they almost constituted a *summoning*: past jeopardy signalling present. She seemed to *see* the child looking up at her from her arms, though she'd never carried Babette in human form. The child's mouth was opening and closing, forming an appeal Lori could not read from lips alone.

Then, like a cinema screen blanked out in mid-movie, the images disappeared, and she was left with only one set of sensations: the street, the sun, the burnt out building ahead.

There was no purpose in putting off the evil moment any longer. She crossed the street, mounted the sidewalk, and without allowing herself to slow her step by a beat stepped through the carbonized door frame into the murk beyond. So quickly dark! So quickly cold! One step out of the sunlight, and she was in another world. Her pace slowed a little now, as she negotiated the maze of debris that lay between front door and the kitchen. Fixed clearly in her mind was her sole intention: to turn up some shred of evidence that would convict Decker. She had to keep all other thoughts at bay: revulsion, grief, fear. She had to be cool and calm. Play Decker's game.

Girding herself, she stepped through the archway.

Not into the kitchen, however: into *Midian*.

She knew the moment it happened where she was – the chill and the dark of the tombs was unmistakable. The kitchen had simply vanished: every tile.

Across the chamber from her stood Rachel, looking up at the roof, distress on her face. For a moment she glanced at Lori, registering no surprise at her presence. Then she returned to watching and listening.

'What's wrong?' Lori said.

'Hush,' Rachel said sharply, then seemed to regret her harshness and opened her arms. 'Come to me, child,' she said.

Child. So that was it. She wasn't in Midian, she was in Babette, seeing with the child's eyes. The memories she'd felt so strongly on the street had been a prelude to a union of minds.

'Is this real?' she said.

'Real?' Rachel whispered. 'Of course it's real . . .'

Her words faltered, and she looked at her daughter with enquiry on her face.

'Babette?' she said.

'No . . .' Lori replied.

'Babette. What have you done?'

She moved towards the child, who backed away from her. Her view through these stolen eyes brought a taste of the past back. Rachel seemed impossibly tall, her approach ungainly.

'What have you done?' she asked a second time.

'I've brought her,' the girl said. 'To see.'

Rachel's face became furious. She snatched at her daughter's arm. But the child was too quick for her. Before she could be caught she'd scooted away, out of Rachel's reach. Lori's mind's eye went with her, dizzied by the ride.

'Come back here,' Rachel whispered.

Babette ignored the instructions, and took to the tunnels, ducking round corner after corner with the ease of one who knew the labyrinth back to front. The route took runner and passenger off the main thoroughfares and into darker, narrower passages, until Babette was certain she was not being pursued. They had come to an opening in the wall, too small to allow adult passage. Babette clambered through, and into a space no larger than a refrigerator, and as cold, which was the child's hideaway. Here she sat to draw breath, her sensitive eyes able to pierce the total darkness. Her few treasures were gathered around her. A doll made of grasses, and crowned with spring flowers; two bird skulls, a small collection of stones. For all her otherness Babette was in this like any child: sensitive, ritualistic. Here was her world. That she'd let Lori see it was no small compliment.

But she hadn't brought Lori here simply to see her hoard. There were voices overhead, close enough to be heard clearly.

'*Who-ee*! Will you look at this shit? You could hide a fuckin' army here.'

'Don't say it, Cas.'

'Shittin' your pants, Tommy?'

'Nope.'

'Sure smells like it.'

'Fuck you.'

'Shut up, the both of you. We've got work to do.'

'Where do we start?'

'We look for any signs of disturbance.'

'There's people here. I feel 'em. Decker was right.'

'So let's get the fuckers out where we can see 'em.'

'You mean . . . *go down*? I ain't going down.'

'No need.'

'So how the fuck do we bring 'em up, asshole?'

The reply wasn't a word but a shot, ringing off stone.

'Be like shootin' fish in a barrel,' somebody said. 'If they won't come up they can stay down there permanent.'

'Saves digging a grave!'

Who are these people? Lori thought. No sooner had she asked the question than Babette was up and clambering into a narrow duct that led off her playroom. It was barely large enough to accommodate her small body; a twinge of claustrophobia touched Lori. But there was compensation. Daylight up ahead, and the fragrance of the open air, which, warming Babette's skin, warmed Lori too.

The passage was apparently some kind of drainage system. The child squirmed through an accumulation of debris, pausing only to turn over the corpse of a shrew that had died in the duct. The voices from overground were distressingly close.

'I say we just start here and open up every damn tomb till we find something to take home.'

'Nothing here I wanna take home.'

'Shit, Pettine, I want *prisoners*! As many of the fuckers as we can get.'

'Shouldn't we call in first?' a fourth speaker now asked. This dissenting voice had not so far been heard in the exchanges. 'Maybe the Chief's got fresh instructions for us.'

'Fuck the Chief,' Pettine said.

'Only if he says *please*,' came the response from Cas.

Amid the laughter that followed there were several other remarks exchanged, obscenities mostly. It was Pettine who silenced the hilarity.

'OK. Let's get the fuck on with it.'

'Sooner the better,' said Cas. 'Ready Tommy?'

'I'm always ready.'

The source of the light Babette was crawling towards now became apparent: a latticed grille in the side of the tunnel.

Keep out of the sun, Lori found herself thinking.

It's all right, Babette's thoughts replied. Clearly this wasn't the first time she'd used the spy hole. Like a prisoner without hope of parole she took what entertainment she could find to ease the passage of time. Watching the world from here was one such distraction, and she'd chosen her vantage point well. The grille offered a view of the avenues but was so placed in the mausoleum wall that direct sunlight did not fall through it. Babette put her face close to the grille, to get a clearer grasp of the scene outside.

Lori could see three of the four speakers. All were in uniform; all – despite their brave talk – looked like men who could think of a dozen better places to be than this. Even in broad daylight, armed to the teeth and safe in the sun, they were ill at ease. It wasn't difficult to guess why. Had they come to take prisoners from a tenement block there'd be none of the half glances and nervous tics on display here. But this was Death's territory, and they felt like trespassers.

In any other circumstances she would have taken some delight in their discomfiture. But not here, not now. She knew what men afraid, and afraid of their fear were capable of.

They'll find us, she heard Babette think.

Let's hope not, her thoughts replied.

But they will, the child said. *The Prophetic says so.*

Who?

Babette's answer was an image, of a creature Lori had glimpsed when she'd gone in pursuit of Boone in the tunnels: the beast with larval wounds, lying on a mattress in an empty cell. Now she glimpsed it in different circumstances, lifted up above the heads of a congregation by two Breed, down whose sweating arms the creature's burning blood coursed. It was speaking, though she couldn't hear its words. Prophecies, she presumed; and amongst them, this scene.

They'll find us, and try to kill us all, the child thought.

And will they?

The child was silent.

Will they, Babette?

The Prophetic can't see, because it's one of those that'll die. Maybe I'll die too.

The thought had no voice, so came as pure feeling, a wave of sadness that Lori had no way to resist or heal.

One of the men, Lori now noticed, had sidled towards his colleague, and was surreptitiously pointing at a tomb to their right. Its door stood slightly ajar. There was movement within. Lori could see what was coming; so could the child. She felt a shudder run down Babette's spine, felt her fingers curl around the lattice, gripping it in anticipation of the horror ahead. Suddenly the two men were at the tomb door, and kicking it wide. There was a cry from within; somebody fell. The lead cop was inside in seconds, followed by his partner, the din alerting the third and fourth to the tomb door.

'Out of the way!' the cop inside yelled. The trooper stepped back and with a grin of satisfaction on his face the arresting officer dragged his prisoner out of hiding, his colleague kicking from behind.

172

Lori caught only a glimpse of their victim, but quick-eyed Babette named him with a thought.

Ohnaka.

'On your knees, asshole,' the cop bringing up the rear demanded, and kicked the legs from under the prisoner. The man went down, bowing his head to keep the sun from breaching the defence of his wide brimmed hat.

'Good work, Gibbs,' Pettine grinned.

'So where's the rest of them?' the youngest of the four, a skinny kid with a coxcomb, demanded.

'Underground, Tommy,' the fourth man announced. 'That's what Eigerman said.'

Gibbs closed in on Ohnaka.

'We'll get fuckface to show us,' he said. He looked up at Tommy's companion: a short, wide man. 'You're good with the questions, Cas.'

'Ain't nobody ever said no to me,' the man replied. 'True or false?'

'True,' said Gibbs.

'You want this man on your case?' Pettine asked Ohnaka. The prisoner said nothing.

'Don't think he heard,' Gibbs said. 'You ask him, Cas.'

'Sure enough.'

'Ask him *hard*.'

Cas approached Ohnaka, reaching down and snatching the brimmed hat from off his head. Instantly, Ohnaka began to scream.

'Shut the fuck up!' Cas yelled at him, kicking him in the belly.

Ohnaka went on screaming, his arms crossed over his bald head to keep the sun off it as he clambered to his feet. Desperate for the succour of the dark he started back towards the open door, but young Tommy was already there to block his way.

'Good man, Tommy!' Pettine hollered. 'Go get him Cas!'

Forced back into the sun, Ohnaka had begun to shudder as though a fit had seized him.

'What the fuck?' said Gibbs.

The prisoner's arms no longer had the strength to protect his head. They fell to his sides, smoking, leaving Tommy to look straight into his face. The boy cop didn't speak. He just took two stumbling steps backwards, dropping his rifle as he did so.

'What are you doin', dickhead?' Pettine yelled. Then he reached and took hold of Ohnaka's arm to prevent him claiming the dropped weapon. In the confusion of the moment it was difficult for Lori to see what happened next, but it seemed Ohnaka's flesh gave way. There was a cry of disgust from Cas, and one of fury from Pettine as he pulled his hand away, dropping a fistful of fabric and dust.

'*What the fuck?*' Tommy shouted. '*What the fuck? What the fuck?*'

'Shut up!' Gibbs told him, but the boy had lost control. Over and over, the same question:

'*What the fuck?*'

Unmoved by Tommy's panic, Cas went in to beat Ohnaka back down to his knees. The blow he delivered did more than he intended. It broke Ohnaka's arm at the elbow, and the limb fell off at Tommy's feet. His shouts gave way to puking. Even Cas backed off, shaking his head in disbelief.

Ohnaka was past the point of no return. His legs buckled beneath him, his body growing frailer and frailer beneath the assault of the sun. But it was his face – turned now towards Pettine – that brought the loudest shouts, as the flesh dropped away and smoke rose from his eye sockets as though his brain were on fire.

He no longer howled. There was no strength in his body left for that. He simply sank to the ground, head thrown back as if to invite the sun's speed, and have the agony over. Before he hit the paving some final stitch in his being snapped with a sound like a shot. His decaying remains flew apart in a burst of blood-dust and bones.

Lori willed Babette to look away, as much for her own sake as that of the child. But she refused to avert her eyes. Even when the horror was over – Ohnaka's body spread in pieces across the avenue – she still pressed her face to the grille, as if to know this death by sunlight in all its particulars. Nor could Lori look away while the child stared on. She shared every quiver in Babette's limbs; tasted the tears she was holding back, so as not to let them cloud her vision. Ohnaka was dead, but his executioners were not finished with their business yet. While there was more to see the child kept watching.

Tommy was trying to wipe spattered puke from the front of his uniform. Pettine was kicking over a frag-ment of Ohnaka's corpse; Cas was taking a cigarette from Gibbs' breast pocket.

'Gimme a light, will you?' he said. Gibbs dug his trembling hand into his trouser pocket for matches, his eyes fixed on the smoking remains.

'Never saw nothin' like that before,' Pettine said, almost casually.

'You shit yourself this time, Tommy?' Gibbs said.

'Fuck you,' came the reply. Tommy's fair skin was flushed red. 'Cas said we should have called the Chief,' he said. 'He was right.'

'What the fuck does Eigerman know?' Pettine com-mented, and spat into the red dust at his feet.

'You see the face on that fucker?' Tommy said. 'You see the way it looked at me? I was near dead, I tell you. He would have had me.'

'What's going on here?' Cas said.

Gibbs had the answer almost right.

'Sunlight,' he replied. 'I heard there's diseases like that. It was the sun got him.'

'No way, man,' said Cas. 'I never seen or heard of nothin' like that.'

'Well we seen and heard it *now*,' said Pettine with more than a little satisfaction. 'It weren't no hallucination.'

'So what do we do?' Gibbs wanted to know. He was having difficulty getting the match in his shaking fingers to the cigarette between his lips.

'We look for more,' said Pettine, 'and we *keep* looking.'

'I ain't,' said Tommy. 'I'm calling the fuckin' Chief. We don't know how many of these freaks there are. There could be hundreds. You said so yourself. Hide a fuckin' army you said.'

'What are you so scared of?' Gibbs replied. 'You saw what the sun did to it.'

'Yeah. And what happens when the sun goes down, fuckwit?' was Tommy's retort.

The match flame burnt Gibbs' fingers. He dropped it with a curse.

'I seen the movies,' Tommy said. 'Things come out at night.'

Judging by the look on Gibbs' face he'd seen the same movies.

'Maybe you *should* call up some help,' he said. 'Just in case.'

Lori's thoughts spoke hurriedly to the child.

You must warn Rachel. Tell her what we've seen.

They know already, came the child's reply.

Tell them anyway. Forget me! Tell them, Babette, before it's too late.

I don't want to leave you.

I can't help you Babette. I don't belong with you. I'm —

She tried to prevent the thought coming, but it was too late.

— I'm normal. The sun won't kill me the way it'll

176

kill you. I'm alive. I'm human. I don't belong with you.

She had no opportunity to qualify this hurried response. Contact was broken instantly – the view from Babette's eyes disappearing – and Lori found herself standing on the threshold of the kitchen.

The sound of flies was loud in her head. Their buzzing was no echo of Midian, but the real thing. They were circling the room ahead of her. She knew all too well what scent had brought them here, egg-laden and hungry; and she knew with equal certainty that after all she'd seen in Midian she couldn't bear to take another step towards the corpse on the floor. There was too much death in her world, inside her head and out. If she didn't escape it she'd go mad. She had to get back into the open air, where she could breathe freely. Maybe find some unremarkable shop girl to talk to about the weather, about the price of sanitary towels; anything as long as it was banal, predictable.

But the flies wanted to buzz in her ears. She tried to swat them away. Still they came *at* her and *at* her, their wings buttered with death, their feet red with it.

'Let me alone,' she sobbed. But her excitement drew them in larger and still larger numbers, rising at the sound of her voice from their dining table out of sight behind the ovens. Her mind struggled to take hold of the reality she'd been thrown back into, her body to turn and leave the kitchen.

Both failed, mind and body. The cloud of flies came at her, their numbers now so large they were a darkness unto themselves. Dimly she realized that such a multiplicity was impossible and that her mind was creating this terror in its confusion. But the thought was too far from her to keep the madness at bay; her reason reached for it, and reached, but the cloud was upon her now. She felt their feet on her arms and face, leaving trails of whatever they'd been dabbling in: Sheryl's blood, Sheryl's bile, Sheryl's sweat and tears. There were so many of them they could not all find flesh to occupy, so they began to force their way between her lips, and crawl up her nostrils and across her eyes.

Once, in a dream of Midian, hadn't the dead come as dust, from all four corners of the world? And hadn't she stood in the middle of the storm – caressed, eroded – and been happy to know that the dead were on the wind? Now came the companion dream: horror to the splendour of the first. A world of flies to match that world of dust; a world of incomprehension and blindness, of the dead without burial, and without a wind to carry them away. Only flies to feast on them, to lay in them and make more flies.

And matching dust against flies, she knew which she favoured; knew, as consciousness went out of her completely, that if Midian died – and she let it – if Pettine and Gibbs and their friends dug up the Nightbreed's refuge, then *she*, dust herself one day, and touched by Midian's condition – would have nowhere to be carried, and would belong, body and soul, to the flies.

Then she hit the tiles.

XVIII

The Wrath of the Righteous

1

For Eigerman bright ideas and excretion were inextricably linked; he did all his best thinking with his trousers around his ankles. More than once, in his cups, he'd explained to any who'd listen that world peace and a cure for cancer could be achieved overnight if the wise and the good would just sit down and take a crap together.

Sober, the thought of sharing that most private of functions would have appalled him. The can was a place for solitary endeavour, where those weighed down by high office could snatch a little time to sit and meditate upon their burdens.

He studied the graffiti on the door in front of him. There was nothing new amongst the obscenities, which was reassuring. Just the same old itches, needing to be scratched. It gave him courage in the face of his problems.

Which were essentially twofold. First, he had a dead man in custody. That, like the graffiti, was an old story. But zombies belonged in the late movie, like sodomy on a lavatory wall. They had no place in the real world. Which brought him onto the second problem: the panicked call from Tommy Caan, reporting that something bad was going down in Midian. To those two, on reflection, he now added a third: Doctor Decker. He wore a fine suit, and he talked fine talk, but there was something unwholesome about him.

Eigerman hadn't admitted the suspicion to himself until now, sitting on the crapper, but it was plain as his dick once he thought about it. The bastard knew more than he was telling: not just about Dead Man Boone, but about Midian and whatever was going on there. If he was setting Shere Neck's finest up for a fall then there'd come a reckoning time, sure as shit, and he'd regret it.

Meanwhile the Chief had to make some decisions. He'd begun the day as a hero, leading the arrest of the Calgary Killer, but instinct told him events could very quickly get out of hand. There were so many imponderables in all of this; so many questions to which he had no answers. There was an easy way out, of course. He could call up his superiors in Edmonton and pass the whole fuck-up along to them to deal with. But if he gave away the problem he also gave the glory. The alternative was to act now – before nightfall, Tommy had kept saying, and how far was that? three, four hours – to root out the abominations of Midian. If he succeeded he'd double his helping of accolades. In one day he'd not only have brought a human evil to justice but scoured the cess-pit in which it had found succour: an appealing notion.

But again the answered questions raised their heads, and they weren't pretty. If the doctors who'd examined Boone and reports coming out of Midian were to be trusted then things he'd only heard in stories were true today. Did he really want to pit his wits against dead men who walked, and beasts that sunlight killed?

He sat, and crapped, and weighed up the alternatives. It took him half an hour, but he finally came to a decision. As usual, once the sweat was over, it looked very simple. Perhaps today the world was not quite the way it had been yesterday. Tomorrow, God willing, it would be its old self: dead men dead, and sodomy on the walls where it belonged. If he didn't seize his chance to become a man of destiny there wouldn't be another, at least not till he was too old to do more than tend his haemorrhoids. This was a God given opportunity to show his mettle. He couldn't afford to ignore it.

With new conviction in his gut he wiped his ass, hauled up his pants, flushed the crapper and went out to meet the challenge head-on.

2

'I want volunteers, Cormack, who'll come out to Midian with me and get digging.'

'How soon do you need them?'

'*Now.* We don't have much time. Start with the bars. Take Holliday with you.'

'What are we telling them it's for?'

Eigerman mused on this a moment: what to *tell*.

'Say we're looking for grave-robbers. That'll get a sizeable turnout. Anyone with a gun and a shovel's eligible. I want 'em mustered in an hour. Less if you can do it.'

Decker smiled as Cormack went on his way.

'You happy now?' Eigerman said.

'I'm pleased to see you've taken my advice.'

'Your advice, shit.'

Decker just smiled.

'Get the fuck out of here,' Eigerman said. 'I've got work to do. Come back when you've found yourself a gun.'

'I just might do that.'

Eigerman watched him leave, then picked up the phone. There was a number he'd been thinking about dialling since he'd made up his mind to go into Midian; a number he hadn't had reason to call in a long time. He dialled it now. In seconds, Father Ashbery was on the line.

'You sound breathless, Father.'

Ashbery knew who his caller was without need of prompting.

'Eigerman.'

'Got it in one. What have you been up to?'

'I've been out running.'

'Good idea. Sweat out the dirty thoughts.'

'What do you want?'

'What do you think I want? A priest.'

'I've done nothing.'

'That's not what I hear.'

'I'm not paying, Eigerman. God forgave me my sins.'

'Not in question.'

'So leave me alone.'

'Don't hang up!'

Ashbery was quick to detect the sudden anxiety in Eigerman's voice.

'Well, well,' he said.

'What?'

'You've got a problem.'

'Maybe both of us do.'

'Meaning?'

'I want you here real quick, with whatever you've got in the way of crucifixes and Holy Water.'

'What for?'

'Trust me.'

Ashbery laughed.

'I'm not at your beck and call any longer, Eigerman. I've got a flock to tend.'

'So do it for them.'

'What are you talking about?'

'You preach the Day of Judgement, right? Well they're warming up for it, over in Midian.'

'Who are?'

'I don't know who and I don't know why. All I know is, we need a little holiness on our side, and you're the only priest I've got.'

'You're on your own, Eigerman.'

'I don't think you're listening. I'm talking serious shit here.'

'I'm not playing any of your damn fool games.'

'I mean it, Ashbery. If you don't come of your own accord, I'll make you.'

'I burned the negatives, Eigerman. I'm a free man.'

'I kept copies.'

There was a silence from the Father. Then:

'You swore.'

'I lied,' came the reply.

'You're a bastard, Eigerman.'

'And you wear lacy underwear. So how soon can you be here?'

Silence.

'Ashbery. I asked a question.'

'Give me an hour.'

'You've got forty-five minutes.'

'Fuck you.'

'That's what I like: a God-fearing lady.'

3

Must be the hot weather, Eigerman thought when he saw how many men Cormack and Holliday had rounded up in the space of sixty minutes. Hot weather always got folks itchy: for fornication maybe, or killing. And Shere Neck being what it was, and fornication not being so easy to get just whenever you wanted it, the hunger to do some shooting was well up today. There were twenty men gathered outside in the sun, and three or four women coming along for the ride; plus Ashbery and his Holy Water.

There'd been two more calls from Midian in that hour. One from Tommy, who was ordered back into the cemetery to help Pettine contain the enemy until reinforcements arrived, the second from Pettine himself, informing Eigerman that there'd been an escape bid made by one of Midian's occupants. He'd slipped away through the main gate while accomplices created a diversion. The nature of this diversion not only explained Pettine's choking as he delivered his report, but also why they'd failed to give chase. Somebody had ignited the tyres of the cars. The conflagration was quickly consuming the vehicles, including the radio upon which the report was being made. Pettine was in the process of explaining that there would be no further bulletins when the airwaves went dead.

Eigerman kept this information to himself, for fear it cooled anyone's appetite for the adventure ahead. Killing was all very fine, but he wasn't so sure there'd be quite so many ready to roll now if it was common knowledge that some of the bastards were ready to fight back.

As the convoy moved off he looked at his watch. They had maybe two and a half hours of good light left before dusk began to settle in. Three quarters of an hour to Midian, which left an hour and three quarters to get these fuckers dealt with before the enemy had night on its side. That was long enough, if they were organized about it. Best to treat it like a regular shake-down, Eigerman supposed. Drive the bastards out into the light and see what happened. If they came apart at the seams, the way piss pants Tommy had kept saying, then that was all the proof a Judge would need that these creatures were unholy as hell. If not – if Decker was lying, Pettine on dope again, and all this a fool's errand – he'd find someone to shoot, so it wasn't all a wasted journey. Might just turn around and put a bullet through the zombie in Cell Five; the man with no pulse and blood on his face.

Either way, he wouldn't let the day end without tears.

PART FIVE

THE GOOD NIGHT

'No sword shall touch you. Unless it be mine'

Lover's Oath
(Anon)

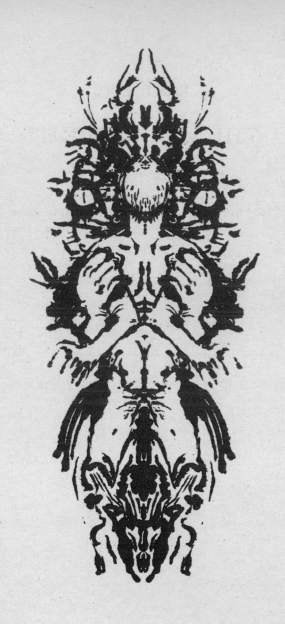

XIX

A Friendless Face

1

Why did she have to wake? Why did there have to be a coming to? Couldn't she just sink and sink, further into the nowhere she'd taken refuge in? But it didn't want her. She rose from it, unwillingly, and into the old pain of living and dying.

The flies had gone. That at least was something. She got to her feet, her body cumbersome; an embarrassment. As she made an attempt to dust the dirt from her clothes she heard the voice calling her name. She hadn't woken of her own accord, it seemed. Someone had called her. For a ghastly moment, she thought the voice was Sheryl's; that the flies had succeeded in their ambition, and driven her to lunacy. But when it came a second time she put another name to it: Babette. The child was calling her. Turning her back on the kitchen she picked up her bag and started through the debris towards the street. The light had changed since she'd made the first crossing; hours had passed while she'd debated with sleep. Her watch, broken in the fall, refused to tell how many.

It was still balmy on the street, but the heat of noon had long passed. The afternoon was winding down. It could not be long until dusk.

She began to walk, not once looking back at the restaurant. Whatever crisis of reality had overcome her there, Babette's voice had called her from it, and she felt oddly buoyant, as though something about the way the world worked had come clear.

She knew what it was, without having to think too hard. Some vital part of her, heart or head or both, had made its peace with Midian and all it contained. Nothing in the chambers had been as agonizing as what she'd confronted in the burnt out building: the loneliness of Sheryl's body, the stench of creeping decay, the inevitability of it all. Against that the monsters of Midian — transforming, re-arranging, ambassadors of tomorrow's flesh and reminders of yesterday's — seemed full of possibilities. Weren't there, amongst those creatures, faculties she envied? The power to fly; to be transformed; to know the condition of beasts; to defy death?

All that she'd coveted or envied in others of her species now seemed valueless. Dreams of the perfected anatomy — the soap opera face, the centrefold body — had distracted her with promises of true happiness. Empty promises. Flesh could not keep its glamour, nor eyes their sheen. They would go to nothing soon.

But the monsters were forever. Part of her forbidden self. Her dark, transforming midnight self. She longed to be numbered amongst them.

There was still much she had to come to terms with; not least their appetite for human flesh, which she'd witnessed first-hand at the Sweetgrass Inn. But she could learn to understand. In a real sense she had no choice. She'd been touched by a knowledge that had changed her inner landscape out of all recognition. There was no way back to the bland pastures of adolescence and early womanhood. She had to go forward. And tonight that meant along this empty street, to see what the coming night had in store.

The idling engine of a car on the opposite side of the road drew her attention. She glanced across at it. Its windows were all wound up — despite the warmth of the air — which struck her as odd. She could not see the driver; both windows and windshield were too thick with grime. But an uncomfortable suspicion was growing in her. Clearly the occupant was waiting for someone. And given that there was nobody else on the street, that someone was most likely her.

If so, the driver could only be one man, for only one knew that she had a reason to be here: Decker.

She started to run.

The engine revved. She glanced behind her. The car was moving off from its parking place, slowly. He had no reason to hurry. There was no sign of life along the street. No doubt there *was* help to be had, if only she knew which direction to run. But the car had already halved the distance between them. Though she knew she couldn't outrun it, she ran anyway, the engine louder and louder behind her. She heard the tyre walls squeal against the sidewalk. Then the car appeared at her side, keeping pace with her yard for yard.

The door opened. She ran on. The car kept its companion pace, the door scraping the concrete.

Then, from within, the invitation.

'Get in.'

Bastard, to be *so* calm.

'Get in, will you, before we're arrested.'

It wasn't Decker. The realization was not a slow burn but a sudden comprehension: it *wasn't* Decker speaking from the car. She stopped running, her whole body heaving with the effort of catching her breath.

The car also stopped.

'Get in,' the driver said again.

'Who . . . ?' she tried to say, but her lungs were too jealous of her breath to provide the words.

The answer came anyway.

'Friend of Boone's.'

Still she hung back from the open door.

'Babette told me how to find you,' the man went on.

'Babette?'

'Will you *get in*? We've got work to do.'

189

She approached the door. As she did so, the man said, 'Don't scream.'

She didn't have the breath to make a sound, but she certainly had the *inclination*, when her eyes fell on the face in the gloom of the car. This was one of Midian's creatures, no doubt, but not a brother to the fabulous things she'd seen in the tunnels. The man's appearance was horrendous, his face raw and red, like uncooked liver. Had it been any other way she might have distrusted it, knowing what she knew about pretenders. But this creature could pretend nothing: his wound was a vicious honesty.

'My name's Narcisse,' he said. 'Will you shut the door please? It keeps the light out. And the flies.'

2

His story, or at least its essentials, took two and a half blocks to tell. How he'd first met with Boone in the hospital; how he'd later gone to Midian, and once more encountered Boone; how together they'd broken Midian's laws, trespassing overground. He had a souvenir of that adventure, he told her; a wound in his belly the like of which a lady should never have to set eyes upon.

'So they exiled you, like Boone?' she said.

'They tried to,' he told her. 'But I hung on there, hoping I could maybe get myself a pardon. Then when the troopers came I thought: well, we brought this on the place. I should try and find Boone. Try and stop what we started.'

'The sun doesn't kill you?'

'Maybe I've not been dead long enough, but no – I can bear it.'

'You know Boone's in prison?'

'Yeah, I know. That's why I got the child to help me find you. I'm thinking together we can get him out.'

190

'How in God's name do we do that?'

'I don't know,' Narcisse confessed. 'But we'd damn well better try. And be quick about it. They'll have people out at Midian by now, digging it up.'

'Even if we can free Boone, I don't see what he can do.'

'He went into the Baptiser's chamber,' Narcisse replied, his finger going to lip and heart. 'He spoke with Baphomet. From what I hear nobody other than Lylesburg ever did that before, and survived. I'm figuring the Baptiser had some tricks to pass on. Something that'll help us stop the destruction.'

Lori pictured Boone's terrified face as he stumbled from the chamber.

'I don't think Baphomet told him anything,' Lori said. 'He barely escaped alive.'

Narcisse laughed.

'He *escaped*, didn't he? You think the Baptiser would have allowed that if there hadn't been a reason for it?'

'All right . . . so how do we get access to him? They'll have him guarded within an inch of his life.'

Narcisse smiled.

'What's so funny?'

'You forget what he *is* now,' Narcisse said. 'He's got powers.'

'I don't *forget*,' Lori replied. 'I simply don't *know*.'

'He didn't tell you?'

'No.'

'He went to Midian because he thought he'd shed blood – '

'I guessed that much.'

'He hadn't, of course. He was guiltless. Which made him meat.'

'You mean he was attacked?'

'Almost killed. But he escaped, at least as far as the town.'

'Where Decker was waiting for him,' Lori said, finishing the story; or beginning it. 'He was damn lucky that none of the shots killed him.'

Narcisse's smile, which had more or less lingered on his face since Lori's remark about Boone being guarded within an inch of his life, disappeared.

'What do you mean . . .' he said, '. . . none of the shots killed him? What do you think took him back to Midian? Why do you think they opened the tombs to him the second time?'

She stared at him blankly.

'I don't follow,' she said, hoping she didn't. 'What are you telling me?'

'He was bitten by Peloquin,' Narcisse said. 'Bitten and infected. The balm got into his blood . . .' He stopped speaking '. . . You want me to go on?'

'Yes.'

'The balm got into his blood. Gave him the powers. Gave him the hunger. And allowed him to get up off the slab and go walking . . .'

His words had grown soft by the end of his statement, in response to the shock on Lori's face.

'He's dead?' she murmured.

Narcisse nodded.

'I thought you understood that,' he said. 'I thought you were making a joke before . . . about his being . . .' The remark trailed into silence.

'This is too much,' Lori said. Her fist had closed on the door-handle, but she lacked the strength to pull on it. '. . . too much.'

'Dead isn't bad,' Narcisse said. 'It isn't even that different. It's just . . . unexpected.'

'Are you speaking from experience?'

'Yes.'

Her hand dropped from the door. Every last ounce of strength had gone from her.

'Don't give up on me now,' Narcisse said.

Dead; all dead. In her arms, in her mind.

'Lori. Speak to me. Say something, if it's only goodbye.'

'How . . . can . . . you *joke* about it?' she asked him.

192

'If it's not funny, what is it? Sad. Don't want to be sad. Smile, will you? We're going to save lover-boy, you and me.'

She didn't reply.

'Do I take silence as consent?'

Still she made no answer.

'Then I do.'

XX

Driven

1

Eigerman had only been to Midian once before,
when providing back up for the Calgary force in
their pursuit of Boone. It had been then that he'd
met Decker – who'd been the hero of that day, risking
his life to try and coax his patient out of hiding. He'd
failed, of course. The whole thing had ended in Boone's
summary execution as he stepped out into plain sight.
If ever a man should have laid down and died, it was
that man. Eigerman had never seen so many bullets in
one lump of meat. But Boone hadn't laid down. At
least not stayed down. He'd gone walkabout, with no
heartbeat and flesh the colour of raw fish.

Sickening stuff. It made Eigerman's hide crawl to
think of it. Not that he was about to admit that fact to
anyone. Not even to his passengers on the back seat,
the priest and the doctor, both of whom had secrets of
their own. Ashbery's he knew. The man liked to dress
in women's dainties, which fact Eigerman had chanced
upon and used as leverage when he'd needed sanctifi-
cation of a sin or two of his own. But Decker's secrets
remained a mystery. His face betrayed nothing, even
to an eye as practised in the recognition of guilt as
Eigerman's.

Re-angling the mirror, the Chief looked at Ashbery,
who shot him a sullen glance.

'Ever exorcize anyone?' he asked the priest.

'No.'

'Ever watch it done?'

Again, 'No.'

'You do *believe* though,' Eigerman said.

'In *what*?'

'In Heaven and Hell, for Christ's sake.'

'Define your terms.'

'Huh?'

'What do you *mean* by Heaven and Hell?'

'Jesus, I don't want a fucking debate. You're a priest, Ashbery. You're supposed to believe in the Devil. Isn't that right, Decker?'

The doctor grunted. Eigerman pushed a little harder.

'Everyone's seen stuff they can't explain, haven't they? Especially doctors, right? You've had patients speaking in tongues – '

'I can't say that I have,' Decker replied.

'Is that right? It's all perfectly scientific, is it?'

'I'd say so.'

'You'd say so. And what would you say about Boone?' Eigerman pressed. 'Is being a fucking zombie scientific too?'

'I don't know,' Decker murmured.

'Well, will you look at this? I've got a priest who doesn't believe in the Devil, and a doctor who doesn't know science from his asshole. That makes me feel real comfortable.'

Decker didn't respond. Ashbery did.

'You really think there's something up ahead, don't you?' he said. 'You're sweating a flood.'

'Don't push, sweetheart,' Eigerman said. 'Just dig out your little book of Exorcisms. I want those freaks sent back wherever the fuck they came from. You're supposed to know how.'

'There are other explanations these days, Eigerman,' Ashbery replied. 'This isn't Salem. We're not going to a burning.'

Eigerman turned his attention back to Decker, floating his next question lightly.

'What do you think, Doc? Think maybe we should try putting the zombie on the couch? Ask him if he ever wanted to fuck his sister?' Eigerman threw a look at Ashbery. 'Or dress in her underwear?'

'I think we *are* going to Salem,' Decker replied. There was an undercurrent in his voice Eigerman hadn't heard before. 'And I also think you don't give a fuck what I believe or don't believe. You're going to burn them out anyway.'

'Right on,' Eigerman said, with a throaty laugh.

'*And* I think Ashbery's right. You're *terrified*.'

That silenced the laugh.

'Asshole,' Eigerman said quietly.

They drove the rest of the way in silence, Eigerman setting a new pace for the convoy, Decker watching the light getting frailer with every moment, and Ashbery, after a few minutes of introspection, leafing through his Book of Prayers, turning the onion-skin pages at speed, looking for the Rites of Expulsion.

2

Pettine was waiting for them fifty yards from the necropolis gate, his face dirtied by smoke from the cars, which were still burning.

'What's the situation?' Eigerman wanted to know.

Pettine glanced back towards the cemetery.

'There's been no sign of movement in there since the escape. But we've *heard* stuff.'

'Like what?'

'Like we're sitting on a termite hill,' Pettine said. 'There's things moving around underground. No doubt about that. You can feel it as much as hear it.'

Decker, who'd travelled in one of the later cars, came across and joined the debate, cutting Pettine off in mid-flow to address Eigerman.

'We've got an hour and twenty minutes before the sun sets.'

'I can count,' Eigerman replied.

'So are we going to get digging?'

'When *I* say so, Decker.'

'Decker's right, Chief,' Pettine said. 'It's sun these bastards are afraid of. I tell you, I don't think we want to be here at nightfall. There's a lot of them down there.'

'We'll be here as long as it takes to clear this shit up,' said Eigerman. 'How many gates are there?'

'Two. The big one, and another on the north-east side.'

'All right. So it shouldn't be difficult to contain them. Get one of the trucks in front of the main gate, and then we'll post men at intervals around the wall just to make sure nobody gets out. Once they're sealed in we make our approach.'

'See you brought some insurance,' Pettine commented, looking at Ashbery.

'Damn right.'

Eigerman turned to the priest.

'You can bless water, right? Make it holy?'

'Yes.'

'So do it. Any water we can find. Bless it. Spread it amongst the men. It may do some good if bullets don't. And you, Decker, stay out of the fucking way. This is police business now.'

Orders given, Eigerman walked down towards the cemetery gates. Crossing the dusty ground he rapidly understood what Pettine had meant by *the termite hill*. There was something going on below ground. He even seemed to hear voices bringing thoughts of premature burial to mind. He'd seen that once; or its consequences. Done the spadework disinterring a woman who'd been heard screaming underground. She'd had reason: she'd given birth and died in her coffin. The child, a freak, had survived. Ended up in an asylum, probably. Or here perhaps, in the earth with the rest of the motherfuckers.

If so, he could count the minutes left of his sick life on his six-fingered hand. Soon as they showed their heads Eigerman would kick them right back where they came from, bullets in their brain. So let them come. He wasn't afraid. Let them come. Let them try and dig their way out.

His heel was waiting.

3

Decker watched the organization of the troops until it began to make him uneasy. Then he withdrew up the hill a little. He loathed being an observer of other men's labour. It made him feel impotent. It made him long to show them *his* power. And that was always a dangerous urge. The only eyes that could stare safely at his murder-hard were eyes about to glaze, and even then he had to erase them when they'd looked, for fear they told what they'd seen.

He turned his back on the cemetery and entertained himself with plans for the future. With Boone's trial over, he'd be free to begin the Mask's work afresh. He looked forward to that with a passion. He'd go further afield from now on. Find slaughtering places in Manitoba and Saskatchewan; or maybe over in Vancouver. He became hot with pleasure just thinking about it. From the briefcase he was carrying he could almost hear Button-Face sigh through his silver teeth.

'*Hush*,' he found himself telling the Mask.

'What's that?'

Decker turned. Pettine was standing a yard from him.

'Did you say something?' the cop wanted to know.

He'll go to the wall, the Mask said.

'Yes,' Decker replied.

'I didn't hear.'

'Just talking to myself.'

Pettine shrugged.

'Word from the Chief. He says we're about to move in. Do you want to give a hand?'

'*I'm ready,*' the Mask said.

'No,' said Decker.

'Don't blame you. Are you just a head-doctor?'

'Yes. Why?'

'Think we might need some medics before too long. They're not going to give up without a fight.'

'I can't help. Don't even like the sight of blood.'

There was laughter from the briefcase, so loud Decker was certain Pettine would hear. But no.

'You'd better keep your distance, then,' he said, and turned away to head back to the field of action.

Decker drew the bag up towards his chest, and held it tight in his arms. From inside he could hear the zipper opening and closing, opening and closing.

'Shut the fuck up,' he whispered.

'*Don't lock me away,*' the Mask whined. '*Not tonight of all nights. If you don't like the sight of blood let me look for you.*'

'I can't.'

'*You owe me,*' it said. '*You denied me in Midian, remember?*'

'I had no choice.'

'*You have now. You can give me some air. You know you'd like it.*'

'I'd be seen.'

'*Soon then.*'

Decker didn't reply.

'*Soon!*' the Mask yelled.

'Hush.'

200

'Just say it.'
'. . . please . . .'
'Say it.'
'Yes. Soon.'

XXI

That Desire

1

Two men had been left on duty at the station to guard the prisoner in Cell Five. Eigerman had given them explicit instructions. They were not on any account to unlock the cell door, whatever noises they heard from within. Nor was any outside agency – Judge, doctor or the Good Lord Himself – to be given access to the prisoner. And to enforce these edicts, should enforcement be necessary, troopers Cormack and Koestenbaum had been given the keys to the arsenal, and carte blanche to use extreme prejudice should the security of the station be in jeopardy. They weren't surprised. Shere Neck would most likely never see another prisoner so certain to find his way into the annals of atrocity as Boone. If he were to be sprung from custody Eigerman's good name would be cursed from coast to coast.

But there was more to the story than that, and both of them knew it. Though the Chief had not been explicit about the condition of the prisoner, rumours had been rife. The man was in some way *freakish*; possessed of powers that made him dangerous, even behind a locked and bolted door.

Cormack was grateful, then, to have been left to guard the front of the station, while Koestenbaum watched the cell itself. The whole place was a fortress. Every window and door sealed. Now it was simply a question of sitting it out, rifle at the ready, until the cavalry returned from Midian.

It wouldn't be long. The kind of human garbage they'd be likely to find at Midian – addicts, perverts, radicals – would be rounded up in a few hours, and the convoy on its way back to relieve the sentinels. Then tomorrow there'd be a force up from Calgary to take possession of the prisoner, and things would settle back into their regular pattern. Cormack wasn't in the policing business to sit and sweat the way he was now – he was in it for the easy feeling that came on a summer night when he could drive down to the corner of South and Emmett, and coerce one of the professionals to put her face in his lap for half an hour. That was what he liked the law for. Not this fortress under siege shit.

'Help me,' somebody said.

He heard the words quite clearly. The speaker – a woman – was just outside the front door.

'Help me, *please.*'

The appeal was so pitiful he couldn't ignore it. Rifle cocked he went to the door. There was no glass in it, not even a spy-hole, so he couldn't see the speaker on the step. But he heard her again. First a sob; then a soft rapping, which was failing even as it came.

'You'll have to go someplace else,' he said. 'I can't help you right now.'

'I'm hurt,' she seemed to say, but he wasn't sure. He put his ear to the door.

'Did ya hear me?' he asked. 'I can't help you. Go on down to the drug store.'

There was not even a sob by way of reply. Only the faintest of breaths.

Cormack liked women; liked to play the boss-man and bread-winner. Even the hero, as long as it didn't cost him too much sweat. It went against the grain not to open the door to a woman begging for help. She'd sounded young, and desperate. It was not his heart that hardened, thinking of her vulnerability. Checking first that Koestenbaum wasn't in sight to witness his defiance of Eigerman's orders, he whispered:

'Hold on.'

And unbolted the door top and bottom.

He'd only opened it an inch and a hand darted through, its thumb slashing his face. The wound missed his eye by a centimetre, but the spurting blood turned half the world red. Semi-blind, he was thrown backwards as the force on the other side of the door threw it open. He didn't let the rifle go, however. He fired, first at the woman (the shot went wide), then at her companion, who ran at him half-crouching to avoid the bullets. The second shot, though as wide as the first, brought blood. Not his target's, however. It was his own boot, and the good flesh and bone inside, that was spattered across the floor.

'Jesus Fucking Christ!'

In his horror he let the rifle drop from his fingers. Knowing he'd not be able to bend and snatch it up again without losing his balance he turned and started to hop towards the desk, where his gun lay.

But Silver Thumbs was already there, swallowing the bullets like vitamin pills.

Denied his defences, and knowing he could not stay vertical for more than a few seconds, he began to howl.

2

Outside Cell Five, Koestenbaum held his post. He had his orders. Whatever happened beyond the door into the station itself he was to stand guard by the cell, defending it from any and every assault. That he was determined to do, however much Cormack yelled.

Grinding out his cigarette he drew the shutter in the cell door aside and put his eyes to the peep-hole. The killer had moved in the last few minutes, edging into the corner by degrees, as if hunted by a patch of weak sunlight that fell through the tiny window high above him. Now he could go no further. He was wedged in the corner, wrapped up in himself. Movement aside, he looked much as he had all along: like wreckage. No danger to anyone.

Appearances deceived, of course; Koestenbaum had been in uniform too long to be naïve about that. But he knew a defeated man when he saw one. Boone didn't even look up when Cormack let out another yelp. He just watched the crawling sunlight from the corner of his eye, and shook.

Koestenbaum slammed the peep-hole shut and turned back to watch the door through which Cormack's attackers – whoever they were – had to come. They'd find him ready and waiting, guns blazing.

He didn't have long to contemplate his last stand, as a blast blew out the lock and half the door with it, shards and smoke filling the air. He fired into the confusion, seeing somebody coming at him. The man was tossing away the rifle he'd used to blow the door, and was raising his hands, which *glinted* as they swept towards Koestenbaum's eyes. The trooper hesitated long enough to catch sight of his assailant's face – like something that should have been under bandages or six feet of earth – then he fired. The bullet struck its target, but slowed the man not a jot, and before he could fire a second time he was up against the wall, with the raw face inches from his. Now he saw all too clearly what glinted in the man's hands. A hook hovered an inch from the gleam of his left eye. There was another at his groin.

'Which do you want to live without?' the man said.

'No need,' said a woman's voice, before Koestenbaum had a chance to choose between sight and sex.

'Let me,' Narcisse said.

'Don't let him,' Koestenbaum murmured. 'Please . . . don't let him.'

The woman came into view now. The parts of her that showed seemed natural enough, but he wouldn't have wanted to lay bets on what she looked like under her blouse. More tits than a bitch, most likely. He was in the hands of freaks.

'Where's Boone?' she said.

There was no purpose in risking his balls, eye or otherwise. They'd find the prisoner with or without his help.

'Here,' he said, glancing back towards Cell Five.

'And the keys?'

'On my belt.'

The woman reached down and took the keys from him.

'Which one?' she said.

'Blue tag,' he replied.

'Thank you.'

She moved past him to the door.

'Wait – ' Koestenbaum said.

'What?'

' – make him let me alone.'

'Narcisse,' she said.

The hook was withdrawn from his eye, but the one at his groin remained, pricking him.

'We have to be quick,' Narcisse said.

'I know,' the woman replied.

Koestenbaum heard the door swing open. He glanced round to see her stepping into the cell. As he looked back the fist came at his face, and he dropped to the floor with his jaw broken in three places.

Cormack had suffered the same summary blow, but he'd been already toppling when it came, and instead of knocking him solidly into unconsciousness it had merely left him in a daze, from which he quickly shook himself. He crawled to the door, and hauled himself, hand over hand, to his foot. Then he stumbled out in the street. The rush of homeward traffic was over, but there were still vehicles passing in both directions, and the sight of a toeless trooper hobbling into the middle of the street, arms raised, was enough to bring the flow of traffic to a squealing halt.

But even as the drivers and their passengers stepped out of the trucks and cars to come to his assistance Cormack felt the delayed shock of his self-wounding closing his system down. The words his helpers were mouthing to him reached his befuddled mind as nonsense.

He thought (hoped) somebody had said:

'*I'll get a gun.*'

But he couldn't be sure.

He hoped (prayed) his lolling tongue had told them where to find the felons, but he was even less sure of that.

As the ring of faces faded around him, however, he realized his seeping foot would have left a trail that would lead them back to the transgressors. Comforted, he passed out.

4

'Boone,' she said.

His sallow body, bared to the waist – scarred, and

missing a nipple – shuddered as she spoke his name. But he didn't look up at her.

'Get him going, will you?'

Narcisse was at the door, staring at the prisoner.

'Not with you yelling I won't,' she told him. 'Leave us alone a little while, huh?'

'No time for fucky fucky.'

'*Just get out.*'

'OK.' He raised his arms in mock surrender. 'I'm going.'

He closed the door. It was just her and Boone now. The living and the dead.

'Get up,' she told him.

He did nothing but shudder.

'Will you get up? We don't have that much time.'

'So leave me,' he said.

She ignored the sentiment but not the fact that he'd broken his silence.

'Talk to me,' she said.

'You shouldn't have come back,' he said, defeat in his every word. 'You put yourself at risk for nothing.'

She hadn't expected this. Anger maybe, that she'd left him to be captured at the Sweetgrass Inn. Suspicion even, that she'd come here with someone from Midian. But not this mumbling, broken creature, slumped in a corner like a boxer who'd fought a dozen too many fights. Where was the man she'd seen at the Inn, changing the order of his very flesh in front of her? Where was the casual strength she'd seen; and the appetite? He scarcely seemed capable of lifting his own head, never mind meat to his lips.

That was the issue, she suddenly understood. That forbidden meat.

'I can still taste it,' he said.

There was such shame in his voice; the human he'd been repulsed by the thing he'd become.

'You weren't answerable,' she told him. 'You weren't in control of yourself.'

209

'I am now,' he replied. His nails dug into the muscle of his forearms, she saw, as though he were holding himself down. 'I'm not going to let go. I'm going to wait here till they come to string me up.'

'That won't do any good, Boone,' she reminded him.

'*Jesus* . . .' The word decayed into tears. 'You know everything?'

'Yes, Narcisse told me. You're dead. So why wish a hanging on yourself? They can't kill you.'

'They'll find a way,' he said. 'Take off my head. Blow out my brains.'

'Don't talk like that!'

'They have to finish me, Lori. Put me out of my misery.'

'I don't want you out of your misery,' she said.

'But I do!' he replied, looking up at her for the first time. Seeing his face, she remembered how many had doted on him, and understood why. Pain could have no more persuasive apologists than his bones, his eyes.

'I want *out*,' he said. 'Out of this body. Out of this life.'

'You can't. Midian needs you. It's being destroyed, Boone.'

'Let it go! Let it all go. Midian's just a hole in the ground, full of things that should lie down and be dead. They know that, all of 'em. They just haven't got the balls to do what's right.'

'Nothing's right,' she found herself saying (how far she'd come, to this bleak relativity), 'except what you feel and know.'

His small fury abated. The sadness that replaced it was profounder than ever.

'I *feel* dead,' he said. 'I *know* nothing.'

'That's not true,' she replied, taking the first steps towards him she'd taken since entering the cell. He flinched as if he expected her to strike him.

'You *know* me,' she said. 'You *feel* me.'

She took hold of his arm, and pulled it up towards

210

her. He didn't have time to make a fist. She laid his palm on her stomach.

'You think you disgust me, Boone? You think you horrify me? You don't.'

She drew his hand up towards her breasts.

'I still want you, Boone. Midian wants you too, but I want you more. I want you cold, if that's the way you are. I want you dead, if that's the way you are. And *I'll* come to you if you won't come to me. I'll let them shoot me down.'

'*No*,' he said.

Her grip on his hand was light now. He could have slipped it. But he chose to leave his touch upon her, with only the thin fabric of her blouse intervening. She wished she could dissolve it at will; have his hand stroking the skin between her breasts.

'They're going to come for us sooner or later,' she said.

Nor was she bluffing. There were voices from outside. A lynch-mob gathering. Maybe the monsters *were* forever. But so were their persecutors.

'They'll destroy us both, Boone. You for what you are. Me for loving you. And I'll never hold you again. I don't want that, Boone. I don't want us dust in the same wind. I want us *flesh*.'

Her tongue had outstripped her intention. She hadn't meant to say it so plainly. But it was said now; and true. She wasn't ashamed of it.

'I won't let you deny me, Boone,' she told him. The words were their own engine. They drove her hand to Boone's cold scalp. She snatched a fist of his thick hair.

He didn't resist her. Instead the hand on her chest closed on the blouse, and he went down onto his knees in front of her, pressing his face to her crotch, licking at it as if to tongue her clean of clothes and enter her with spit and spirit all in one.

She was wet beneath the fabric. He smelt her heat for him. Knew what she'd said was no lie. He kissed her cunt, or the cloth that hid her cunt, over and over and over.

'Forgive yourself, Boone,' she said.

He nodded.

She took tighter hold on his hair, and pulled him away from the bliss of her scent.

'*Say it*,' she told him. '*Say you forgive yourself.*'

He looked up from his pleasure, and she could see before he spoke the weight of shame had gone from his face. Behind his sudden smile she met the monster's eyes, *dark*, and darkening still as he delved for it.

The look made her ache.

'Please . . .' she murmured, '. . . love me.'

He pulled at her blouse. It tore. His hand was through the gap in one smooth motion, and beneath her bra for her breast. This was madness of course. The mob would be upon them if they didn't get out quickly. But then madness had drawn her into this circle of dust and flies in the first place; why be surprised that her journey had brought her round to this *new* insanity? Better this than life without him. Better this than practically anything.

He was getting to his feet, teasing her tit from hiding, putting his cold mouth to her hot nipple, flicking it, licking it, tongue and teeth in perfect play. Death had made a lover of him. Given him knowledge of clay, and how to rouse it; made him easy with the body's mysteries. He was everywhere about her, working his hips against hers in slow grinding circles – trailing his tongue from her breasts to the sweat-bowl between her clavicles, and up along the ridge of her throat to her chin, thence to her mouth.

Only once in her life had there been such wrenching hunger in her. In New York, years before, she'd met and fucked with a man whose name she'd never known, but whose hands and lips seemed to know her better than herself.

212

'Have a drink with me?' she'd said, when they'd unglued themselves.

He'd told her *no* almost pityingly, as though someone so ignorant of the rules was bound for grief. So she'd watched him dress and leave, angry with herself for asking, and with him for such practised detachment. But she'd dreamt of him a dozen times in the weeks after, revisiting their squalid moments together, hungry for them again.

She had them here. Boone was the lover of that dark corner, perfected. Cool and feverish, urgent and studied. She knew his name this time; but he was still strange to her. And in the fervour of his possession, and in her heat for him, she felt that other lover, and all the lovers who'd come and gone before him, burned up. It was only their ash in her now – where their tongues and cocks had been – and she had power over them completely.

Boone was unzipping himself. She took his length in her hand. Now it was his turn to sigh, as she ran her fingers along the underside of his erection, up from his balls to where the ring of his circumcision scar bore a nugget of tender flesh. She stroked him there, tiny movements to match the measure of his tongue back and forth between her lips. Then, on the same sudden impulse, the teasing time was over. He was lifting her skirt, tearing at her underwear, his fingers going where only hers had been for too long. She pushed him back against the wall; pulled his jeans down to mid-thigh. Then, one arm hooked around his shoulders, the other hand enjoying the silk of his cock before it was out of sight, she took him inside. He resisted her speed, a delicious war of want which had her at screaming pitch in seconds. She was never so open, nor had ever needed to be. He filled her to overflowing.

Then it really began. After the promises, the proof. Bracing his upper back against the wall he angled himself so as to throw his fuck up into her, her weight its own insistence. She licked his face. He grinned. She spat in it. He laughed and spat back.

'*Yes,*' she said. '*Yes. Go on. Yes.*'

All she could manage were affirmatives. Yes to his spittle; yes to his cock; yes to this life in death, and joy in life in death forever and ever.

His answer was honey-hipped; wordless labour, teeth clenched, brow ploughed. The expression on his face made her cunt spasm. To see him shut his eyes against her pleasure; to know that the sight of her bliss took him too close to be countenanced. They had such power, each over each. She demanded his motion with motion of her own, one hand gripping the brick beside his head so she could raise herself along his length then impale herself again. There was no finer hurt. She wished it could never stop.

But there was a voice at the door. She could hear it through her whining head.

'*Quickly.*'

It was Narcisse.

'*Quickly.*' Boone heard him too; and the din behind his voice as the lynchers gathered. He matched her new rhythm; up to meet her descent.

'Open your eyes,' she said.

He obeyed, grinning at the command. It was too much for him, meeting her eyes. Too much for her, meeting his. The pact struck, they parted till her cunt only sucked at the head of his cock – so slicked it might slip from her – then closed on each other for one final stroke.

The joy of it made her cry out, but he choked her yell with his tongue, sealing their eruption inside their mouths. Not so below. Undammed after months, his come overflowed and ran down her legs, its course colder than his scalp or kisses.

It was Narcisse who brought them back from their world of two into that of many. The door was now open. He was watching them without embarrassment.

'Finished?' he wanted to know.

Boone wiped his lips back and forth on Lori's, spreading their saliva from cheek to cheek.

'For now,' he said, looking only at her.

'So can we get going?' Narcisse said.

'Whenever. Wherever.'

'Midian,' came the instant reply.

'Midian then.'

The lovers drew apart. Lori pulled up her underwear. Boone tried to get his cock, still hard, behind his zip.

'There's quite a mob out there,' Narcisse said. 'How the hell are we going to get past them?'

'They're all the same – ' Boone said, ' – all afraid.'

Lori, her back turned to Boone, felt a change in the air around her. A shadow was climbing the walls to left and right, spreading over her back, kissing her nape, her spine, her buttocks and what lay between. It was Boone's darkness. He was in it to its length and breadth.

Even Narcisse was agog.

'Holy Shit,' he muttered, then flung the door wide to let the night go running.

5

The mob was itching for fun. Those with guns and rifles had brought them from their cars; those with the luck to have been travelling with rope in their trunks were practising knots; and those without rope or guns had picked up stones. For justification they needed to look no further than the spattered remains of Cormack's foot, spread on the station floor. The leaders of the group – who'd established themselves immediately by natural selection (they had louder voices and more powerful weapons) – were treading this red ground when a noise from the vicinity of the cells drew their attention.

Somebody at the back of the crowd started shouting: *'Shoot the bastards down!'*

It was not Boone's shadow the leaders' target-hungry eyes first alighted upon. It was Narcisse. His ruined face brought a gasp of disgust from several of the throng, and shouts for his dispatch from many more.

'Shoot the fucker!

'Through the heart!'

The leaders didn't hesitate. Three of them fired. One of them hit the man, the bullet catching Narcisse in the shoulder and passing straight through him. There was a cheer from the mob. Encouraged by this first wounding they surged into the station in still greater numbers, those at the back eager to see the bloodletting, those at the front mostly blind to the fact that their target had not shed a single drop. He hadn't fallen either; that they *did* see. And now one or two acted to put that to rights, firing a volley at Narcisse. Most of the shots went wide, but not all.

As the third bullet struck home, however, a roar of fury shook the room, exploding the lamp on the desk and bringing dust from the ceiling.

Hearing it one or two of those just crossing the threshold changed their minds. Suddenly careless of what their neighbours might think they began to dig their way out into the open air. It was still light on the street; there was warmth to cancel the chill of fear that ran down every human spine, hearing that cry. But for those at the head of the mob there was no retreat. The door was jammed. All they could do was stand their ground and aim their weapons, as the roarer emerged from the darkness at the back of the station.

One of the men had been a witness at the Sweetgrass Inn that morning, and knew the man who now came into sight as the killer he'd seen arrested. Knew his name too.

'That's him!' he started to yell. 'That's Boone!'

216

The man who'd fired the first shot to strike Narcisse aimed his rifle.

'*Bring him down!*' somebody shouted.

The man fired.

Boone had been shot before; and shot; and shot. This little bullet, entering his chest and nicking his silent heart, was nothing. He laughed it off and kept coming, feeling the change in him as he breathed it out. His substance was fluid. It broke into droplets and became something new; part the beast he'd inherited from Peloquin, part a shade warrior, like Lylesburg; part Boone the lunatic, content with his visions at last. And oh! the pleasure of it, feeling this possibility liberated and forgiven; the pleasure of bearing down on this human herd and seeing it break before him.

He smelt their heat, and hungered for it. He saw their terror, and took strength from it. They stole such authority for themselves, these people. Made themselves arbiters of good and bad, natural and unnatural, justifying their cruelty with spurious laws. Now they saw a simpler law at work, as their bowels remembered the oldest fear: of being *prey*.

They fled before him, panic spreading throughout their unruly ranks. The rifles and the stones were forgotten in the chaos, as howls for blood became howls for escape. Trampling each other in their haste, they clawed and fought their way into the street.

One of the riflemen stood his ground, or else was rooted to it in shock. Whichever, the weapon was dashed from his grip by Boone's swelling hand, and the man flung himself into the throng of people to escape further confrontation.

Daylight still ruled the street outside, and Boone was loath to step into it, but Narcisse was indifferent to such niceties. With the route cleared he made his way out into the light, weaving through the fleeing crowd unnoticed, until he reached the car.

There was some regrouping of forces going on, Boone

could see. A knot of people on the far sidewalk – comforted by the sunlight, and their distance from the beast – talking heatedly together as though they might rally. Dropped weapons were being claimed from the ground. It could only be a matter of time before the shock of Boone's transformation died away and they renewed their assault.

But Narcisse was swift. He was in the car and revving it by the time Lori reached the door. Boone held her back, the touch of his shadow, (which he trailed like smoke) more than enough to cancel any lingering fear she might have had of his reworked flesh. Indeed, she found herself imagining what it would be like to fuck with him in this configuration; to spread herself for the shadow and the beast at its heart.

The car was at the door now, squealing to a halt in a cloud of its own fumes.

'*Go!*' Boone said, pitching her through the door, his shadow covering the sidewalk to confound the enemy's sights. With reason. A shot blew out the back window even as she threw herself into the car; a barrage of stones followed.

Boone was at her side already, and slamming the door.

'They're going to come after us!' Narcisse said.

'Let them,' was Boone's response.

'To Midian?'

'It's no secret now.'

'True.'

Narcisse put his foot down, and the car was away.

'We'll lead them to Hell,' said Boone, as a quartet of vehicles began to give chase, 'if that's where they want to go.'

His voice was guttural from the throat of the creature he'd become, but the laugh that followed was Boone's laugh, as though it had always belonged to this beast; a humour more ecstatic than his humanity had room for, that had finally found its purpose and its face.

XXII

Triumph of the Mask

1

If he never saw another day like today, Eigerman thought, he'd have little to complain to the Lord about, when he was eventually called. First the sight of Boone in chains. Then bringing the baby out to meet the cameras, knowing his face would be on the cover of every newspaper across the country tomorrow morning. And now this: the glorious sight of Midian in flames.

It had been Pettine's notion, and a damn good one, to pour lighted gasoline down the gullets of the tombs, to drive whatever was underground up into the light. It had worked better than either of them had anticipated. Once the smoke began to thicken and the fires to spread, the enemy had no choice but to exit their cess-pit into the open air, where God's good sun took many of them apart at a stroke.

Not all however. Some of them had time to prepare for their emergence, protecting themselves against the light by whatever desperate means they could. Their invention was in vain. The pyre was sealed: gates guarded, walls manned. Unable to escape skyward with wings and heads covered against the sun, they were driven back into the conflagration.

In other circumstances Eigerman might not have allowed himself to enjoy the spectacle as openly as he did. But these creatures weren't human – that much was apparent even from a safe distance. They were miscreated fuckheads, no two the same, and he was sure the saints themselves would have laughed to see them bested. Putting down the Devil was the Lord's own sport.

But it couldn't last forever. Night would soon be falling. When it did their strongest defence against the enemy would drop out of sight, and the tide might turn. They'd have to leave the bonfire to burn overnight, and at dawn return to dig the survivors out of their niches and finish them off. With crosses and holy water securing the walls and gates there'd be little chance of any escaping before daybreak. He wasn't sure what power was working to subdue the monsters: fire, water, daylight, faith: all, or some combination of these. It didn't matter. All that concerned him was that he had the power to crack their heads.

A shout from down the hill broke Eigerman's train of thought.

'You've got to stop this!'

It was Ashbery. It looked like he'd been standing too close to the flames. His face was half-cooked, basted in sweat.

'Stop what?' Eigerman yelled back.

'This massacre.'

'I see no massacre.'

Ashbery was within a couple of yards of Eigerman, but he still had to shout over the noise from below: the din of the freaks and the fires punctuated now and again by louder dins as the heat broke a slab, or brought a mausoleum down.

'They don't stand a chance!' Ashbery hollered.

'They're not supposed to,' Eigerman pointed out.

'But you don't know who's down there! Eigerman! . . . *You don't know who you're killing!'*

The Chief grinned.

'I know damn well,' he said, a look in his eyes that Ashbery had only ever seen in mad dogs. 'I'm killing the dead, and how can that be wrong? Eh? *Answer me,*

Ashbery. How can it be wrong to make the dead lie down and *stay dead*?'

'There's children down there, Eigerman,' Ashbery replied, jabbing a finger in the direction of Midian.

'Oh yes. With eyes like headlamps! And teeth! You seen the teeth on those fuckers? That's the Devil's children, Ashbery.'

'You're out of your mind.'

'You haven't got the balls to believe that, have you? You haven't got balls at all!'

He took a step towards the priest, and caught hold of the black cassock.

'Maybe you're more like *them* than us,' he said. 'Is that what it is, Ashbery? Feel the call of the wild, do you?'

Ashbery wrested his robes from Eigerman's grip. They tore.

'All right . . .' he said, 'I tried reasoning with you. If you've got such God-fearing executioners, then maybe a man of God can stop them.'

'You leave my men alone!' Eigerman said.

But Ashbery was already half way down the hill, his voice carried above the tumult.

'*Stop*!' he yelled. '*Lay down your weapons*!'

Centre-stage in front of the main gates he was visible to a good number of Eigerman's army, and though few, if any, had stepped into a church since their wedding or their baptism they listened now. They wanted some explanation of the sights the last hour had provided; sights they'd happily have fled from but that some urge they'd barely recognize as their own kept them at the wall, childhood prayers on their lips.

Eigerman knew their loyalty was only his by default. They didn't obey him because they loved the law. They obeyed because they were more afraid of retreating in front of their companions than of doing the job. They obeyed because they couldn't defy the ant-under-the-magnifying-glass fascination of watching helpless things go bang. They obeyed because obeying was simpler than not.

Ashbery might change their minds. He had the robes, he had the rhetoric. If he wasn't stopped he might still spoil the day.

Eigerman took his gun from his holster, and followed the priest down the hill. Ashbery saw him coming; saw the gun in his hand.

He raised his voice still louder.

'This isn't what God wants!' he yelled. 'And it's not what you want either. You don't want innocent blood on your hands.'

Priest to the bitter end, Eigerman thought, laying on the guilt.

'Shut your mouth, faggot,' he hollered.

Ashbery had no intention of doing so; not when he had his audience in the palm of his hand.

'They're not animals in there!' he said. 'They're people. And you're killing them just because this lunatic tells you to.'

His words carried weight, even amongst the atheists. He was voicing a doubt more than one had entertained but none had dared express. Half a dozen of the non-uniformed began to retire towards their cars, all enthusiasm for the extermination drained. One of Eigerman's men also withdrew from his station at the gate, his slow retreat becoming a run as the chief fired a shot in his direction.

'*Stand your ground*!' he bellowed. But the man was away, lost in the smoke.

Eigerman turned his fury back on Ashbery.

'Got some bad news,' he said, advancing towards the priest.

Ashbery looked to right and left for someone willing to defend him, but nobody moved.

'You going to watch him kill me?' he appealed. 'For God's sake, won't somebody help me?'

Eigerman levelled his gun. Ashbery had no intention

222

of attempting to outrun the bullet. He dropped to his knees.

'Our Father . . .' he began.

'You're on your own, cocksucker,' Eigerman purred. 'Nobody's listening.'

'Not true,' somebody said.

'Huh?'

The prayer faltered.

'*I'm* listening.'

Eigerman turned his back on the priest. A figure loomed in the smoke ten yards from him. He pointed the gun in the newcomer's direction.

'Who are you?'

'Sun's almost set,' the other said.

'One more step and I'll shoot you.'

'So shoot,' said the man, and took a step towards the gun. The tatters of smoke that clung to him blew away, and the prisoner in Cell Five walked into Eigerman's sights, his skin bright, his eyes brighter. He was stark naked. There was a bullet hole in the middle of his chest and more wounds besides, decorating his body.

'Dead,' Eigerman said.

'You bet.'

'Jesus Lord.'

He backed off a step, and another.

'Ten minutes maybe, before sundown,' Boone said. 'Then the world's ours.'

Eigerman shook his head.

'You're not getting me,' he said. 'I won't let you get me!'

His backward steps multiplied and suddenly he was away at speed, not looking behind him. Had he done so, he would have seen that Boone was not interested in pursuit. He was moving instead towards the besieged gates of Midian. Ashbery was still on the ground there.

'*Get up,*' Boone told him.

223

'If you're going to kill me, do it will you?' Ashbery said. 'Get it over with.'

'Why should I kill you?' Boone said.

'I'm a priest.'

'So?'

'You're a monster.'

'And you're not?'

Ashbery looked up at Boone.

'Me?'

'There's lace under the robe,' Boone said.

Ashbery pulled together the tear in his cassock.

'Why hide it?'

'Let me alone.'

'Forgive yourself,' Boone said. 'I did.'

He walked on past Ashbery to the gates.

'Wait!' the priest said.

'I'd get going if I were you. They don't like the robes in Midian. Bad memories.'

'I want to see,' Ashbery said.

'Why?'

'Please. Take me with you.'

'It's your risk.'

'I'll take it.'

2

From a distance it was hard to be sure of what was going on down at the cemetery gates, but of two facts the doctor was sure: Boone had returned, and somehow bested Eigerman. At the first sight of his arrival Decker had taken shelter in one of the police vehicles. There he sat now, briefcase in hand, trying to plot his next action.

It was difficult, with two voices each counselling different things. His public self demanded retreat, before events became any more dangerous.

Leave now, it said. *Just drive away. Let them all die together.*

There was wisdom in this. With night almost fallen, and Boone there to rally them, Midian's hosts might still triumph. If they did, and they found Decker, his heart would be ripped from his chest.

But there was another voice demanding his attention.

Stay, it said.

The voice of the Mask, rising from the case on his lap.

You've denied me here once already, it said.

So he had, knowing when he did it there'd come a time for repaying the debt.

'Not now,' he whispered.

Now, it said.

He knew rational argument carried no weight against its hunger; nor did pleading.

Use your eyes, it said. *I've got work to do.*

What did it see that he didn't? He stared out through the window.

Don't you see her?

Now he did. In his fascination with Boone, naked at the gates, he'd missed the other newcomer to the field: Boone's woman.

Do you see the bitch? the Mask said.

'I see her.'

Perfect timing, eh? In this chaos who's going to see me finish her off? Nobody. And with her gone there'll be no-one left who knows our secret.

'There's still Boone.'

He'll never testify, the Mask laughed. *He's a dead man, for Christ's sake. What's a zombie's word worth, tell me that?*

'Nothing,' Decker said.

Exactly. He's no danger to us. But the woman is. Let me silence her.

'Suppose you're seen?'

Suppose I am, the Mask said. *They'll think I was one of Midian's clan all along.*

'Not you,' Decker said.

The thought of his precious Other being confused with the degenerates of Midian nauseated him.

'You're pure,' he said.

Let me prove it, the Mask coaxed.

'Just the woman?'

Just the woman. Then we'll leave.

He knew the advice made sense. They'd never have a better opportunity of killing the bitch.

He started to unlock the case. Inside, the Mask grew agitated.

Quickly or we'll lose her.

His fingers slid on the dial as he ran the numbers of the lock.

Quickly, damn you.

The final digit clicked into place. The lock sprang open.

Ol' Button Face was never more beautiful.

3

Though Boone had advised Lori to stay with Narcisse, the sight of Midian in flames was enough to draw her companion away from the safety of the hill and down towards the cemetery gates. Lori went with him a little way, but her presence seemed to intrude upon his grief, so she hung back a few paces, and in the smoke and deepening twilight was soon divided from him.

The scene before her was one of utter confusion. Any attempt to complete the assault on the necropolis had ceased since Boone had sent Eigerman running. Both his men and their civilian support had retreated from around the walls. Some had already driven away, most likely fearing what would happen when the sun sank over the horizon. Most remained however, prepared to beat a retreat if necessary, but mesmerized by the spectacle of destruction. Her gaze went from one to another, looking for some sign of what they were feeling, but every face was blank. They looked like death masks, she thought, wiped of response. Except that she *knew* the dead now. She walked with them, talked with them. Saw them feel and weep. Who then were the *real* dead? The silent hearted, who still knew pain, or their glassy-eyed tormentors?

A break in the smoke uncovered the sun, teetering on the rim of the world. The red light dazzled her. She closed her eyes against it.

In the darkness, she heard a breath a little way behind her. She opened her eyes, and began to turn, knowing harm was coming. Too late to slip it. The Mask was a yard from her, and closing.

She had seconds only before the knife found her, but it was long enough to see the Mask as she'd never seen it before. Here was the blankness on the faces she'd studied perfectly perfected; the human fiend made myth. No use to call it *Decker*. It wasn't Decker. No use to call it anything. It was as far beyond names as she was beyond power to tame it.

It slashed her arm. Once, and again.

There were no taunts from it this time. It had come only to despatch her.

The wounds stung. Instinctively she put her hand to them, her motion giving him opportunity to kick the legs from under her. She had no time to cushion her fall. The impact emptied her lungs. Sobbing for breath, she turned her face to the ground to keep it from the knife. The earth seemed to shudder beneath her. Illusion, surely. Yet it came again.

She glanced up at the Mask. He too had felt the tremors, and was looking towards the cemetery. His distraction would be her only reprieve; she had to take it. Rolling out of his shadow she got to her feet. There

227

was no sign of Narcisse, or Rachel; nor much hope of help from the death-masks, who'd forsaken their vigil and were hurrying away from the smoke as the tremors intensified. Fixing her eyes on the gate through which Boone had stepped, she stumbled down the hill, the dusty soil dancing at her feet.

The source of the agitation was Midian. Its cue, the disappearance of the sun, and with it the light that had trapped the Breed underground. It was their noise that made the ground shake, as they destroyed their refuge. What was below could remain below no longer.

The Nightbreed were rising.

The knowledge didn't persuade her from her course. Whatever was loose inside the gate she'd long ago made her peace with it, and might expect mercy. From the horror at her back, matching her stride for stride, she could expect none.

There were only the fires from the tombs up ahead to light her way now, a way strewn with the debris of the siege: petrol cans, shovels, discarded weapons. She was almost at the gates before she caught sight of Babette standing close to the wall, her face terror stricken.

'*Run!*' she yelled, afraid the Mask would wound the child.

Babette did as she was told, her body seeming to melt into beast as she turned and fled through the gates. Lori came a few paces after her, but by the time she was over the threshold the child had already gone, lost down the smoke filled avenues. The tremors here were strong enough to unseat the paving stones, and topple the mausoleums, as though some force underground – Baphomet, perhaps, Who Made Midian – was shaking its foundations to bring the place to ruin. She hadn't anticipated such violence; her chances of surviving the cataclysm were slim.

But better to be buried in the rubble than succumb to the Mask. And be flattered, at the end, that Fate had at least offered her a choice of extinctions.

XXIII

The Harrowing

1

In the cell back at Shere Neck memories of Midian's labyrinth had tormented Boone. Closing his eyes against the sun he'd found himself lost here, only to open them again and find the maze echoed in the whirls of his fingertips and the veins on his arms. Veins in which no heat ran; reminders, like Midian, of his shame.

Lori had broken that spell of despair, coming to him not begging but *demanding* he forgive himself.

Now, back in the avenues from which his monstrous condition had sprung, he felt her love for him like the life his body no longer possessed.

He needed its comfort, in the pandemonium. The Nightbreed were not simply bringing Midian down, they were erasing all clue to their nature or keepsake of their passing. He saw them at work on every side, labouring to finish what Eigerman's scourge had begun. Gathering up the pieces of their dead and throwing them into the flames; burning their beds, their clothes, anything they couldn't take with them.

These were not the only preparations for escape. He glimpsed the Breed in forms he'd never before had the honour to see: unfurling wings, unfolding limbs. One becoming many (a man, a flock); many becoming one (three lovers, a cloud). All around, the rites of departure.

Ashbery was still at Boone's side, agog.

'Where are they going?'

'I'm too late,' Boone said. 'They're leaving Midian.'

The lid of a tomb ahead flew off, and a ghost form rose like a rocket into the night sky.

'Beautiful,' Ashbery said. 'What are they? Why have I never known them?'

Boone shook his head. He had no way to describe the Breed that were not the old ways. They didn't belong to Hell; nor yet to Heaven. They were what the species he'd once belonged to could not bear to be. The *un*-people; the *anti*-tribe; humanity's sack unpicked and sewn together again with the moon inside.

And now, before he'd a chance to know them – and by knowing them, know *himself* – he was losing them. They were finding transport in their cells, and rising to the night.

'Too late,' he said again, the pain of this parting bringing tears to his eyes.

The escapes were gathering momentum. On every side doors were being thrown wide, and slabs over-turned, as the spirits ascended in innumerable forms. Not all flew. Some went as goat or tiger, racing through the flames to the gate. Most went alone, but some – whose fecundity neither death nor Midian had slowed – went with families of six or more, their littlest in their arms. He was witnessing, he knew, the passing of an age, the end of which had begun the moment he'd first stepped on Midian's soil. He was the maker of this devastation, though he'd set no fire and toppled no tomb. He had brought men to Midian. In doing so, he'd destroyed it. Even Lori could not persuade him to forgive himself that. The thought might have tempted him to the flames, had he not heard the child calling his name.

She was only human enough to use words; the rest was beast.

'*Lori*,' she said.

'What about her?'

'The Mask has her.'

The Mask? She could only mean Decker.

'*Where?*'

2

Close, and closer still.

Knowing she couldn't outpace him she tried instead to out*dare* him, going where she hoped he would not. But he was too hot for her life to be shaken off. He followed her into territory where the ground erupted beneath their feet, and smoking stone rained around them.

It was not his voice that called her, however.

'Lori! This way!'

She chanced a desperate look, and there – *God love him*! – was Narcisse, beckoning. She veered off the pathway, or what was left of it, towards him, ducking between two mausoleums as their stained glass blew, and a stream of shadow, pricked with eyes, left its hiding place for the stars. It was like a piece of night sky itself, she marvelled. It belonged in the heavens.

The sight slowed her pace by an all but fatal step. The Mask closed the gap between them and snatched at her blouse. She threw herself forward to avoid the stab she knew must follow, the fabric tearing as she fell. This time he had her. Even as she reached for the wall to haul herself to her feet she felt his gloved hand at her nape.

'*Fuckhead?*' somebody shouted.

She looked up to see Narcisse at the other end of the passage between the mausoleums. He'd clearly caught Decker's attention. The hold on her neck was relaxing. It wasn't enough for her to squirm free, but if Narcisse could only keep up his distraction he might do the trick.

'*Got something for you,*' he said, and took his hands from his pocket to display the silver hooks on his thumbs.

He struck the hooks together. They sparked.

Decker let Lori's neck slip from his fingers. She slid out of his reach and began to stumble towards Narcisse. He was moving down the passage towards her, or rather towards *Decker*, on whom his eyes were fixed.

'Don't – ' she gasped. 'He's dangerous.'

Narcisse heard her – he *grinned* at the warning – but he made no reply. He just moved on past her to intercept the killer.

Lori glanced back. As the pair came within a yard of each other the Mask dragged a second knife, its blade as broad as a machete, from his jacket. Before Narcisse had a chance to defend himself the butcher delivered a swift downward stroke that separated Narcisse's left hand from his wrist in a single cut. Shaking his head, Narcisse took a backward step, but the Mask matched his retreat, raising the machete a second time and bringing it down on his victim's skull. The blow divided Narcisse's head from scalp to neck. It was a wound even a dead man could not survive. Narcisse's body began to shake, and then – like Ohnaka, trapped in sunlight – he came apart with a crack, a chorus of howls and sighs emerging, then taking flight.

Lori let out a sob, but stifled anything more. There was no time to mourn. If she waited to shed a single tear the Mask would claim her, and Narcisse's sacrifice would have been for nothing. She started to back away, the walls shaking to either side of her, knowing she should simply run but unable to detach herself from the sight of the Mask's depravity. Rooting amid the carnage he skewered half of Narcisse's head on the finer of his blades, then rested the knife on his shoulder, trophy and all, before renewing his pursuit.

Now she ran, out of the shadow of the mausoleums

and back onto the main avenue. Even if memory could have offered a guide to her whereabouts all the monuments had gone to the same rubble; she could not tell north from south. It was all one in the end. Whichever way she turned the same ruin, and the same pursuer. If he would come after her forever and forever – *and he would* – what was the use of living in fear of him? Let him have his sharp way. Her heart beat too hard to be pressed any further.

But even as she resigned herself to his knife the stretch of paving between her and her slaughterer cracked open, a plume of smoke shielding her from the Mask. An instant later the whole avenue opened up. She fell. Not to the ground. There was no ground. But into the earth –

3

' – falling!' the child said.

The shock of it almost toppled her from Boone's shoulders. His hands went up to support her. She took fiercer hold of his hair.

'Steady?' he said.

'Yes.'

She wouldn't countenance Ashbery accompanying them. He'd been left to fend for himself in the maelstrom, while they went looking for Lori.

'Ahead,' she said, directing her mount. 'Not very far.'

The fires were dying down, having devoured all they could get their tongues to. Confronted with cold brick all they could do was lick it black, then gutter out. But the tremors from below had not ceased. Their motions still ground stone on stone. And beneath the reverberations there was another sound, which Boone didn't so much hear as *feel*: in his gut and balls and teeth.

The child turned his head with her reins.

'That way,' she said.

The diminishing fires made progress easier; their brightness hadn't suited Boone's eyes. Now he went more quickly, though the avenues had been ploughed by the quake and he trod turned earth.

'How far?' he asked.

'*Hush*,' she told him.

'What?'

'Stand still.'

'You hear it too?' he said.

'Yes.'

'What is it?'

She didn't answer at first, but listened again.

Then she said:

'*Baphomet*.'

In his hours of imprisonment he'd thought more than once of the Baptiser's chamber; of the cold time he'd spent witness to the divided God. Hadn't it spoken prophecies to him? whispered in his head and demanded he listen? It had seen this ruin. It had told him Midian's last hour was imminent. Yet there'd been no accusations, though it must have known that it spoke to the man responsible. Instead it had seemed almost *intimate*, which had terrified him more than any assault. He could not be the confidant of divinities. He'd come to appeal to Baphomet as one of the newly dead, requesting a place in the earth. But he'd been greeted like an actor in some future drama. Called by another name, even. He'd wanted none of it. Not the auguries; not the name. He'd fought them, turning his back on the Baptiser; stumbling away, shaking the whispers from his head.

In that he'd not succeeded. At the thought of Baphomet's presence its words, and that name, were back like Furies.

You're Cabal, it had said.

He'd denied it then; he denied it now. Much as he pitied Baphomet's tragedy, knowing it couldn't escape this destruction in its wounded condition, he had more urgent claims upon his sympathies.

He couldn't save the Baptiser. But he could save Lori.

'She's there!' the child said.

'Which way?'

'Straight ahead. Look!'

There was only chaos visible. The avenue in front of them had been split open; light and smoke poured up through the ruptured ground. There was no sign of anything living.

'I don't see her,' he said.

'She's underground,' the child replied. 'In the pit.'

'Direct me then.'

'I can't go any further.'

'Why not?'

'Put me down. I've taken you as far as I can.' A barely suppressed panic had crept into her voice. '*Put me down*,' she insisted.

Boone dropped to his haunches, and the child slid off his shoulders.

'What's wrong?' he said.

'I mustn't go with you. It's not allowed.'

After the havoc they'd come through, her distress was bewildering.

'What are you afraid of?' he said.

'I can't look,' she replied. 'Not at the Baptiser.'

'It's here?'

She nodded, retreating from him as new violence opened the fissure ahead even wider.

'Go to Lori,' she told him. 'Bring her out. You're all she has.'

Then she was gone, two legs becoming four as she fled, leaving Boone to the pit.

Lori's consciousness flickered out as she fell. When she came round, seconds later, she was lying half way up, or down, a steep slope. The roof above her was still intact, but badly fractured, the cracks opening even as she watched, presaging total collapse. If she didn't move quickly she'd be buried alive. She looked towards the head of the slope. The cross tunnel was open to the sky. She began to crawl towards it, earth cascading down on her head, the walls creaking as they were pressed to surrender.

'*Not yet . . .*' she murmured. '*Please, not yet . . .*'

It was only as she came within six feet of the summit that her dazed senses recognized the slope. She'd carried Boone up this very incline once, away from the power that resided in the chamber at the bottom. Was it still there, watching her scrabblings? Or was this whole cataclysm evidence of its departure: the architect's farewell? She couldn't feel its surveillance, but then she could feel very little. Her body and mind functioned because instinct told them to. There was life at the top of the slope. Inch by wracking inch she was crawling to meet it.

Another minute and she reached the tunnel, or its roofless remains. She lay on her back for a time, staring up at the sky. With her breath regained she got to her feet and examined her wounded arm. The cuts were gummed up with dirt, but at least the blood had ceased to flow.

As she coaxed her legs to move something fell in front of her, wet in the dirt. Narcisse looked up at her with half a face. She sobbed his name, turning her eyes to meet the Mask. He straddled the tunnel like a gravedigger then dropped down to join her.

The spike was aimed at her heart. Had she been stronger it would have struck home, but the earth at the head of the slope gave way beneath her backward step and she had no power to keep herself from falling, head over heels, back down the incline –

Her cry gave Boone direction. He clambered over upended slabs of paving into the exposed tunnels, then through the maze of toppled walls and dying fires towards her. It was not her figure he saw in the passage ahead, however, turning to meet him with knives at the ready.

It was the doctor, at last.

From the precarious safety of the slope Lori saw the Mask turn from her, diverted from its purpose. She had managed to arrest her fall by catching hold of a crack in the wall with her good hand, which did its duty long enough for her to glimpse Boone in the passageway above. She'd seen what the machete had done to Narcisse. Even the dead had their mortality. But before she could utter any word of warning to Boone a wave of cold power mounted the slope behind her. Baphomet had not vacated its flame. It was there still, its grasp unpicking her fingers from the wall.

Unable to resist it, she slid backwards down the slope, into the erupting chamber.

The ecstasies of the Breed hadn't tainted Decker. He came at Boone like an abattoir worker to finish a slaughter he'd been called from: without flourish, without passion.

It made him dangerous. He struck quickly, with no signal of his intention. The thin blade ran straight through Boone's neck.

To disarm the enemy Boone simply stepped away from him. The knife slid through Decker's fingers, still caught in Boone's flesh. The doctor made no attempt to claim it back. Instead he took a two-handed grip on the skull splitter. Now there was some sound from him: a low moan that broke into gasps as he threw himself forward to despatch his victim.

Boone ducked the slicing blow, and the blade embedded itself in the tunnel wall. Earth spattered them both as Decker pulled it free. Then he swung again, this time missing his target's face by a finger length.

Caught off balance, Boone almost fell, and his downcast eyes chanced on Decker's trophy. He couldn't mistake that maimed face. Narcisse; cut up and dead in the dirt.

'*You bastard*!' he roared.

Decker paused for a moment, and watched Boone. Then he spoke. Not with his own voice, but with someone else's; a grinning whine of a voice.

'You can die,' it said.

As he spoke he swung the blade back and forth, not attempting to touch Boone, merely to demonstrate his authority. The blade whined like the voice; the music of a fly in a coffin, to and fro between the walls.

Boone retreated before the display, with mortal terror in his gut. Decker was right. The dead *could* die.

He drew breath, through mouth and punctured throat. He'd made a near fatal error, staying human in the presence of the Mask. And why? From some absurd idea that this final confrontation should be man to man; that they'd trade words as they fought, and he'd undo the doctor's ego before he undid his life.

It wouldn't be that way. This wasn't a patient's revenge on his corrupted healer: this was a beast and a butcher, tooth to knife.

He exhaled, and the truth in his cells came forth like honey. His nerves ran with bliss; his body throbbed as it swelled. In life he'd never felt so alive as he did at these moments, stripping off his humanity and dressing for the night.

'*No more . . .*' he said, and let the beast come from him everywhere.

Decker raised his machete to undo the enemy before the change had been completed. But Boone didn't wait. Still transforming, he tore at the butcher's face, taking off the mask – buttons, zipper and all – to uncover the infirmities beneath.

Decker howled at being revealed, putting his hand up to his face to half cover it against the beast's stare.

Boone snatched the mask up from the ground, and began to tear it apart, his claws shredding the linen. Decker's howls mounted. Dropping his hand from his face he began to swipe at Boone with insane abandon. The blade caught Boone's chest, slicing it open, but as it returned for a second cut Boone dropped the rags and blocked the blow, carrying Decker's arm against the wall with such force he broke the bones. The machete fell to the ground, and Boone reached out for Decker's face.

The steep howl stopped as the claws came at him. The mouth closed. The features slackened. For an instant Boone was looking at a face he'd studied for hours, hanging on its every word. At that thought his hand went from face to neck and he seized Decker's windpipe, which had funded so many lies. He closed his fist, his claws piercing the meat of Decker's throat. Then he pulled. The machinery came out in a wash of blood. Decker's eyes widened, fixed on his silencer. Boone pulled again, and again. The eyes glazed. The body jerked, and jerked, then started to sag.

Boone didn't let it drop. He held it as in a dance, and undid the flesh and bone as he'd undone the mask, clots of Decker's body striking the walls. There was only the dimmest memory of Decker's crimes against him in his head now. He tore with a Breed's zeal, taking monstrous satisfaction in a monstrous act. When he'd done his worst he dropped the wreckage to the earth, and finished the dance with his partner underfoot.

There'd be no rising from the grave for this body. No

hope of earthly resurrection. Even in the full flood of his attack Boone had withheld the bite that would have passed life after death into Decker's system. His flesh belonged only to the flies, and their children; his reputation to the vagaries of those who chose to tell his story. Boone didn't care. If he never shrugged off the crimes Decker had hung around his neck it scarcely mattered now. He was no longer innocent. With this slaughter he became the killer Decker had persuaded him he was. In murdering the prophet he made the prophecy true.

He let the body lie, and went to seek Lori. There was only one place she could have gone: down the slope into Baphomet's chamber. There was pattern in this, he saw. The Baptiser had *brought* her here, unknitting the ground beneath her feet so as to bring Boone after.

The flame its divided body occupied threw a cold glamour up into his face. He started down the slope towards it, dressed in the blood of his enemy.

XXIV

Cabal

1

Lost in the wasteland, Ashbery was found by a light, flickering up from between the fractured paving stones. Its beams were bitterly cold, and sticky in a way light had no right to be, adhering to his sleeve and hand before fading away. Intrigued, he tracked its source from one eruption to another, each point brighter than the one before.

A scholar in his youth, he would have known the name Baphomet had somebody whispered it to him, and understood why the light, springing from the deity's flame, exercised such a claim upon him. He would have known the deity as god and goddess in one body. Would have known too how its worshippers had suffered for their idol, burned as heretics, or for crimes against nature. He might have feared a power that demanded such homage; and wisely.

But there was nobody to tell him. There was only the light, drawing him on.

2

The Baptiser was not alone in its chamber, Boone found. He counted eleven members of the Breed around the walls, kneeling blindfolded with their backs to the flame. Amongst them, Mister Lylesburg and Rachel.

On the ground to the right of the door lay Lori. There was blood on her arm, and on her face, and her eyes were closed. But even as he went to her aid the thing in the flame set its eyes on him, turning him round with an icy touch. It had business with him, which it was not about to postpone.

'Approach,' it said. 'Of your own free will.'

He was afraid. The flame from the ground was twice the size it had been when last he'd entered, battering the roof of the chamber. Fragments of earth, turned to either ice or ash, fell in a glittering rain and littered the floor. Standing a dozen yards from the flame the assault of its energies was brutal. Yet Baphomet *invited* him closer.

'You're safe,' it said. 'You came in the blood of your enemy. It'll keep you warm.'

He took a step towards the fire. Though he'd suffered bullet and blade in his life since death, and felt none of them, he felt the chill from Baphomet's flame plainly enough. It pricked his nakedness; made frost patterns on his eyes. But Baphomet's words were no empty promise. The blood he wore grew hot as the air around him grew colder. He took comfort from it, and braved the last few steps.

The weapon, Baphomet said. *Discard it.*

He'd forgotten the knife in his neck. He drew it out of his flesh and threw it aside.

Closer still, the Baptiser said.

The flame's fury concealed all but glimpses of its freight, but enough to confirm what his first encounter with Baphomet had taught him: that if this deity had made creatures in its own image then he'd never set eyes on them. Even in dreams, nothing that approached the Baptiser. It was one of one.

Suddenly some part of it reached for him, out of the flame. Whether limb, or organ, or both he had no chance to see. It snatched at his neck and hair and pulled him towards the fire. Decker's blood didn't

242

shield him now; the ice scorched his face. Yet there was no fighting free. It immersed his head in the flame, holding him fast. He knew what this was the instant the fire closed around his head: *Baptism*.

And to confirm that belief, Baphomet's voice in his head.

You are Cabal, it said.

The pain was mellowing. Boone opened his mouth to draw breath, and the fire coursed down his throat and into his belly and lungs, then through his whole system. It carried his new name with it, baptizing him inside out.

He was no longer Boone. He was Cabal. An alliance of many.

From this cleansing on he would be capable of heat and blood and making children: that was in Baphomet's gift, and the deity gave it. But he would be frail too, or frailer. Not just because he bled, but because he was charged with purpose.

I must be hidden tonight, Baphomet said. *We all have enemies, but mine have lived longer and learned more cruelty than most. I will be taken from here and hidden from them.*

Now the presence of the Breed made sense. They'd remained behind to take a fraction of the Baptiser with them and conceal it from whatever forces came in pursuit.

This is your doing, Cabal, Baphomet said. *I don't accuse you. It was bound to happen. No refuge is forever. But I charge you —*

'Yes?' he said. 'Tell me.'

Rebuild what you've destroyed.

'A new Midian?'

No.

'What then?'

You must discover for us in the human world.

'Help me,' he said.

243

I can't. From here on, it's you must help me. You've undone the world. Now you must re-make it.

There were shudders in the flame. The Rites of Baptism were almost over.

'How do I begin?' Cabal said.

Heal me, Baphomet replied. *Find me, and heal me. Save me from my enemies.*

The voice that had first addressed him had changed its nature utterly. All trace of demand had gone from it. There was only this prayer to be healed, and kept from harm, delivered softly at his ear. Even the leash on his head had been slipped, leaving him free to look left and right. A call he hadn't heard had summoned Baphomet's attendants from the wall. Despite their blindfolds they walked with steady steps to the edge of the flame, which had lost much of its ferocity. They'd raised their arms, over which shrouds were draped, and the flame wall broke as pieces of Baphomet's body were dropped into the travellers' waiting arms, to be wrapped up instantly and put from sight.

This parting of piece from piece was agonizing. Cabal felt the pain as his own, filling him up until it was almost beyond enduring. To escape it he began to retreat from the flame.

But as he did so the one piece yet to be claimed tumbled into view in front of his face. Baphomet's head. It turned to him, vast and white, its symmetry fabulous. His entire body rose to it: gaze, spittle and prick. His heart began to beat, healing its damaged wing with its first throb. His congealed blood liquefied like a saint's relics, and began to run. His testicles tightened; sperm ran up his cock. He ejaculated into the flame, pearls of semen carried up past his eyes to touch the Baptiser's face.

Then the rendezvous was over. He stumbled out of the fire as Lylesburg – the last of the adherents in the chamber – received the head from the flames and wrapped it up.

Its tenants departed, the flame's ferocity redoubled. Cabal stumbled back as it unleashed itself with terrifying vigour –

On the ground above, Ashbery felt the force build, and tried to retreat from it, but his mind was full of what he'd spied upon, and its weight slowed him. The fire caught him, sweeping him up as it hurtled heavenward. He shrieked at its touch, and at the aftertaste of Baphomet that flooded his system. His many masks were burned away. The robes first, then the lace he'd not been able to pass a day of his adult life without wearing. Next the sexual anatomy he'd never much enjoyed. And finally, his flesh, scrubbing him clean. He fell back to earth more naked than he'd been in his mother's womb, and blind. The impact smashed his legs and arms beyond repair.

Below, Cabal shook himself from the daze of revelation. The fire had blown a hole in the roof of the chamber, and was spreading from it in all directions. It would consume flesh as easily as earth or stone. They had to be out of here before it found them. Lori was awake. From the suspicion in her eyes as he approached it was plain she'd seen the Baptism, and feared him.

'It's me,' he told her. 'It's still me.'

He offered her a hand. She took it, and he pulled her to her feet.

'I'll carry you,' he said.

She shook her head. Her eyes had gone from him to something on the floor behind him. He followed her gaze. Decker's blade lay close to the fissure, where the man he'd been before the Baptism had cast it aside.

'You want it?' he said.

'Yes.'

Shielding his head from the debris he retraced his steps and picked it up.

'Is he dead?' she asked, as he came back to her.

'He's dead.'

There was no sign of the corpse to verify his claim. The tunnel, collapsing on itself, had already buried him, as it was burying all of Midian. A tomb for the tombs.

With so much already levelled it wasn't difficult to find their way out to the main gates. They saw no sign of Midian's inhabitants on their way. Either the fire had consumed their remains, or rubble and earth covered them.

Just outside the gate, left where they could not fail to find it, was a reminder for Lori of one whom she prayed had escaped unharmed. Babette's doll – woven from grasses, and crowned with spring flowers – lay in a small ring of stones. As Lori's fingers made contact with the toy it seemed she saw one final time through the child's eyes – a landscape moving by as somebody speeded her away to safety. The glimpse was all too brief. She had no time to pass a prayer for good fortune along to the child before the vision was startled from her by a noise at her back. She turned to see that the pillars which had supported Midian's gates were beginning to topple. Cabal snatched her arm as the two stone slabs struck each other, teetered head to head like matched wrestlers, then fell sideways to hit the ground where moments before Lori and Cabal had stood.

3

Though he had no watch to read the hour, Cabal had a clear sense – Baphomet's gift, perhaps – of how long they had until daybreak. In his mind's eye he could see the planet, like a clock face decorated with seas, the magical divide of night from day creeping around it.

He had no fear of the sun's appearance on the horizon. His Baptism had given him a strength denied his brothers and sisters. The sun wouldn't kill him. This he knew without question. Undoubtedly it would be a discomfort to him. Moonrise would always be a more welcome sight than daybreak. But his work wouldn't be confined to the night hours. He wouldn't need to hide his head from the sun the way his fellow Breed were obliged to. Even now they'd be looking for a place of refuge before morning broke.

He imagined them in the sky over America, or running beside its highways, groups dividing when some amongst them grew tired, or found a likely haven: the rest moving on, more desperate by the moment. Silently he wished them safe journeys and secure harbour.

More: he promised he would find them again with time. Gather them up and unite them as Midian had done. Unwittingly, he'd harmed them. Now, he had to heal that harm, however long it took.

'I have to start tonight,' he told Lori. 'Or their trails will be cold. Then I'll never find them.'

'You're not going without me, Boone.'

'I'm not Boone any longer,' he told her.

'Why?'

They sat on the hill overlooking the necropolis, and he recited to her all he'd learned at the Baptism. Hard lessons, which he had too few words to communicate. She was weary, and shivering, but she wouldn't let him stop.

'Go on . . .' she'd kept saying, when he'd faltered. 'Tell me everything.'

She knew most of it. She'd been Baphomet's instrument as much as he, or more. Part of the prophecy. Without her he'd never have returned to Midian to save it, and to fail. The consequence of that return and that failure was the task before him.

Yet she revolted.

'You can't leave me,' she said. 'Not after all that's happened.'

She put her hand on his leg.

'Remember the cell . . .' she murmured.

He looked at her.

'You told me to forgive myself. And it was good advice. But it doesn't mean I can turn my back on what happened here. Baphomet; Lylesburg; all of them . . . I destroyed the only home they ever had.'

'*You* didn't destroy it.'

'If I'd never come here, it'd still be standing,' he replied. 'I have to undo that damage.'

'So take me with you,' she said. 'We'll go together.'

'It can't be that way. You're alive, Lori. I'm not. You're still human. I'm not.'

'You can change that.'

'What are you saying?'

'You can make me the same as you. It's not difficult. One bite and Peloquin changed you forever. So change *me*.'

'I can't.'

'You *won't* you mean.'

She turned the point of Decker's blade in the dirt.

'You don't want to be with me. Simple as that, isn't it?' She made a small, tight-lipped smile. 'Haven't you got the guts to say it?'

'When I've finished my work . . .' he answered. 'Maybe then.'

'Oh, in a hundred years or so?' she murmured, tears beginning. 'You'll come back for me then will you? Dig me up. Kiss me all over. Tell me you would have come sooner, but the days just kept *slipping by*.'

'*Lori*.'

'Shut up,' she said. 'Don't give me any more excuses. They're just insults.' She studied the blade, not him. 'You've got your reasons. I think they stink, but you

248

keep hold of them. You're going to need something to cling to.'

He didn't move.

'What are you waiting for? I'm not going to tell you it's all right. Just go. I never want to set eyes on you again.'

He stood up. Her anger hurt, but it was easier than tears. He backed away three or four paces, then – understanding that she wouldn't grant him a smile or even a look – he turned from her.

Only then did she glance up. His eyes were averted. It was now or never. She put the point of Decker's blade to her belly. She knew she couldn't drive it home with only one hand, so she went on to her knees, wedged the handle in the dirt, and let her body weight carry her down onto the blade. It hurt horribly. She yelled in pain.

He turned to find her writhing, her good blood pouring out into the soil. He ran back to her, turning her over. The death spasms were already in her.

'*I lied*,' she murmured. 'Boone . . . I lied. You're all I ever want to see.'

'Don't die,' he said. 'Oh God in Heaven, don't die.'

'So stop me.'

'I don't know how.'

'Kill me. Bite me . . . give me the balm.'

Pain twisted up her face. She gasped.

'Or let me die, if you can't take me with you. That's better than living without you.'

He cradled her, tears dropping onto her face. Her pupils were turning up beneath her lids. Her tongue was twitching at her lips. In seconds, she'd be gone, he knew. Once dead, she'd be beyond his power of recall.

'Is . . . it . . . *no*?' she said. She wasn't seeing him any longer.

He opened his mouth to provide his answer, raising her neck to his bite. Her skin smelled sour. He bit deep into the muscle, her blood meaty on his tongue, the balm rising in his throat to enter her bloodstream. But the shudders in her body had already ceased. She slumped in his embrace.

He raised his head from her torn neck, swallowing what he'd taken. He's waited too long. Damn him! She was his mentor and his confessor, and he'd let her slip from him. Death had been upon her before he'd had time to turn sting into promise.

Appalled at this last and most lamentable failure he laid her down on the ground in front of him.

As he drew his arms out from beneath her she opened her eyes.

'I'll never leave you,' she said.

XXV

Abide with Me

1

I t was Pettine who found Ashbery, but it was Eigerman who recognized the remnants for the man they'd been. The priest still had life in him, a fact — given the severity of his injuries — that verged on the miraculous. Both his legs were amputated in the days following, and one of his arms up to mid-bicep. He didn't emerge from his coma after the operations, nor did he die, though every surgeon opined that his chances were virtually zero. But the same fire that had maimed him had lent him an unnatural fortitude. Against all the odds, he endured.

He was not alone through the nights and days of unconsciousness. Eigerman was at his side twenty hours out of every twenty-four, waiting like a dog at a table for some scrap from above, certain that the priest could lead him to the evil that had undone both their lives.

He got more than he bargained for. When Ashbery finally rose from the deep, after two months of teetering on extinction, he rose voluble. Insane, but voluble. He named Baphomet. He named Cabal. He told, in the hieroglyphs of the hopelessly lunatic, of how the Breed had taken the pieces of their divinity's body and hidden them. More than that. He said he could find them again. Touched by the Baptiser's fire, and its survivors, he wanted the touch again.

'I can smell God,' he'd say, over and over.

251

'Can you take us to Him?' Eigerman asked.

The answer was always yes.

'I'll be your eyes then,' Eigerman volunteered. 'We'll go together.'

Nobody else wanted the evidence Ashbery offered, there were too many nonsenses to be accounted for as it was, without adding to the burden on reality. The authorities gladly let Eigerman have custody of the priest. They deserved each other, was the common opinion. Not one sane cell between them.

Ashbery was utterly dependent on Eigerman: incapable, at least at the beginning, of feeding, shitting or washing without help. Repugnant as it was to tend the imbecile, Eigerman knew Ashbery was a God-given gift. Through him he might yet revenge himself for the humiliations of Midian's last hours. Coded in Ashbery's rantings were clues to the enemy's whereabouts. With time he'd decipher them.

And when he did — oh *when he did* — there would come such a day of reckoning the Last Trump would pale beside.

2

The visitors came by night, stealthily, and took refuge wherever they could find it.

Some revisited haunts their forebears had favoured; towns under wide skies where believers still sang on Sunday, and the picket fences were painted every spring. Others took to the cities: to Toronto, Washington, Chicago, hoping to avoid detection better where the streets were fullest, and yesterday's corruption today's commerce. In such a place their presence might not be noticed for a year, or two or three. But not forever. Whether they'd taken refuge in city canyon or bayou or dustbowl none pretended this was a permanent residence. They would be discovered in time, and rooted out. There was a new frenzy abroad, particularly amongst their old enemies the Christians, who were a daily spectacle, talking of their martyr and calling for purges in His name. The moment they discovered the Breed in their midst the persecutions would begin again.

So, discretion was the by-word. They would only take meat when the hunger became crippling, and only then victims who were unlikely to be missed. They would refrain from infecting others, so as not to advertise their presence. If one was found, no other would risk exposure by going to their aid. Hard laws to live by, but not as hard as the consequences of breaking them.

The rest was patience, and they were well used to that. Their liberator would come eventually, if they could only survive the wait. Few had any clue as to the shape he'd come in. But all knew his name.

Cabal, he was called. *Who Unmade Midian.*

Their prayers were full of him. *On the next wind, let him come. If not now, then tomorrow.*

They might not have prayed so passionately had they known what a sea-change his coming would bring. They might not have prayed at all had they known they prayed to themselves. But these were revelations for a later day. For now, they had simpler concerns. Keeping the children from the roofs at night; the bereaved from crying out too loud; the young in summer from falling in love with the human.

It was a life.

Clive Barker's previous novel was WEAVE-WORLD. The following pages are taken from the early part of that novel.

THE SUIT OF LIGHTS

1

The day Cal stepped out into was humid and stale. It could not be long before the summer let fall take its toll. Even the breeze seemed weary, and its condition was contagious. By the time Cal reached the vicinity of Rue Street his feet felt swollen in his shoes and his brain in his skull.

And then, to add insult to injury, he couldn't find the damn street. He'd made his way to the house the previous day with his eyes on the birds rather than on the route he was following, so he had only an impressionistic notion of its whereabouts. Knowing he could well wander for several hours and not find the street, he asked the way from a gaggle of six-year-olds, engaged in war games on a street corner. He was confidently re-directed. Either through ignorance or malice, however, the directions proved hopelessly incorrect, and he found himself in ever more desperate circles, his frustration mounting.

Any sixth sense he might have hoped for – some instinct that would lead him unerringly to the region of his dreams – was conspicuous by its absence.

It was luck then, pure luck, that brought him finally to the corner of Rue Street, and to the house that had once belonged to Mimi Laschenski.

2

Suzanna had spent much of the morning attempting to do as she had promised Doctor Chai: notifying Uncle

Charlie in Toronto. It was a frustrating business. For one thing, the small hotel she'd found the previous night only boasted a single public telephone, and other guests wanted access to it as well as she. For another, she had to call round several friends of the family until she located one who had Charlie's telephone number, all of which took the best part of the morning. When, around one, she finally made contact, Mimi's only son took the news without a trace of surprise. There was no offer to drop his work and rush to his mother's bedside; only a polite request that Suzanna call back when there was 'more news'. Meaning, presumably, that he didn't expect her to ring again until it was time for him to send a wreath. So much for filial devotion.

The call done, she rang the hospital. There was no change in the patient's condition. She's hanging on, was the duty nurse's phrase. It conjured an odd image of Mimi as mountaineer, clinging to a cliff-face. She took the opportunity to ask about her grandmother's personal effects, and was told that she'd come into hospital without so much as a nightgown. Most probably the vultures Mrs Pumphrey had spoken of would by now have taken anything of worth from the house – the tall-boy included – but she elected to call by anyway, in case she could salvage anything to make Mimi's dwindling hours a little more comfortable.

She found a small Italian restaurant in the vicinity of the hotel to lunch in, then drove to Rue Street.

3

The back yard gate had been pushed closed by the removal men, but left unbolted. Cal opened it, and stepped into the yard.

If he had expected some revelation, he was disappointed. There was nothing remarkable here. Just parched chickweed sprouting between the paving stones, and a litter of chattels the trio had discarded as worthless. Even the shadows, which might have hidden some glory, were wan and unsecretive.

Standing in the middle of the yard – where all of the mysteries that had overturned his sanity had been unveiled – he doubted for the first time, *truly* doubted, that anything had in fact happened the previous day.

Maybe there would be something inside the house, he told himself; some flotsam he could cling to that would bear him up in this flood of doubt.

He crossed the ground where the carpet had lain, to the back door. The removal men had left it unlocked; or else vandals had broken in. Either way, it stood ajar. He stepped inside.

At least the shadows were heavier within; there was some room for the fabulous. He waited for his eyes to accommodate the murk. Was it really only twenty-four hours since he'd been here, he thought, as his sharpening gaze scanned the grim interior; only yesterday that he'd entered this house with no more on his mind than catching a lost bird? This time he had so much more to find.

He wandered through to the hallway, looking everywhere for some echo of what he'd experienced the day before. With every step he took his hopes fell further. Shadows there were, but they were deserted. The place was shorn of miracles. They'd gone when the carpet was removed.

Half way up the stairs he halted. What was the use of going any further? It was apparent he'd missed his chance. If he was to rediscover the vision he'd glimpsed and lost he'd have to search elsewhere. It was mere doggedness, therefore – one of Eileen's attributes – that made him continue to climb.

At the top of the stairs the air was so leaden it made drawing breath a chore. That, and the fact that he felt like a trespasser today – unwelcome in this tomb –

made him anxious to confirm his belief that the place had no magic to show him, then get gone.

As he went to the door of the front bedroom something moved behind him. He turned. The labourers had piled several articles of furniture at the top of the stairs, then apparently decided they weren't worth the sweat of moving any further. A chest of drawers, several chairs and tables. The sound had come from behind this furniture. And now it came again.

Hearing it, he imagined rats. The sound suggested several sets of scurrying paws. Live and let live, he thought: he had no more right to be here than they did. Less, perhaps. They'd probably occupied the house for rat generations.

He returned to the job at hand, pushed open the door, and stepped into the front room. The windows were grimy, and the stained lace curtains further clogged the light. There was a chair overturned on the bare boards, and three odd shoes had been placed on the mantelpiece by some wit. Otherwise empty.

He stood for a few moments and then, hearing laughter in the street and needing its reassurance, crossed to the window and drew the curtain aside. But before he found the laughter's source he forsook the search. His belly knew before his senses could confirm it that somebody had entered the room behind him. He let the curtain drop and looked around. A wide man in late middle-age, dressed too well for this dereliction, had joined him in the half-light. The threads of his grey jacket were almost iridescent. But more eye-catching still, his smile. A practised smile, belonging on an actor, or a preacher. Whichever, it was the expression of a man looking for converts.

'Can I be of help?' he said. His voice was resonant, and warm, but his sudden appearance had chilled Cal.

'Help me?' he said, floundering.

'Are you perhaps interested in purchasing property?' the other man said.

'Purchasing? No . . . I . . . was just . . . you know . . . looking around.'

'It's a fine house,' said the stranger, his smile as steady as a surgeon's handshake, and as antiseptic. 'Do you know much about houses?' The line was spoken like its predecessors, without irony or malice. When Cal didn't reply, the man said: 'I'm a salesman. My name's Shadwell.' He teased the calf-skin glove from his thick-fingered hand. 'And yours?'

'Cal Mooney. Calhoun, that is.'

The bare hand was extended. Cal took two steps towards the man – he was fully four inches taller than Cal's five foot eleven – and shook hands. The man's cool palm made Cal aware that he was sweating like a pig.

The handshake broken, friend Shadwell unbuttoned his jacket, and opened it, to take a pen from his inside pocket. This casual action briefly revealed the lining of the Salesman's garment, and by some trick of the light it seemed to shine, as though the fabric were woven of mirrored threads.

Shadwell caught the look on Cal's face. His voice was feather-light as he said:

'Do you see anything you like?'

Cal didn't trust the man. Was it the smile or the calf-skin gloves that made him suspicious? Whichever, he wanted as little time in the man's company as possible.

But there *was* something in the jacket. Something that caught the light, and made Cal's heart beat a little faster.

'Please . . .' Shadwell coaxed. 'Have a look.'

His hand went to the jacket again, and opened it.

'Tell me . . .' he purred, '. . . if there's anything there that takes your fancy.'

This time, he fully opened the jacket, exposing the lining. And yes, Cal's first judgement had been correct. It *did* shine.

'I am, as I said, a salesman,' Shadwell was explaining.

261

'I make it a Golden Rule always to carry some samples of my merchandise around with me.'

Merchandise. Cal shaped the word in his head, his eyes still fixed on the interior of the jacket. What a word that was: *merchandise*. And there, in the lining of the jacket, he could almost see that word made solid. Jewellery, was it, that gleamed there? Artificial gems with a sheen that blinded the way only the fake could. He squinted into the glamour, looking to make sense out of what he saw, while the Salesman's voice went about its persuasions:

'Tell me what you'd like and it's yours. I can't say fairer than that, can I? A fine young man like you should be able to pick and choose. The world's your oyster. I can see that. Open in front of you. Have what you like. Free, gratis and without charge. You tell me what you see in there, and the next minute it's in your hands . . .'

Look away, something in Cal said; nothing comes free. Prices must be paid.

But his gaze was so infatuated with the mysteries in the folds of the jacket that he couldn't have averted his eyes now if his life depended upon it.

'. . . tell me . . .' the Salesman said, '. . . what you see . . .'

Ah, *there* was a question –

'. . . and it's yours.'

He saw forgotten treasures, things he'd once upon a time set his heart upon, thinking that if he owned them he'd never want for anything again. Worthless trinkets, most of them; but items that awoke old longings. A pair of X-ray spectacles he'd seen advertised at the back of a comic book (see thru walls! impress your friends!) but had never been able to buy. There they were now, their plastic lens gleaming, and seeing them he remembered the October nights he'd lain awake wondering how they worked.

And what was that beside them? Another childhood

fetish. A photograph of a woman dressed only in stiletto heels and a sequinned G-string, presenting her over-sized breasts to the viewer. The boy two doors down from Cal had owned that picture, stolen it from his uncle's wallet, he'd claimed, and Cal had wanted it so badly he thought he'd die of longing. Now it hung, a dog-eared memento, in the glittering flux of Shadwell's jacket, there for the asking.

But no sooner had it made itself apparent than it too faded, and new prizes appeared in its place to tempt him.

'What is it you see, my friend?'

The keys to a car he'd longed to own. A prize pigeon, the winner of innumerable races, that he'd been so envious of he'd have happily abducted –

'. . . just tell me what you see. Ask, and it's yours . . .'

There was so much. Items that had seemed – for an *hour*, a *day* – the pivot upon which his world turned, all hung now in the miraculous store-room of the Salesman's coat.

But they were fugitive, all of them. They appeared only to evaporate again. There was something else there, which prevented these trivialities from holding his attention for more than moments. What it was, he couldn't yet see.

He was dimly aware that Shadwell was addressing him again, and that the tone of the Salesman's voice had altered. There was some puzzlement in it now, tinged with exasperation.

'Speak up, my friend . . . why don't you tell me what you want?'

'I can't . . . quite . . . *see* it.'

'Then try harder. Concentrate.'

Cal tried. The images came and went, all insignificant stuff. The mother-lode still evaded him.

'You're not trying,' the Salesman chided. 'If a man

wants something badly he has to zero in on it. Has to make sure it's clear in his head.'

Cal saw the wisdom of this, and re-doubled his efforts. It had become a challenge to see past the tinsel to the real treasure that lay beyond. A curious sensation attended this focusing; a restlessness in his chest and throat, as though some part of him were preparing to be gone; out of him and along the line of his gaze. Gone into the jacket.

At the back of his head, where his skull grew the tail of his spine, the warning voices muttered on. But he was too committed to resist. Whatever the lining contained, it teased him, not quite showing itself. He stared and stared, defying its decorum until the sweat ran from his temples.

Shadwell's coaxing monologue had gained fresh confidence. Its sugar coating had cracked and fallen away. The nut beneath was bitter and dark.

'Go on . . .' he said. 'Don't be so damn weak. There's something here you want, isn't there? Very badly. Go on. Tell me. *Spit it out*. No use waiting. You wait, and your chance slips away.'

Finally, the image was coming clear –

'*Tell me and it's yours.*'

Cal felt a wind on his face, and suddenly he was flying again, and wonderland was spread out before him. Its deeps and its heights, its rivers, its towers – all were displayed there in the lining of the Salesman's jacket.

He gasped at the sight. Shadwell was lightning swift in his response.

'What is it?'

Cal stared on, speechless.

'*What do you see?*'

A confusion of feelings assailed Cal. He felt elated, seeing the land, yet fearful of what he would be asked to give (was *already* giving, perhaps, without quite

264

knowing it) in return for this peep-show. Shadwell had harm in him, for all his smiles and promises.

'*Tell me . . .*' the Salesman demanded.

Cal tried to keep an answer from coming to his lips. He didn't want to give his secret away.

'*. . . what do you see?*'

The voice was so hard to resist. He wanted to keep his silence, but the reply rose in him unbidden.

'I . . .' (*Don't say it*, the poet warned), 'I see . . .' (*Fight it. There's harm here.*) 'I . . . see . . .'

'He sees the Fugue.'

The voice that finished the sentence was that of a woman.

'Are you sure?' said Shadwell.

'Never more certain. Look at his eyes.'

Cal felt foolish and vulnerable, so mesmerized by the sights still unfolding in the lining he was unable to cast his eyes in the direction of those who now appraised him.

'He *knows*,' the woman said. Her voice held not a trace of warmth. Even, perhaps, of humanity.

'You were right then,' said Shadwell. 'It's been here.'

'Of course.'

'Good enough,' said Shadwell, and summarily closed the jacket.

The effect on Cal was cataclysmic. With the world – *the Fugue*, she'd called it – so abruptly snatched away he felt weak as a babe. It was all he could do to stand upright. Queasily, his eyes slid in the direction of the woman.

She was beautiful: that was his first thought. She was dressed in reds and purples so dark they were almost black, the fabric wrapped tightly around her upper body so as to seem both chaste, her ripeness bound and sealed, and, in the act of sealing, eroticized. The same paradox informed her features. Her hair-line had been shaved back fully two inches, and her eyebrows totally removed, which left her face eerily innocent of expression. Yet her flesh gleamed as if oiled, and though the shaving, and the absence of any scrap of make-up to flatter her features, seemed acts in defiance of her beauty, her face could not be denied its sensuality. Her mouth was too sculpted; and her eyes – umber one moment, gold the next – too eloquent for the feelings there to be disguised. What feelings, Cal could only vaguely read. Impatience certainly, as though being here sickened her, and stirred some fury Cal had no desire to see unleashed. Contempt – for him most likely – and yet a great focus upon him, as though she saw through to his marrow, and was preparing to congeal it with a thought.

There were no such contradictions in her voice however. It was steel and steel.

'How long?' she demanded of him. 'How long since you saw the Fugue?'

He couldn't meet her eyes for more than a moment. His gaze fled to the mantelpiece, and the tripod's shoes.

'Don't know what you're talking about,' he said.

'You've seen it. You saw it again in the jacket. It's fruitless to deny it.'

'It's better you answer,' Shadwell advised.

Cal looked from mantelpiece to door. They had left it open. 'You can both go to Hell,' he said quietly.

Did Shadwell laugh? Cal wasn't certain.

'We want the carpet,' said the woman.

'It belongs to us, you understand,' Shadwell said. 'We have a legitimate claim to it.'

'So, if you'd be so kind . . .' the woman's lip curled at this courtesy, '. . . tell me where the carpet's gone, and we can have the matter done with.'

'Such easy terms,' the Salesman said. 'Tell us, and we're gone.'

Claiming ignorance would be no defence, Cal thought; *they* knew that *he* knew, and they wouldn't be persuaded otherwise. He was trapped. Yet dangerous as things had become, he felt inwardly elated. His tormentors had confirmed the existence of the world he'd glimpsed: the Fugue. The urge to be out of their presence as fast as possible was tempered by the desire to play them along, and hope they'd tell him more about the vision he'd witnessed.

'Maybe I did see it,' he said.

'No *maybe*,' the woman replied.

'It's hazy . . .' he said. 'I remember *something*, but I'm not quite sure what.'

'You don't know what the Fugue is?' said Shadwell.

'Why should he?' the woman replied. 'He came on it by luck.'

'But he saw,' said Shadwell.

'A lot of Cuckoos have some sight, it doesn't mean they *understand*. He's lost, like all of them.'

Cal resented her condescension, but in essence she was right. Lost he was.

'What you saw isn't your business,' she said to him. 'Just tell us where you put the carpet, then forget you ever laid eyes on it.'

'I don't *have* the carpet,' he said.

The woman's entire face seemed to darken, the pupils of her eyes like moons barely eclipsing some apocalyptic light.

From the landing, Cal heard again the scuttling sounds he'd previously taken to be rats. Now he wasn't so sure.

'I won't be polite with you much longer,' she said. 'You're a thief.'

'No – ' he protested.

'*Yes*. You came here to raid an old woman's house and you got a glimpse of something you shouldn't.'

'We shouldn't waste time,' said Shadwell.

Cal had begun to regret his decision to play the pair along. He should have run while he had half a chance. The noise from the other side of the door was getting louder.

'Hear that?' said the woman. 'Those are some of my sister's bastards. Her by-blows.'

'They're vile,' said Shadwell.

He could believe it.

'Once more,' she said. 'The carpet.'

And once more he told her. 'I don't have it.' This time his words were more appeal than defence.

'Then we must make you tell,' said the woman.

'Be careful, Immacolata,' said Shadwell.

If the woman heard him, she didn't care for his warning. Softly, she rubbed the middle and fourth fingers of her right hand against the palm of her left, and at this all but silent summons her sister's children came running.

The Hellbound Heart
Clive Barker

The classic novella filmed as *Hellraiser*.

At last he had solved the puzzle of Lemarchand's box. He was standing on the threshold of a new world of heightened sensations.

In moments the Cenobites – who had dedicated an eternity to the pursuit of sensuality – would be here. They would reveal the dark secrets that would transform him for ever.

But with the exquisite pleasure would come pain beyond imagining. To escape his hideous tormentors and return to this world, he would need the help of his brother's wife Julia, the woman who loved him. But most of all he would need blood.

'A real marrow-melter . . . it plays on the darkest fears and fantastical obsessions of the human psyche: chilling and compelling.'   *Scotsman*

ISBN: 0 00 647065 3

Coldheart Canyon
Clive Barker

A Hollywood ghost story

After a run of failed movies, superstar Todd Pickett elects to have extensive surgery in a desperate bid to regain his lost beauty. The procedure goes horribly, grotesquely wrong. Hiding from his fans, and from the press he knows will tear his reputation apart if they find out about his operation, Todd takes refuge in a place that no map of Hollywood has ever described: Coldheart Canyon.

Here, nursing his wounds and his desperation, he discovers what the history of the Dream Factory has long concealed: a world somewhere between life and death, reality and illusion, where the great legends of a forgotten Hollywood are waiting to educate him in the bitter business of life after fame.

'The great imaginer of our time'   QUENTIN TARANTINO

'A powerful and fascinating writer with a brilliant imagination . . . an outstanding storyteller'   J G BALLARD

'Clive Barker is so good that I am literally tongue-tied'
STEPHEN KING

0 00 651040 X

Everville
Clive Barker

Five years ago, in his bestseller *The Great and Secret Show*, Clive Barker mesmerised millions of readers worldwide with an extraordinary vision of human passions and possibilities. Welcome to a new volume in that epic adventure. Welcome to *Everville*.

On a mountain peak, high above the city of Everville, a door stands open: a door that opens onto the shores of the dream-sea Quiddity. And there's not a soul below who'll not be changed by that fact ...

Phoebe Cobb is about to forget her old life and go looking for her lost lover Joe Flicker in the world on the other side of that door; a strange, sensual wonderland the likes of which only Barker could make real.

Tesla Bombeck who knows what horrors lurk on the far side of Quiddity, must solve the mysteries of the city's past if she is to keep those horrors from crossing the threshold.

Harry D'Amour, who has tracked the ultimate evil across America, will find it conjuring atrocities in the sunlit streets of Everville.

Step into Everville's streets, and enter a world like no other ...

'Clive Barker is so good I am almost tongue-tied. What Barker does makes the rest of us look like we've been asleep for the last ten years . . . His stories are compulsorily readable and original. He is an important, exciting and enormously saleable writer.'
Stephen King

ISBN 0 00 647225 7